Downward Spiral

Gary Barocsi

Rival Publishing—Phoenix, AZ
ISBN: 978-0-578-70826-3
Library of Congress Control Number: 2020911230
Title: Downward Spiral
Author: Gary Barocsi
Digital distribution | 2020
Paperback | 2020

This is a work of fiction. The characters, names, incidents, places, and dialogue are products of the author's imagination, and are not to be construed as real.

Author photo credit: Angel Ray
Cover art painted by Gary Barocsi

Dedication

For my Mother who has always been there for me.

Chapter One

On May fourth 1975 Donald McKay was born in Bowling Green Kentucky. His parents owned a farm and were overjoyed at the birth of their son. They had been married five years and this was their first child. Alice, Donald's Mother was convinced she was unable to bare children, so her pregnancy was quite a surprise. Her and her husband Donald Sr. were high school sweethearts and always wanted a big family. They were married at a young age, fresh out of high school. Alice had big dreams of a fairy tale wedding. She imagined her and Donald married with a big house, white picket fence, three or four children, a dog and all that. Though things were not as she had imagined (they never are) life was good. They owned their farm outright. It was passed down from Donald's parents. His Mother had died giving birth to him. His Father was killed in a farming accident when a young Donald Sr. was only seventeen years old.

Growing up Donald Sr. worked hard, learning everything there was to know about farming from his father. Tobacco was the cash crop of Kentucky and Donald Sr. grew up learning all the ins and outs about growing tobacco from his Father. He was by no means a rich man but he had everything he needed and could afford to provide an upper middle class life for his wife and child. He was free from financial burdens that most farmers faced as he had inherited his farm and all the equipment. So he didn't have the stress of paying a mortgage or loans on tractors or other expensive tools of the trade. He only had to pay repairs and wages of the farm hands some who had been around since his Father.

Though the life was not as Alice had dreamed it was still good. Now that they had a new baby boy to share their love and raise to carry on the family farm one more aspect of the dream was fulfilled.

The first years of Donald Jr.'s life were uneventful, normal by all definitions of the word. At age five he started school. He came home every day to chores learning the family business of farming just as his father had before him. By age ten he was quite the helping hand on the farm. That was also the age he was when he met Jimmy. Jimmy is the eleven year old boy who lived on the farm next door. A product of a broken home Jimmy didn't have it as good as young Donnie. His Mother and Father had divorced when he was only six years old. All his siblings were split up. The boys stayed with their father and the girls went with their Mother. Jimmy was the baby of the family.

Jimmy came from a huge family, His Father had seven brothers and sisters, who all had kids of their own. So every now and then some cousin from one of Jimmy's Aunts or Uncles would spend a summer on the farm, usually as a form of punishment. When their parents had enough and their kids kept getting into trouble at school or with the law, off to their Uncles farm they went. They came from all over. Jimmy had relatives all across the United States.

When a kid was sent to the farm for the summer they were never happy. Nothing could be more unpleasant to a teen from a big city than being sent to a farm for a season of hard labor. Waking up at the crack of dawn and being worked all day. This was the family's idea of the ideal punishment. Just what was needed to straighten out an unruly teenager hell bent on not wanting to go to school or doing drugs, getting caught stealing or whatever. Uncle James was always willing to take in the niece or nephew and put them to work. As you know there is never a shortage of work on a farm. Especially Jimmy's farm they had cows, chickens and acres and acres of crops. Any time Jimmy's dad could get some free labor he was all over it. Free labor for him and a much needed break for his brothers and sisters and the kids are being punished. It was a win-win in everyone's eyes. Well everyone but the kid of course. Just to go from a Huge Metropolis full of people to a small farming community was torture enough for most teens full of piss and vinegar, but to add hard labor to the mix made it pure hell for most of them.

One summer when Donnie was around thirteen Jimmy introduced him to his cousin Danny. Danny was a sixteen year old. He was from California. He was skinny, his head was shaved bald and he wore suspenders and steel toed boots. His Mother had sent him to the farm for the summer because she didn't like the group of friends he was hanging around with. A bunch of skinheads in some white supremacist gang she was certain would wind him up in prison or dead. So off to the farm he was sent to see if a summer of hard labor would straighten him out. Jimmy and Danny showed up at Donnie's house and knocked on the door.

"Hey, what's up Jimmy?" Donnie asked as he answered the door.

"Oh nothing, I just wanted to introduce you to my cousin Danny from California. He'll be staying the summer at my house."

"Nice to meet you," Donnie said as he reached out and shook Danny's hand.

"Same here," Danny said shaking Donnie's hand. "What do you guys do for kicks out here? This place is dead."

"There's a movie theater in town and a bowling alley with some video games," Donnie said.

"Man, this place sucks," Danny said.

"Me and Donnie here have been piling up wood to build a fort out by the tree line. Wanna help us?" Jimmy asked.

"Yeah I'm pretty good at building stuff, I guess I could help you guys out."

"Cool," Jimmy said.

"How we gonna get the wood from the barn to the tree line? Looks pretty far," Danny asked.

"My Dad lets me drive the truck on the farm we can load it in there. We got some good plywood from our old barn we tore down last year" Donnie said.

The boys walked over to the barn and looked at the pile of wood." Man, you guys got a lot of wood here," Danny said surprised.

"We've been planning this for a long time, collecting two by fours and any wood we could get our hands on," Donnie said.

"You should have plenty," Danny said.

"I got a couple boxes of nails and some hammers in the barn," Donnie said.

"I can't believe we're finally going to build it! We've had the spot picked out for a long time," Jimmy said excitedly.

"You guys come back after supper and we'll start hauling the wood."

"Sounds good," Danny said.

After the boys had eaten, they met up at Donnie's house and started loading the pick-up truck with all the wood they had piled up behind the barn. They had amassed quite a bit of wood. By time they were done the whole pick-up bed was full. They drove to the tree line separating the two farms.

"Hey, this is a good spot," Danny said.

"Yeah it's hidden from the road and far from the house," Donnie said.

"Why don't we build a tree house?" Danny asked as they unloaded the wood.

"We wanted too at first but it's way too much work, we decided a fort would be easier."

The boys unloaded the truck when Jimmy threw down the last piece he clapped his hands together and said," Well that's it. I got some pallets at my house we can lay down as a floor. We'll bring them with us tomorrow."

"Yeah, it's getting late there is not much more we can do today," Donnie said.

"Alright, we'll meet up tomorrow after supper and go over the plan and start building," Danny said.

Danny and Jimmy took off walking through the tree line separating the two properties. Donnie drove the truck back to the house and got ready for bed.

For the next two weeks the boys met after supper and worked. They sawed and hammered away constructing their fort. Danny had some construction knowledge he'd learned in a class at school. He also helped his dad add onto their house and learned a lot from him. Donnie and Jimmy were very impressed at how much he knew. They quickly realized they never would have done this without him. If they did, it would have never been as good. On the fifteenth day construction was complete and the boys were amazed on their accomplishment.

The next day the boys met at the fort. Danny had a black backpack over one of his shoulders. "I have a surprise for you guys," he said taking the backpack off and putting it on the floor. "Actually I have a couple surprises for you two," he said unzipping the pack. He reached in and pulled out a can of white spray paint. He started shaking it vigorously. 'We need to christen this place," he said and walked to the back wall of the fort and spray painted a big swastika on it. He walked back to the pack and reached inside. Like a magician pulling a rabbit out of a hat he pulled out a six pack of beer.

"Ta–da," He said with a smile.

"Where did you get that?" Donnie asked with his eyes wide.

"I stole it from a store when I went to go buy the paint."

"Alright Danny!" yelled Jimmy pulling one of the cans off the plastic rings and handing it to Donnie. He pulled off another one for himself.

Danny pulled a beer off for himself and popped the top. Donnie and Jimmy followed his lead popping open their cans as well. Danny raised his can of beer in the air and walked over to the boys. They all clinked their cans together, "White Power!" Danny yelled and they all took a big drink."

"After we drink this beer I got one more surprise for you guys," Danny said before taking another big chug from his can. The boys sat around and drank the beer. When it was gone Danny returned to the backpack and started digging around inside. He pulled out what looked like a broken pen with a wire hanging off one end.

"What's that?" Donnie asked.

"What do you think it is?"

"I don't know."

Danny dug in his backpack some more and pulled out a little black bottle. He started shaking the bottle. You could hear liquid sloshing back and forth inside the little bottle.

"Here's a hint," He said tossing the little bottle to Donnie. Donnie caught the bottle and studied it. He squinted his eyes and read the writing to himself.

"Ink?" Donnie asked with a confused look on his face.

"It's a tattoo machine, huh?" Jimmy asked.

"Yep, I got a friend out in Cally, his older brother went to prison for a few years. When he got out he showed us how to make these. I figured I'd give you guys tattoos to mark the occasion."

"We don't have electricity out here," Donnie said.

"We don't need it," Danny said. He started digging around in the bag again. "Ah ha there it is," He said and pulled out a square battery about the size of one of the beer cans. "This will power it," he said putting it down on the makeshift table the boys made from milk crates and a board.

"A battery, will that work?"

"Of course it will," He said as he rolled up his sleeve, showing a tattoo on his arm." How do you think I got this?" He asked.

"Wow!" The boys said as they gawked in amazement at Danny's tattooed arm.

"Did that hurt?" Jimmy asked.

"Not as bad as you might think. It's more of a sting than anything else. It does hurt a little though."

"Did you tattoo that yourself?" Donnie asked.

"No, my buddy did it. He tattooed me and I tattooed him. What do you guys think do you want tattoos?"

"I do!" Jimmy said.

"I don't know. My Dad would beat my ass," Donnie said.

"He won't even know as long as you don't walk around naked."

Donnie just looked at him.

"You don't walk around without a shirt a lot do you?" Danny asked.

"No, I always wear a shirt unless I'm taking a bath or swimming or something," Donnie said

"Well there you go he'll never know unless you take a bath with him. You don't have a pool do you?' Danny asked.

"I wish," Donnie said. "I love to swim."

"Well your Dad will never find out then. So are you in or out?" Danny asked nudging Donnie's arm a little.

Donnie looked at Danny, looked at the tattoo machine then at Jimmy and back to Danny. "What the hell I'm in."

"Alright!" Jimmy yelled. "Let's do it!"

"What should we get?" Donnie asked.

"What else?" Danny asked nodding his head towards the spray painted wall at the back of the fort. "My parents got mad cause they said I was in a gang. I'll show them I'll start my own gang here. It will be cool you guys will see."

Jimmy and Donnie looked at each other and smiled with the excitement of a couple of dumb kids. A few minutes later both of them had a swastika on their right arm just like Danny. They both felt proud like they were part of something now, almost like they were blood brothers or something. Donnie and Jimmy were so happy. This summer was the best.

Donnie was careful to keep his tattoo hidden from his parents. The summer was going by day by day the boys met at the fort and hung out. They told stories. Danny's the one who had all the stories. He told them about his friends in California. He told them about girls he dated. Every once in a while he'd go into some tangent about Adolf Hitler and white supremacy, but all the boys seemed to ask about or really listen to was the stories about the girls. All the other nonsense just went in one ear and out the other.

The boys really looked up to Danny though, as most impressionable young boys look up to older kids. They had fun playing cards and every now and then Danny would surprise them with a six pack of beer, not very often but once in a while. The boys seemed inseparable, that is after chores were finished and supper. Sometimes they would spend the night out in the fort and see if they could stay up all night. Of course they always feel asleep. They had fun though, telling ghost stories and playing games. One day Jimmy showed up to the fort without Danny. Donnie didn't really think much of it until he noticed Jimmy seemed to be acting kind of strange. He just had this weird look on his face. Donnie was confused. "What's up Jimmy, is something wrong?" Donnie asked concerned. "Where's Danny?"

"He's gone."

"Gone? What do you mean?"

"He's gone, his parents showed up last night and they left for California first thing this morning. He told me to tell you goodbye and thanks for being a good friend. He said he'd write us when he got home and see how we are doing."

"Wow, we've been hanging out so much I kinda forgot he was just here for the summer. I never really thought about him going back to California."

"Yeah, it was a surprise to him too. They just showed up. We wanted to come over and see you but it was late and they left so early we couldn't."

The boys just sat in silence for a moment not knowing what to say. Finally Donnie broke the silence.

"I guess it's getting close to school starting, about three weeks or so."

"Man this summer went by fast."

"Yeah, it went by crazy fast."

The boys hung out in the fort after supper, but it wasn't the same. As the days past they met at the fort less and less. It wasn't long and summer was over and they went back to school.

Chapter Two

Donald and Jimmy were still close friends. They palled around at school and always ate lunch together. Sometimes on weekends they would spend the night at the fort. One night the boys met up at the fort both toting their sleeping bags.

"Check it out," Jimmy said. "We got a postcard from Danny," He said as he pulled the postcard out of his back pocket.

"What did he say?"

"Not much really, just that everything is good and he's hoping to come visit us in the summer, if he can. Here, you wanna read it?"

"Yeah, let me see it," Donnie said as he grabbed the post card from Jimmy's hand. He read it silently to himself. "He said he'd write. I really didn't think he was going to. I thought he'd forget all about us once he was back in California with his friends."

"He will. I doubt we'll ever see or hear from him again."

The boys went to school day in and day out, working on their dad's farms. They'd spend the occasional night at the fort on the weekend. They played games and talked about school. They talked about kids and teachers they didn't like. Being teenage boys they talked about girls, of course. They'd go back and forth telling each other who they liked and who they thought liked them.

The school year went on as usual, typical small town life. School and work ate up most of the boy's time and before they knew it the school year was coming to an end. It was summer again and the boys were glad about that. They hung out at the fort more often. They stayed up late playing cards and board games. They told jokes and went on about girls they had crushes on. Then one day Jimmy heard something outside the fort.

"Shhhh! You hear that?" Jimmy said tilting his head like a dog.

Donnie looked at him and laughed. "You're hearing things," He said with a little laugh.

"Shut up and listen."

Donnie got quiet and listened. "I do hear something, its music."

"Yeah it's getting louder."

The boys got up and went out the fort door. They saw a car approaching the fort with rock music blasting out the windows leaving a trail of dust on the farm road behind it. The car stopped and the door opened and out popped Danny. The boys were shocked. They ran over to greet him.

"What's up guys," Danny said giving the boys bear hugs.

"What are you doing here?" Donnie asked.

"I told you guys I was gonna come see you."

"You drove all the way down here to visit?" Jimmy asked.

"Well there is a little more to it than that," Danny said waving at the car, motioning someone to get out.

The boys just looked at the car confused.

"Last week my Aunt called my dad to get Jimmy's Dad's number," He said, once again motioning to the car. "She started asking me about the farm and told me she wanted to send her daughter there to teach her a lesson. She was going to send her here on a bus, but I offered to drive her if she'd give me some gas money. I really didn't think she'd do it but she said okay and here we are." He motioned to the car again. "She's a little pissed off, she don't want to be here at all. I think the only reason my Aunt agreed to me bringing her is cause I asked what if she just gets off on the next stop." He motioned to the car one more time this time yelling, "Come here!"

The cars passenger side door open and a young girl about fifteen or sixteen stepped out. Donnie looked at her and his jaw nearly hit the ground." Man she's beautiful," Donnie whispered to Danny.

"I guess she is kind of cute, I never really gave it much thought, her being my cousin and all," Danny said. "Tracy, this is your cousin Jimmy and his best friend Donnie."

"Hey," She said unenthused.

"Where did you get the wheels?" Jimmy asked excitedly.

"I bought it. Well, I'm buying it off my buddy's older brother. It's cool as hell, huh?"

"Heck yeah!" Donnie said.

"It's a '78 Camero. It's a little dinged up in a few spots but she runs great. I've been working at this carwash after school. I've already gave him Five Hundred dollars, another Five and it's all mine."

"That's awesome," Jimmy said. Tracy just rolled her eyes as to say who cares.

"I'm gonna take her to your house, your Dad is expecting us sometime today."

"He never said anything to me," Jimmy said.

Danny just shrugged his shoulders and said," I'll be right back." He and Tracy got in the car and drove off.

"Man, your cousin sure is pretty."

"Whatever."

"You don't think so?"

"She's my cousin!"

"She's still pretty."

"I guess, I was more impressed with the car," Jimmy said. "It looks and sounds fast."

"Yeah it is cool."

It wasn't long and the boys heard the rumble of the Camero's V8 coming up the dirt road by the farm. Danny pulled up to the fort and got out.

"I can't believe this is yours," Donnie said.

"I know I've had it for almost two months now and I can hardly believe it myself."

"How did you talk your parents into letting you drive all the way out here?" Jimmy asked

"They have been real cool to me now that I'm staying out of trouble and have a job. Plus I've had my license for a year and a half already. I drive my Mom around all the time, she hates to drive. It also didn't hurt that my Mom is real close to my Aunt Deb and she really needed a way to get Tracy down here. She keeps getting in trouble at school and when she got caught shoplifting that was the final straw."

"She sure is pretty. How old is she?" Donnie asked smiling.

"She's fifteen I think, but relax Romeo, she's a real bitch. She had nothing but a crappy attitude the whole way here."

"You weren't too happy about coming here either, if I remember right."

"Yeah, but I didn't take it out on anybody else."

"Yeah, but you didn't have anybody to take it out on."

"I guess you're right. Either way I'm just glad to not be cooped up in the car with her anymore," Danny said. He opened the trunk of the

10

car. "Check this out," He said as he pulled out a twelve pack of beer from under a blanket. "It's warm. It's been in the trunk for twelve hundred miles."

"We have plenty of ice at the house." Jimmy said.

"We'll put it on ice and drink tonight. I'm going to have to leave tomorrow, the next day at the very latest."

"Wow I thought you'd stay at least a week," Donnie said.

"I can't. I have a job to get back to. I gotta keep up on the payments if I wanna keep the car. The dude is cool enough to let me drive it before it's paid off. I don't want to mess that up."

"That makes sense," Donnie said.

"I'll drive you home Jimmy so you can get ice and I gotta get some sleep. Sound good?"

"Yeah, let's go," Jimmy said." I'll be back in a little while Donnie."

"Alright, I'll go to the barn and get an old ice chest we have stored in there."

Later that evening the boys all met up at the fort to drink some cold beer and catch up on what's been going on with each other over the past year.

"What's up with your hair?" Donnie asked Danny.

"It's pretty long, huh?" Danny said. "I'm not a skin anymore. I'm still friends with some of the guys but with work and all. I'm just doing my own thing now."

"It's real long for only growing it a year," Jimmy said.

"Yeah, my hair grows real fast it always has. I don't know why but it grows fast."

"No more praising Hitler and preaching white power and all that?" Donnie asked.

"Nah, I mean don't get me wrong I'm proud to be white and all, but the whole idea of stereo typing people by race seems kind of silly to me anymore."

"What changed your mind?" Jimmy asked.

"I work with these guys at the carwash who are Mexican and Black and this Asian cat and I learn all kinds of shit from them. Most of them go to college and are really smart. The Asian dude really blows my mind how smart he is. I've asked him what the hell he's doing working at a carwash and he told me he does it cause he's bored. He doesn't even need the money. He builds computers or writes code for computer programs or something like that I couldn't possibly begin to understand."

"So he goes to work just for the hell of it?"

"Yeah, he says it helps him unwind. He doesn't have to think, it gives him something to do but his brain gets a rest. When he sits around he can't stop thinking computer shit."

"Weird."

"In a way but it kind of makes sense if you think about it."

"I guess."

"Man I got a buzz off this beer," Donnie said.

"Yeah I do too. I don't drink very often. I'm usually driving my mom around or at work. I never really have any free time to drink," Danny said.

"I wish you could stay longer," Donnie said.

"Yeah, me too," Jimmy said.

"Yeah, I'd like to, but I can't."

"We know it's just nice having you around again, that's all."

"Well let's enjoy it while I'm here."

The next day Danny took off for California. The boys met up at the fort to hang out for a while. They got to the fort and just sat there in silence for a moment. Finally Jimmy broke the silence. "My cousin wants to come over and check out our fort. I told her I had to check with you first."

"Yeah, she can come."

"I'm sure she just wants a place to hide from my dad now and then. If he sees her sitting around too much he'll put her to work. He's good at finding something for you to do."

"That's okay. How do you like her? Is she cool?"

"This is the first time I met her, she seems alright. She's real quiet."

"Does she have a boyfriend?"

"I don't know! I told you she hardly even talks. You can ask her yourself. I'll bring her with me tomorrow."

The next day, just as he said, Jimmy showed up at the fort with Tracy in-tow. Donnie was already there. He was in nice, clean clothes with his hair combed neatly and a big smile on his face. Jimmy took one look at him and rolled his eyes. "Tracy this is Donnie, Donnie Tracy."

"Nice to meet you, Tracy," Donnie said as he stepped forward and extended his hand to her. She grabbed his hand and they shook.

"Nice to meet you too," Tracy said in a sweet little voice that melted Donnie's heart.

"So, you're from Arizona?" Donnie asked.

"Yeah, I live in Sunnyslope, it's a little area in North Phoenix."

"You like it there?"

"Yeah, all my friends are there. I've lived there my whole life."

"I bet you wish you were there right now."

"Yeah I do! This place sucks. I hate waking up at the crack of dawn to do this and do that. That's all my Uncle does is work, work, work. It gets kind of old after a while."

"Well you can come hang out with us anytime you want."

"That's awesome. I need a place to hideout sometimes."

"This place is good for that. You can come here anytime you need to get away. It doesn't matter if we are here or not, right Jimmy?"

"Yeah whatever, I don't care," Jimmy said kind of distracted. "Crap! I gotta go to the house I forgot to do something I'll be back in a little while. You wanna come with me Tracy?"

"I'll just stay here if that's alright."

"Yeah you can stay," Donnie interrupted.

"I'll be back," Jimmy said once again rolling his eyes heading out the door.

Tracy sat there looking around the room. She saw beer cans lying all over and a big swastika painted on the wall, "What do you guys do out here party all the time?"

"No, Danny brought that beer with him."

"Got any left?"

Donnie looked down at the ground wishing to himself they had saved a couple beers. "No, we drank it all last night with Danny."

"Oh well, I have this," Tracy said as she pulled a baggie of marijuana from her bra. "Do you smoke?" She asked.

"I never have."

"We can smoke some if you want, but you can't tell Jimmy. If it gets back to my Uncle he'll surely tell my parents and I'll be in big trouble."

"I won't tell him. I promise," Donnie said as he made an x over his heart.

Tracy took some rolling papers out of the baggie and rolled a joint. She put the joint in her mouth and reached in her pocket. She wiggled around a bit working her hand into the pocket of her tight jeans as the joint dangled from her mouth. Donnie couldn't help staring as her breasts jiggling as she wiggled. She noticed him looking and smiled. Donnie got red in the face. She got the lighter out and lit the joint. She took a big toke and handed it to Donnie. "You gotta hold it in," She muttered trying not to exhale.

Donnie took the joint and put it to his lips and inhaled deeply. He immediately started coughing uncontrollably. Tracy burst out laughing. "Try it again inhale slower this time and try to hold it in," She said with a little giggle at the end.

Donnie took another drag without coughing this time. He exhaled a big plume of smoke and then the coughing came, not as bad though.

"There you go you got it," She said with a big smile.

Next thing they knew they were both rolling around on the floor laughing. They were telling each other stories from school and jokes and just laughing away. After about twenty minutes of stories and giggling Jimmy popped in the door. He looked at the two of them on the floor. "What the hell are you guys doing?" He asked. They both looked up at him and froze not knowing what to say. They looked at each other and started cracking up. "Are you guys high?" He asked. "Is that pot I smell?"

It wasn't long and they were all sitting around the table smoking another joint. They were all laughing and carrying on in the smoke filled fort. Then Tracy looked at Jimmy all serious and said, "You better not say anything to your Dad about me having weed."

"What? And get my ass beat for smoking it with you?" he said.

Tracy just looked at him a moment and they all burst out laughing again as they did throughout the night.

The next day Donnie walked into the fort and Tracy was there. She was sitting at the table playing a game of solitaire with an old deck of cards.

"Hi Donnie, I hope you don't mind me hanging out in here when you guys are not here. I just need to hide out sometimes, you know?"

"No problem. You can hang out anytime."

"Oh yeah, you said that yesterday. I'm kind of a space cadet sometimes."

14

"That's okay I am too."

"You're cute Donnie. I bet all the girls at school are after you. Do you have a girlfriend?"

"Nnno, no girlfriend," Donnie stuttered, blushing, his face as red as a tomato.

Tracy scooted her chair closer to Donnie and grabbed his hand, giving it a little squeeze. "Maybe I could be your girlfriend," She said in her sweet little voice as she laid her head on Donnie's shoulder.

"Yeah, okay, I means yes," Donnie said, stuttering nervously.

Tracy giggled and hugged his arm tightly. "Relax," She said as she gave him a little kiss on the cheek. The next thing you know she was sitting on his lap and they were making out. Donnie slipped his hand under her shirt. He happily noticed she wasn't wearing a bra. He caressed one of her breasts as he kissed her deeply. Just then Jimmy came barging in the door.

"Oh man," He exclaimed. "Come up for air you two. My dad is looking for you. He seems pretty pissed off," Jimmy said looking toward Tracy.

"Oh well," Tracy said as she fixed her shirt and got off Donnie's lap.

Jimmy just looked at her in disbelief. He didn't know what to say to that. He sat there a moment, thinking to himself. "Well you'd better come back with me and see what he wants. The longer you wait the madder he is going to get. I'm just saying…"

"You better go. I don't want you getting into trouble," Donnie said interrupting Jimmy.

"Okay, let's go," Tracy said in a frustrated tone. She pecked Donnie on the lips and said, "I'll be back in a little while."

Tracy and Jimmy left the fort. Donnie just sat there with a big grin on his face. He couldn't believe what just happened. He waited and waited but Tracy did not return. Finally it got so late he walked back to his house and went to bed.

He went to the fort for the next three days. He waited and waited again but she never showed. On the fourth day he decided he had, had enough. He walked through the tree line and headed towards Jimmy's house. He made his way up to the porch. He climbed the few stairs and knocked on the door. Jimmy answered the door. "What's up Donnie?" He asked.

"Where have you guys been?"

"We've been busy. My dad has been working us like dogs. Tracy is grounded. I told her just to work hard and be nice for a few days and my dad will ease up on her."

"How long is she grounded for?"

"I don't know he didn't really say. I stayed here to help her get things done. I should have came and told you what was going on."

"Yeah that would have been nice."

"Well I thought you'd figure she was in trouble. Sorry I should have made it over. We've just been working so hard I've been tired."

"That's okay. Where is she? Can you go get her?"

"I better not, she's grounded. Give it a couple more days and we'll meet you at the fort. Trust me, I know my dad."

"Okay, come to the fort on Saturday."

"Saturday sounds good. If she still can't come I'll be there and let you know what's going on. I'll see you then."

"Alright," Donnie said disappointedly. He turned and stepped off the porch as the door shut behind him. He heard a tapping on an upstairs window. He looked up to see Tracy staring down at him. She held up her index finger signaling for him to wait. She disappeared from the glass pane. Shortly after she returned and Donnie heard the window sliding open slowly. She only opened it a few inches. A paper airplane came flying out of the window and landed nose first into the ground. He hurried over to the plane and unfolded it.

Meet me at the fort

10 pm

Bring a sleeping bag

Tracy

He looked up at the window with a big smile. He nodded his head and gave Tracy a thumbs up. He took off running towards the tree line. He was grinning from ear to ear. He ran all the way home. He was so excited. He got home and was out of breath. He sat on his own porch for a minute to calm down. He pulled out the note and read it again. He chuckled to himself thinking what the hell was I running for?

Dinner time came and went. Donnie went and took a bath. He got out of the tub and got dressed. He went to his room and waited. He paced back and forth looking at the clock every five minutes. It was only 8:45 time was crawling. He took out his sleeping bag and unrolled it on his bed. He then went downstairs. He dug around in a kitchen drawer where he found some candles and a box of matches. He went to the refrigerator opened the door and took four Mountain Dews out and headed back upstairs.

He laid the box of matches, the candles and the sodas on the sleeping bag. He opened his nightstand drawer and pulled out a flashlight. He clicked it on and off making sure it worked. He then pulled his watch out of the same drawer and clasped it to his wrist. He read the time 8:58 and sighed. "Screw it," he said to himself out loud as he rolled the downstairs items into the sleeping bag. He snatched up the flashlight, threw the sleeping bag over his shoulder and headed out to the fort.

He arrived at the fort and looked at his watch. "Damn it," He muttered under his breath, it was only 9:17. He unrolled the sleeping bag and put the sodas and candles on the table. He picked up the box of matches pulled one out and lit it. He used the match light to find a partial candle left over from the last sleepover at the fort. He found it and lit it. He just sat at the table staring at the flame.

He was so anxious to see Tracy. He paced back and forth in the small fort. To make matters worse he caught himself glancing at his watch every five minutes again. "A watched clock never moves," He said to himself and continued pacing. It didn't do any good he continued to torture himself with his repeated eyeing of the watch. Finally it was 9:59 and Donnie was staring at the watch. Watching the dots blink counting down the seconds. The watch changed to 10:00 and Donnie threw a fist in the air in celebration. His celebration is short lived when he realizes he's not waiting for 10:00 he's waiting for Tracy, who still isn't there.

He goes back to pacing. He looked like an expectant Father inside a hospital waiting room, back and forth, to and fro. He doesn't want to but he looks at his watch again, it reads 10:21. He thought he heard a noise so he got really quiet and listened. He heard footsteps approaching the fort and Tracy popped her head in the door. "Sorry I took so long. Have you been waiting long?" She asked.

"No not long," He said trying to play it cool.

"I had a hard time sneaking out. The quieter I tried to be the louder I was. At least it seemed that way to me."

"Why are you whispering?"

"Oh," Tracy laughed. "I forgot I don't have to be quiet anymore." They both started laughing.

"I brought some sodas from my house if you are thirsty," Donnie said pointing to the Mountain Dew cans on the table.

"Cool, Mountain Dew is my favorite," She said as she popped the top of one of the cans and took a drink. "You have been here a while."

"Why do you say that?"

"I'm sure this soda was colder than this when you got here," She said and took another drink.

"You got me. I've been here about an hour."

"Yeah?" She said as she walked closer to him. "Were you that anxious to see me?"

Donnie was thankful the candlelight hid how much he was blushing. "Yeah, I was......" Before he could finish his sentence she was kissing him. They laid down on the sleeping bag and continued to make out.

"Have you ever done it before?" Tracy asked

"Have you?"

"I asked you first."

"No, I haven't" Donnie said sounding kind of embarrassed.

"That's okay."

"Have you?"

"Only twice, last summer, I had a boyfriend from school."

"What happened to him?"

"His dad got a job and he moved away. They moved to Connecticut."

"That sucks."

"Yeah, I cried for a whole week."

"Do you still talk to him?"

"He used to write me but, he hasn't in a long time. He probably forgotten all about me by now I'm sure."

"Do you miss him?"

18

She kissed him long and hard. "You're my boyfriend now." With that being said they were at it again, making out on the sleeping bag, rolling around. She pulled his shirt over his head in between kisses. He slid his hand under her shirt and was surprised to feel a bra. He slipped his hand under the bra feeling her soft breast. As he moved his hand he felt something. He pulled his hand out from under her shirt. Pinched between two of his fingers was a cellophane bag dangling back and forth.

"Oh, I forgot I still have a little weed left. Want to smoke some?"

"Maybe later," He said tossing the baggie to the side. He peeled her shirt off and started fumbling around with the clasp on the back of the bra.

"Let me help," she whispered, unfastening the bra with ease. Donnie's eyes got wide as the bra dropped down, revealing two perky breasts lit by the shimmering flame of the candle. He goes in kissing her neck, working his way down to her nipple. 'Bip,bip,bip,bip,' he hears as he pulls to the side the top of her button fly jeans. He continues to kiss her breasts occasionally working his way to her neck and back. He slid his hand down feeling her smooth silk panties. She arches her back and he slides her Levi's down her legs. She tackles him, rolling him on his back and unfastens his belt and pants, pulling them off. She laid down on top of him and started kissing him hard and deeply as she reached down and pulled his boxer shorts down with one hand.

He slid his hands down her back hooking his thumbs in the elastic of her panties and slid them over her ass. She stood up letting the panties fall to her ankles stepping one foot out and kicking them away with the other. She knelt down and pulled Donnie's boxers down and over his feet tossed them to the side and said, "We won't be needing those." She laid back down on top of him and started kissing him some more. Sensing he didn't know what to do, she rolled him over on top of her. She reached down and grabbed his penis and inserted it inside herself. She whispered into his ear. "Push it in me." Donnie obeyed and after about five or six pumps he let out a moan. She pulled him tight to her, kissed his ear and whispered, "Don't worry I'm on the pill."

"I'm not worried about anything right now." He said.

Tracy laughed and said," Congratulations, you're not a virgin anymore."

"That was awesome," He said and kissed her.

They got dressed. "Do you want to smoke the rest of my weed?" Tracy asked.

"No I'm good."

"Well can I leave it here in the fort?"

"Are you leaving?"

"Yes, I have to. I gotta sneak back in. I can't risk falling asleep out here and getting caught."

"Okay," He said as he grabbed the baggie out of her hand. He opened the lid to a Monopoly board game and put it inside. "It will be in here," He said as he put the lid back on and put the box back on the shelf made of stacked milk crates.

"Cool," She said. She grabbed her soda off the table and took a big drink finishing what was left in the can. "I gotta go," She said.

He grabbed her and kissed her. "Come and see me as soon as you can."

"I will," She said and took off out the door.

Donnie just leaned back in his chair with his hands on the back of his head and just smiled.

Chapter Three

The next day Donnie woke up feeling like a million bucks. His mother made a big breakfast and he finished all his chores early. He was having a great day. Of course it couldn't compare to yesterday but it was a good start. He made his way down to the fort. He brought a roll of trash bags and some cleaning supplies. He figured the fort was due for a good cleaning.

He started picking up beer cans and trash off the floor. He reached out for what he thought was a crumbled up piece of paper. When he grabbed it he felt it was soft to the touch. He quickly realized they were Tracy's panties. He held them up to his face inhaling deeply through his nose. He smelled the intoxicating aroma of Tracy's perfume.

"What are you doing," A loud voice asked from the door behind him. Donnie startled nearly jumped out of his skin.

"Na..nothing," Donnie said hiding his hand behind his back.

It's Jimmy. "What are you hiding back there?" He asked as he walked over to him. Jimmy quickly reached behind Donnie's back and snatched the panties from his grip. He took one look at them and his eyes got wide. His mouth fell open in disbelief. "Did you?..."

Donnie looked him in the eye and just nodded his head yes. He could feel his face was red and he was smiling from ear to ear.

"When?"

"Last night, she snuck out of the house and met me here."

"Bullshit, I would have heard her."

"I swear."

"You guys did it?"

"Yes we did. But don't tell her I told you."

"I won't, what was it like?"

"It was frickin' awesome! I don't even know how to explain it."

"I can't believe my dad didn't hear her sneaking out, or sneaking back in."

"He didn't. I'm so happy he didn't. I can't believe it! I had sex."

"You're lucky," Jimmy said giving Donnie a little punch in the arm.

"I'm lucky you showed up. Now you can help me clean this pig sty up."

"I suppose." Jimmy said as he started picking up cans. They got the fort cleaned up and went their separate ways.

A couple days later Tracy showed up at the fort. The boys were already there playing cards. "Hey guys what's up?" She asked. "Hey boyfriend," She said and kissed Donnie on the cheek and smiled. She sat down at the table. "What are you playing?" She asked.

"Rummy," Jimmy said concentrating on his cards. Donnie just sat there staring at Tracy with love in his eyes. "It's your turn," Jimmy said waving his hand in front of Donnie's face, trying to break the spell.

Donnie just ignored him staring into Tracy's eyes and smiling. He laid his cards down on the table. He stood up and walked over to Tracy. He knelt down and kissed her. Not just a peck either, a full on French tongue twister. One of those I just got back from the war type kisses. "I'm outta here," Jimmy said as he tossed his cards onto the table in disgust.

"Jimmy don't go!" Tracy yelled as the door shut. "Let's smoke some weed!"

It was no use he had stormed off and was probably halfway home by now.

"Let him go. I want to be alone with you," Donnie said. He started kissing her and rubbing on her. They made their way down to the floor, onto the sleeping bag. It was laid out on the floor still. It looked like a shrine with unlit candles place around it. Donnie had even brought a pillow from the house.

"Wow, you cleaned this place up."

"I can't have our little love nest looking a mess."

"Our love nest, I like that," Tracy said and giggled.

They peeled their clothes off and had sex again. When they were done they laid there holding each other. "What did you mean when you said you were on the pill?" Donnie asked.

"Birth control pills, my parents freaked out when they found out I had sex. They made me go to the doctor. They insisted I get put on birth control."

"How did they know? I mean how did they find out you had sex?"

"My boyfriend had given me a note at school and my mom found it in my pants when she did the laundry. It was pretty obvious reading the note."

"Were your parents mad?"

"My dad was, but my mom was a little more understanding. She got my dad to come around after a while. After a month or so he let me leave the house again."

"A month, holy crap!"

"Yeah I spent a lot of last summer cooped up at home being lectured on diseases and teen age pregnancy," Tracy said. "That's how I mastered the art of sneaking out of the house."

They smoked the rest of the pot from the Monopoly game. They sat at the table laughing and talking for the next couple hours. "You know I found your underwear when I was cleaning up."

"I thought you might want to keep them as a souvenir."

"Oh, you aren't getting them back," Donnie said. They both started laughing. After a while they said their goodbyes and headed home for the night.

That summer went by fast. Donnie was having the time of his life. Then the day came. The day he'd been dreading had arrived. Tracy showed up at the fort with a sad look on her face. She was holding a letter. She stood there looking at Donnie not saying a word.

"What's the matter?"

"My parents are coming to get me and take me back to Phoenix."

"When?"

"They will be here this weekend."

Donnie just looked at her and a tear rolled down his cheek. Almost ready to start crying herself, Tracy said, "Don't do that you're gonna make me start crying." They hugged each other tightly and both started balling like a couple of babies. They cried like the world was coming to an end. Finally Tracy pulled away. "This is stupid. We have two whole days, let's not waste them crying," She said wiping the tears off her cheeks.

"I love you," Donnie said.

"You do?"

"I really do."

"I love you too Donnie."

They stayed at the fort as much as they could for the next two days. Then one day she was gone. Donnie was devastated. He mopped around the house doing his chores in a daze of depression. About a week passed and he received a postcard in the mail. It had a picture of a giant cactus that fell on a car crushing it in the driveway. He turned it over and read it.

Hey Donnie,

Everything is good, started school

Miss you something awful! Love you. Love Tracy.

The card was neatly typed. It was short but he didn't care he was just happy to hear from her. He pinned it on the wall next to his bed. They wrote back and forth for a while. At first the letters came often they seemed to be writing each other every day. Donnie saved all the letters he kept them in a shoe box, he had quite a few. As time went on the letters came further and further apart. After a while they stopped coming all together. He thought about Tracy all the time. After writing her three times and not getting a letter back he stopped writing.

Donnie brought the box of letters out to the fort and every once in a while he would go and read them. He would reminisce about him and Tracy. He missed her so much. Donnie and Jimmy were still good friends but other than school they didn't hang out as often. He had plenty of time to think about Tracy.

Jimmy had met a girl at school. He spent most of his time with her. Donnie would still eat lunch with Jimmy at school. The only difference was Brenda was always there. Brenda was Jimmy's girlfriend and Donnie liked her, they got along fine. Just every now and then they would start playing kissy face and Donnie finally understood how Jimmy felt during the summer. He was now the third wheel.

One day after school Donnie was done with his chores early. He was bored and whenever he got bored he always thought of Tracy. He decided he'd go read some old letters and walked out to the fort. He walked into the fort and almost had a heart attack when a girl started screaming at the top of her lungs. It was Brenda. Donnie had walked in on them having sex.

"Sorry," Donnie said covering his eyes with his hands. He could hear them scurrying around trying to get their clothes on. Jimmy was laughing the whole time.

Donnie could hear Brenda smacking Jimmy. "It's not funny," She said as she gave him one more hit to the chest and stormed out the fort. Donnie uncovered his eyes and he and Jimmy just burst out laughing.

"Way to go Jimmy!"

"Yeah we've been getting it on for a few weeks now."

"You know one day I came out here and was lying down and thought the pillowcase smelled like laundry soap. I thought that was weird."

"She makes me wash it every time, the sleeping bag too. If I don't she won't lay on it."

"That's a Small price to pay."

"Hell, I'd knit one every time if that's what it took," Jimmy said. They both burst out laughing.

"I better go catch up with her," Jimmy said and ran out the door.

Chapter Four

After the incident at the fort, Donnie didn't go there often. When he did he made sure he was loud and would announce he was there before he entered. The school year seemed long and drawn out. Jimmy was always with Brenda so they didn't hang out after school or on weekends like they used to. Whenever Donnie wasn't working or doing homework he drove himself crazy thinking about Tracy. He wondered what she was doing. He was beginning to think she had forgotten all about him.

One day Donnie came home from school and he noticed an envelope on the kitchen table. He picked it up and seen it was addressed to him. There was no return address on the envelope. He slid his finger under the flap and ripped the envelope open. Happy Birthday was written on the front of a card with a picture of a birthday cake under the letters. He opened the card and a piece of paper fell out onto his lap. "Wishing you a joyous day and hoping all your birthday wishes come true." He read out loud, quietly to himself. Then he read the last two words these were handwritten, Love Tracy. She remembered my birthday he thought to himself and smiled.

He picked up the paper from his lap. It was lined paper and looked as if it was torn from a small notebook. He unfolded it and read. I haven't forgotten you Donnie! I have a lot going on right now. I got myself in trouble. I will send you an address to write me as soon as I can, Love Tracy. He stared at the note for a moment. His mind began to race. He started thinking of all different kinds of scenarios. Then he got excited. If she was in trouble maybe her parents would send her back to the farm, he thought.

He looked at the birthday card again. It had slipped his mind that his birthday was so close. He was so busy with school and working on the farm and thinking about Tracy he simply forgot. He couldn't believe he had basically forgotten about his own birthday. Then he started to worry about Tracy. He wondered what kind of trouble she was in. He tossed and turned that night until he finally fell asleep.

The next day he woke up and got ready for school. He ate breakfast and headed to school. He saw Jimmy and Brenda and asked, "Have you heard anything about Tracy?"

"No, why is something wrong?"

"I don't know. She sent me a birthday card with a note saying she was in some kind of trouble."

"I haven't heard anything."

"I was hoping her parents would send her back here for the summer again."

"My Dad hasn't said anything to me. Not that he tells me anything anyway."

"I'm worried about her. Let me know if you hear anything, okay?"

"I will. I wouldn't worry you know how girls are everything is a big deal. It's probably nothing."

"Hey, I'm right here you know!" Brenda said and punched Jimmy in the arm.

"Yeah she probably broke a nail or something." Donnie said and laughed a little. He tried to be lighthearted but deep down he felt it was a little more serious than that.

Donnie's birthday arrived. His parents had gotten him a cake. It was his favorite chocolate cake with chocolate frosting. They also gave him a card. When he opened the card a crisp new one hundred dollar bill went floating to the floor. "Wow, a hundred bucks!" Donnie exclaimed.

"You deserve it son. You're a big help around here and you're doing good in school."

"Thanks Dad."

"We are very proud of you," Donnie's Mother said as she leaned in and kissed him on the cheek.

"Thanks Mom."

"No work today son, you enjoy yourself," Donnie's Father said as he rustled Donnie's hair.

After dinner Donnie went to the fort. He told Jimmy he'd meet him there earlier at school that day. When he arrived at the fort Jimmy was already there. "Happy Birthday buddy," Jimmy said as he lit the one and five shaped candles on the top of an odd shaped cake. It was tall but not very long and not very wide. It didn't look like it would fit in any cake pan Donnie ever saw.

"Blow out the candles and cut you a piece," Jimmy said as he handed Donnie a knife. "I made it myself," He added. "Don't forget to make a wish."

Donnie closed his eyes and blew out the two candles. After a short pause, to make his wish he opened his eyes. Donnie raised the knife to cut a piece of cake. The knife cut through the top layer of frosting with ease. Suddenly the knife hit something hard. Donnie pushed the knife attempting to cut the odd shaped cake. Dit, dit, dit, dit the knife sounded like a saw cutting through a two by four. Jimmy started to laugh. Donnie scraped the knife across the cake revealing it was actually a twelve pack of beer. Jimmy had wrapped the box in tin foil and frosted it.

"That was a good one," Donnie said, "How'd you get the beer?"

"Brenda's brother bought it for me. He told me about the tin foil and frosting trick too."

"Where is Brenda?"

"I thought it should just be us bros for your birthday."

"Cool."

"Speaking of Brenda, her friend said you were cute and wants to meet you."

"Who's her friend?"

"Gina."

"Gina Miller?"

"Yeah, I think that's her name, the one that was talking to Brenda last week at lunch."

"She's actually good looking."

"Yeah, she's cute and she's got pretty big tits for a fifteen year old."

"Yeah but I don't know."

"You gotta quit with this Tracy thing. I get it you lost your virginity to her and you love her and all that. But face it, you never know if you're gonna see her again."

"I'll see her again."

"Look man, I'm just telling you how it is. You don't know for sure you'll ever see her again."

"I know I will someday."

"Maybe someday, but what about now, Do you think she's putting her life on hold for you?"

"No, I guess not. You're probably right."

"Of course I am. If you see Tracy again you can get back with her. It's not like I'm asking you to marry Gina."

"Yeah, you're right."

"I wish we had some money we could go out on a double date."

"We do," Donnie said as he reached in his pocket and pulled out the hundred dollar bill.

"Whoa, where did you get that?"

"Birthday money," Donnie said.

"I can't have you spending your birthday money on me and Brenda."

"Why not, what else am I going to spend it on?"

"I don't know it don't seem right."

"It's my money. Besides, I need you to borrow your Dad's truck. You know my Dad only lets me drive on the farm."

"Alright, I'll set it up," Jimmy said as he dumped the twelve pack of beer into the ice chest. As the cans fell into the chest, water splashed up and hit him on the face. Donnie started to laugh. Jimmy spit and wiped his face with the sleeve of his shirt. "Damn it, we've been yapping so long the ice is all melted."

"I'll go get some from the house," Donnie said as he headed towards the door still chuckling a little bit.

"Hurry back."

"I will."

Fifteen minutes later Donnie showed back up at the fort with a trash bag of ice, a couple cans of Mountain Dew and some real birthday cake. "Jimmy," he yelled. "Where are you?" There was no answer. He was gone. I wonder where he went he thought to himself. Donnie put the sodas into the chest with the beers floating on the icy water. He ripped open the thrash bag of ice and dumped it over the cans.

"Ten minutes later Jimmy came through the door huffing and puffing. Clearly he ran all the way to his house and back. "I called Brenda and told her to call Gina. She said she would." He said in between deep breaths.

"Cool, you want a piece of cake?"

"Hell yeah, I do."

"Let's play rummy while the beer chills."

"Okay, I'm going to run back to the house in about a half an hour and call Brenda back."

"Sounds good, there's some cold soda in with the beer. I thought I'd bring some so my parents wouldn't wonder what the ice was for."

"Good thinking, I'm dying of thirst from running," he said and got a can of soda from the chest. The boys sat down and played cards for the next thirty minutes. Then Jimmy went running off to his house again. He returned huffing and puffing again. He had another trash bag with some ice in it over his shoulder. He opened the chest grabbed a beer and threw it to Donnie. He grabbed another one and wiped it across his forehead. "Whew," he said as he popped the top and took a drink of the cold beer. "It's all set," he said as he dragged the ice chest to the door. "Double date tomorrow night," Jimmy said, still a little out of breath.

"Tomorrow," Donnie said surprised.

"Yeah, Brenda called Gina and she said she could go out tomorrow, it's Saturday. I asked my Dad if I could use the truck tomorrow and he said yes." Jimmy popped open the drain on the side of the ice chest hanging out the doorway. He dumped the bag of ice into it as the water trickled out the door.

"Where we gonna take 'em?"

"I don't know we got all night to figure that out, don't worry."

"That's true," Donnie said as he took another drink of beer and lit a candle sitting on the table. They stayed up late drinking beer, playing games and trading stories.

They woke up the next morning a little hung over. Jimmy started shaking out the sleeping bag and rolling it up.

"What are you doing?"

"I'm taking this home to wash it, just in case," he said with a wink. "I'll go home and check the old man's newspaper and see what movies are playing."

"Okay, I'm going home to eat some breakfast. I kind of have a headache."

"Me too, meet me back here in a couple of hours."

"Okay."

The boys went home and ate. Jimmy checked the paper, washed the sleeping bag and gathered up a few odds and ends he thought might be useful at the fort. He showed up at the fort to find Donnie was already there. He was busy cleaning the place up.

"Wow, it looks good in here," Jimmy said as he placed a box on the table.

"What's in the box?"

"Oh not much, some old sheets, a blanket, some candles and some batteries."

"Good job, we need all that stuff. Did you bring the paper?"

"No, my Dad would rip my head off if I took his paper. I read it though."

"Did you find any good movies?"

"Yeah, there is a comedy, 'Weekend at Bernie's' starts at six."

"Sounds good, did you talk to Brenda at all?"

"No, her folks get pissed if I call before ten."

"Do they know you guys are doing it?"

"I don't know. I never thought about that. Why are you asking me that?"

"Never mind, what time should we go?"

"I think we should pick the girls up by four. That way we can go eat somewhere before the movie starts. What do you think?"

"I think four is perfect."

"I was gonna come and clean this place up, but you beat me to it."

"This fort was a good idea."

"The best idea we ever had. I'm going back home. When I come back do you want me to pick you up here or at your house?"

"Pick me up at the house. What do you think about three?"

"Yeah three, three thirty the latest," Jimmy said and glanced at his watch. "I'm going back home to iron out all the details with Brenda. Be ready to go at three."

"I'll be ready, see you then."

Jimmy pulled up to Donnie's house at three twenty. Donnie was ready and waiting on the porch. Donnie climbed into the cab of the pickup. "Man you smell good." Donnie said grinning.

"I used some of my Dad's after shave," Jimmy said as he took off down the dirt driveway. He left a trail of dust in his path. He made it to the road and turned right, heading to Brenda's house.

"I can't believe how smooth this is going. It was all on such short notice."

"Yeah, weird huh?" Just as soon as Jimmy got the words out of his mouth, boom! wap,wap,wap,wap. "Oh man, I guess we spoke too soon."

"What is it?"

"A flat tire," Jimmy muttered as he pulled the old Ford to the side of the road. "Don't worry my old man always has two spares. He keeps one underneath and one in the bed of the truck, always"

They got out of the truck. Jimmy leans the bench seat forward and grabs the jack and four way from behind the seat. He goes to the back right side of the truck. He squats down and starts loosening the lug nuts on the flat. Donnie starts positioning the jack under the truck and starts jacking it up. Jimmy notices out of the corner of his eye something flapping in the breeze. He walked over to a big rock on the side of the road and caught in the weeds in front of the rock he sees a twenty dollar bill. "All right," Jimmy yelled as he snatched up the bill from the weeds. "Check out what I found."

"Damn, that thing is dirty," Donnie said eyeing the bill Jimmy was holding up. "It looks like it's been there for ten years."

"It probably has."

"Luckiest flat tire I ever heard of."

"I'll say, looks like we can split the cost of the date now."

The boys drove to Brenda's house and picked her up. She gave them directions to Gina's house and they drove there. They all squeezed into the cab of the truck. They stopped and ate at a fast food restaurant, nothing fancy. Once they finished eating they headed to the movies.

Gina was shy, she didn't say much at all. The movie was funny and they all enjoyed it very much. Afterwards they all piled into the pickup and drove to the fort. They arrived at about 8:30 that's when Gina finally began to speak. "This place is cool," she said. "Did you guys build this?"

"Yeah, we built it with the help of Jimmy's cousin Danny."

"It looks well built, real sturdy," Gina said looking around and at the ceiling.

"My cousin knew construction, he was a big help," Jimmy said as he grabbed a sheet and started tacking it up.

"What are you doing?" Donnie asked.

"I'm hanging up a divider so we can have a little privacy," Jimmy said and gave Donnie a wink. "You guys can have this side and we'll go over there," He said as he took Brenda by the hand and led her back behind the sheet.

Donnie and Gina just sat there in an uncomfortable silence staring at their hands. Finally Gina broke the silence. "Wanna make out?" She asked awkwardly.

"Sure" Donnie said surprised.

Donnie moved closer to Gina and started to kiss her. He moved his hand up under her shirt and started sliding it up her side. Her arm quickly came down pushing his arm away. "Mmmt Mmm," she mumbled in the middle of a kiss. Not two seconds later they heard a loud smack from behind the sheet.

"I'm not doing that," Brenda yelled. "They are right there," she said as she came storming out from behind the sheet obviously mad. "Come on Gina let's go," she said shaking her head.

"Okay," Gina said shrugging her shoulders at Donnie as she followed Brenda out of the fort. A few seconds later the boys heard the truck door slam shut.

"I had to try," Jimmy said.

Donnie just started laughing. He tried to laugh quietly but couldn't. He hoped Brenda didn't hear him laughing. A minute later the horn started to honk. "I'm coming! Hold your horses!" Jimmy yelled out to the truck. "Are you coming with me to take the girls home?"

"I think it would be rude not to, don't you?"

"Yeah, it would. Maybe you can at least get a goodnight kiss."

"You think so?"

"Sure, a goodnight kiss is customary after a date," Jimmy said as he pulled his key ring out of his pocket and jingled them at Donnie. "Let's go."

They all piled into the pickup again. They dropped Brenda off first and then Gina. Donnie got a goodnight kiss and got back in the truck.

"See, it's tradition to kiss goodnight after a date," Jimmy said smugly.

"I already kissed her at the fort, dummy."

"I didn't know. Is she a good kisser?"

"Yeah, I liked it."

Jimmy pulled up to Donnie's house. "I'll see you tomorrow, buddy," He said as he stopped the truck.

"Alright, have a goodnight and thanks."

"You too, we'll have to do it again sometime when Brenda calms down."

Chapter Five

Once again it was summer. Jimmy and Brenda and Donnie and Gina are together quite a bit. They go to Gina's house a lot. Gina doesn't live on a farm she lives in a neighborhood. Her dad works at the coal mine and is hardly ever home. Her mom is there being a stay at home mom. They hang out at Gina's often because she has a pool. It's nothing fancy, just an above ground four foot pool, but it's a pool none the less.

They spend most of the summer either swimming at Gina's or hanging out at the fort. Despite Donnie's efforts he can't get Gina to have sex with him. He doesn't mind all that much. He likes her and enjoys hanging out with her playing kissy face and swimming at her house with Jimmy and Brenda. Gina's mother is very nice. She often made them sandwiches and lemonade when they came over to swim. That summer went by fast as summers tend to do when you're young and having fun.

School started back up without a hitch. Back to the same old routine school, chores and hanging out at the fort. Sometimes all of them would be there. Other times a couple would want the fort to themselves for a day. It was never Donnie and Gina of course. More often than not it would just be Donnie and Jimmy at the fort playing games and either complaining or bragging about what their girl would or wouldn't do.

"How's it going with Gina?" Jimmy asked.

"Okay, I guess."

"She still won't let you...you know?"

"Nah, but I did get to second base with her the other day."

"Hey progress is good."

"I guess. I still miss Tracy though."

"She hasn't written or anything?"

"Not a word."

"You're just gonna have to face in man. You are probably never going to see or hear from her again," Jimmy said in a serious tone.

Hell I probably won't ever hear from her again and she's my cousin."

"I hope you're wrong."

"I do too, but that's how it is man."

"I know."

The next day Brenda showed up at school with a guy nobody knew. He had long hair past his shoulders. He was wearing a Van Halen shirt with the sleeves cut off and he had a hole in one of the knees of his jeans. He had a little peach fuzz mustache and it looked like he had an earring in his left ear.

"This is my cousin Bobby," Brenda said. "It's his first day. He and his folks just moved down from Florence." Everyone said hi and introduced themselves to Bobby.

"Florence, that's up by Ohio isn't it?" Donnie asked.

"Yeah it's right by the border. Cincinnati is only about eight miles away," Bobby said.

"Why did you guys move down here?" Jimmy asked.

"My dad lost his job and Uncle David, I mean Brenda's Dad, said he could get him hired on at the mine."

"He and his folks are going to stay at my house for a while," Brenda said.

"It sucks having to move I bet," Donnie said.

"Yeah, I had to leave all my friends and start a new school and all that jazz. I'm going to miss going to the city, Cincinnati was a lot of fun."

"It's only about three and a half hours away," Brenda said.

"Yeah, if you have a car," Jimmy said.

"I have a car," Bobby said. Everyone just looked at him surprised for a moment, everyone, except for Brenda of course.

"What kind of car do you have?" Donnie asked.

"I have a '70 Chevelle," Bobby said with a smile. "My Grandfather left it to me when he died. It is a sweet ride."

"I can't wait to see it," Jimmy said.

"After school I'll give you guys a ride home and you can check it out."

After school they all met in the parking lot. There it was bigger than life, a shiny red Chevelle with black racing stripes running down the hood and trunk. The Crager rims let off a brilliant shine in the afternoon sun. Jimmy and Donnie just stood there in amazement staring at the car. Jimmy rubbed his hand across the roof, licked his lips and said, "Man this is right off the pages of Hot Rod Magazine."

Bobby opened the driver side door, got in and started the car. Vrooom, blub, blub, blub the eight cylinder motor came to life. He revved the engine a couple of times for good measure. "Get in!" He yelled over the rumble of the glass pack mufflers. They all piled into the car. Bobby put the car in gear and dumped the clutch. The tires lit up, smoke poured from the wheel wells and the car jetted across the parking lot.

"Woo Hoo!" Jimmy yelled out the window. "This thing is fast," he said looking in Bobby's direction. The rest of the group were in the back seat. They felt as if their heads were glued to the head rest. Bobby dropped them all off at their houses one by one.

The next day, Jimmy drove everybody crazy talking about the car. Every other word out of his mouth was Chevelle or car or hot rod. After a week of getting rides home the thrill was gone and things were back to normal. Bobby had no problem getting girls being one of the few boys at school with a car. It didn't take long for him to be too busy to drive the four of them home. He always had a date after school or something. He didn't hang out with the group much.

The school year flew by and before Donnie knew it, it was his birthday again. This time his parents took him to get his driver's license. He got his traditional cake and a new stereo for his room, but his license was his favorite present. Now he could borrow the truck and go to town or to Gina's house or wherever, with his father's permission of course.

Donnie realized he didn't get a card from Tracy this year. He began to think Jimmy was right after all, He would never see her again. He thought about her often. He cared a lot for Gina, but he still loved Tracy. She was in his heart.

Summer rolled around again, no more school for three months. The two couples were together often. They went to the movies, hung out at the fort and of course went swimming at Gina's house. One day they were at Gina's swimming. It was actually more like making out in chest high water. In between kisses Gina looked Donnie in the eye and asked, "Do you think we can have the fort to ourselves tonight?"

"I'm sure we can, we let them have it to themselves all the time," Donnie said motioning to Jimmy and Brenda with his head.

"Good I have a surprise for you," Gina said and gave him a peck on the lips. She swam to the ladder and climbed out of the pool. She started walking to the house. Donnie couldn't help but stare at her butt in her bikini bottoms shaking across the yard. She stopped at some lawn chairs by the door and grabbed one of the towels hanging on one of them. She started drying herself off.

"Hey wait for me," Brenda yelled across the yard. She swam to the ladder and climbed out and ran to Gina. Brenda dried herself as the girls talked and giggled. They soon both disappeared into the back door of the house. Donnie swam to Jimmy on the other side of the pool.

"How come chicks can never go to the bathroom by themselves?" Donnie asked.

"I don't know, it's just one of those things I guess," Jimmy said and got a big smile on his face as he looked at Donnie.

"Why are you smiling like that?" Donnie asked. "You're weirding me out."

"No reason," He said again with the smile.

"What?"

"Alright, but you can't say that I told you or Brenda will kick my ass."

"I won't, you know that."

"I bet when you swam over here you were going to tell me you need the fort tonight, weren't you?"

"Yeah, Gina said she has a surprise for me. How did you know?"

"Oh, she has a surprise for you all right. You have any idea what that surprise might be?"

"I don't know, late birthday present maybe? I don't know"

"She's gonna have sex with you dummy."

"Bullshit."

"Gina told Brenda she is going all the way with you tonight," Jimmy said smiling from ear to ear. "She got a couple condoms from Brenda and everything."

"Yeah!" Donnie yelled pumping his fist down from the air splashing Jimmy in the face.

"Shut the hell up," Jimmy muttered under his breath. "Gina told Brenda not to tell me and Brenda told me not to tell you."

"Relax they're inside they can't hear me." Just then as if they were on cue the door flew open and the girls came running across the yard giggling away.

"Mums the word," Jimmy whispered to Donnie as the two boys admired the girls' chests bouncing as they ran across the grass to the pool.

"No way!" The Yankees don't stand a chance this year!" Jimmy yelled giving Donnie a wink, pretending to be in the middle of a conversation.

"You're crazy, they are going all the way." Donnie said pretending to argue back. The girls got back in the pool and swam to their boyfriends.

"We have the fort to ourselves," Donnie whispered in Gina's ear.

"She smiled. "Do you think you can pick me up around 7 O' Clock?"

"I gotta ask my Dad, but I'm sure I can."

Later that evening Donnie ate dinner, got cleaned up and drove to Gina's house to pick her up. He was both nervous and excited. He pulled up to Gina's house and was surprised to see her on the porch swing waiting for him. She got off the swing and grabbed a bag that was next to her and ran down the steps and over to the truck. She opened the door and said, "You're right on time."

"I wouldn't keep you waiting."

"Awe, you're sweet," She said and climbed in the passenger door. She scooched across the bench seat and gave him a peck on the cheek. She took the big canvass bag off her shoulder and sat it between them on the seat. Donnie looked at the bag and back at her then put the truck in gear and drove off.

"Did you eat dinner?" Gina asked.

"Yeah, I ate with my folks before I came."

"I brought some leftovers in case you were hungry."

They pulled onto the farm property and drove up to the fort. "You get out and wait here and I'm going to drop the truck off and walk back."

"Alright," she said and got out of the truck.

The last thing Donnie needed was for his Dad to come barging in the fort needing the keys to the truck for something. He drove the truck to the house and hung the keys on the hook by the door. He walked out to the fort. He pushed the fort door open to find Gina sitting at the table with a cupcake. She lit the single candle stuck in the cupcake and yelled, "Surprise!"

"What's all this for?" Donnie asked.

"I never got you anything for your birthday."

"You didn't need to get me anything."

"Well I wanted to. I know it was three weeks ago but I had to get you something. Now hurry up and blow the candle out and make a wish."

Donnie closed his eyes and blew the candle out. He made a wish. He felt guilty because he wished for Tracy to come back. He really liked Gina, she's smart, pretty and real sweet. None of that changed his feelings for Tracy though. He felt bad for wishing for Tracy but that's what he always wished for. He couldn't get it out of his head.

"What did you wish for?"

"I can't tell you."

"I know I was just testing you," she said and smiled. "I think I might know anyway," she said as she handed him a small wrapped present. It was about the size of a cigarette pack. He pulled the bow off the top of it and put it on the table. He tore off the colorful wrapping paper and pulled the box out. He broke the tape with his fingernail and took the lid off. He flipped the box upside down into his other hand. Whatever it was it was wrapped in tissue paper. He unfolded the tissue paper and looked confused.

"A condom?" He said confused.

Gina took the bow off the table. She leaned back in her chair and stuck the bow to the front of her shorts.

"You mean..." he stopped in mid-sentence to Gina nodding her head. He did his best to act surprised so Gina didn't know Brenda and Jimmy had spilled the beans. In a way he was surprised because he didn't know how Gina was going to go about it.

"Just give me about Five minutes to get ready and come back in."

"Okay," Donnie said as he got up and exited the fort, condom in hand. "Let me know when you are ready." He stood outside the fort with the door cracked so he could hear her call.

"Okay, you can come in!" She yelled.

He entered the fort and was immediately hit with the sweet smell of perfume. He gazed around the room seeing a dozen scented candles shimmering. His eyes caught sight of her lying on the sleeping bag. She looked beautiful in white, lacy lingerie with her hair down. His heart started to race as he stepped toward her peeling off his shirt. He thought his erection was going to tear through his jeans. He knelt down and kind of crawled over her and they started to kiss. He let his weight down on the sleeping bag next to her and they kissed some more.

"Are you sure you want to do this?" He asked, his voice shaking a bit.

"I'm sure," she whispered in his ear. Her hot breath sent tingles down his spine. He started kissing her more running his hand down her side over her hip. He grabbed a handful of ass as he moved his mouth to her neck and kissed his way up to her ear. She giggled a little as he nibbled on her earlobe. He slid his hand around her hip cupping her crotch in his hand. He could feel the warmth of her through the silk and lace panties. She moaned a little as he squeezed and slid his palm up to her belly button. She grabbed a fistful of hair on the back of his head. She pulled his face to hers and shoved her tongue in his mouth. He moved his hand down under her panties and inserted his finger in her. She gasped between kisses as he slid his finger up over her clit.

He pulled back from her onto his knees. He popped the buttons on the fly of his jeans, still gripping the condom in his left fist. She arched her back and slid her panties off and peeled off the lacy top. Donnie stood up fumbling around. He couldn't get his pants off fast enough. He pulled his pants down to his ankles and almost fell on his face. He tried to pull his foot out without realizing he hadn't taken his shoes off yet. He couldn't help staring at her naked body which didn't help him undress.

He fumbled around some more and kicked his shoes off. He finally got all of his clothes off. He crawled back over her and started to kiss her again. He got in between her legs and leaned in and kissed her again. This time she pulled away. "Don't forget the condom," she said.

"Oh yeah," he said. He got back to his knees. Now she was the one staring at his rock hard erection as he struggled with the condom wrapper. His palms were all sweaty and he couldn't get a grip on the package to open it. She noticed his frustration and took the condom from his hand. She put it up to her mouth and ripped the package open with her teeth.

"Why didn't I think of that?"

"You're just nervous. We both are."

She pulled the condom out of the package and tried to put it on him. She realized she had it backwards and turned it around. "See nervous," she said and rolled the condom down his penis. He winced a little worried he was going to ejaculate just from that. He laid her back gently and started to kiss her. He needed to calm down a little. He knew if he stuck it in her now it would be over before it started. He kissed her neck and worked his way down to her breasts. He kissed her breasts and sucked on her nipples until he didn't feel so sensitive down there.

Once he was confident he wouldn't orgasm the second he entered her, he kissed his way back up to her lips. He spread her legs apart and got between them. He grabbed his penis and guided it in her. It felt so good. She bit her lip and let out a high pitched squeal. "Are you okay?" He whispered in her ear. She just nodded her head yes not saying a word. He pulled out and went in again two or three more times and let out a little yell of his own. That was it he just laid there huffing and puffing still inside her.

"Sorry I was so fast," he said between breaths.

"You did fine," she said and kissed him.

"Did it feel good?"

"Honestly it kind of hurt more than anything else."

"I'm sorry."

"Don't be, it's not your fault," she said giving him a tight squeeze as he lay on top of her. "I did my homework, I know a girls first time is not very enjoyable."

Donnie got up on his knees. "Oh shit," he said as he looked down and saw the condom was off.

"What?" She asked worried.

"Blood," he said as he pulled the condom out of her hoping she wouldn't notice.

"That's normal too, don't worry," she said as she got up and went to her canvass bag. She dug around in it and pulled out a silky little robe and put it on. She reached in again and pulled out some baby wipes. She turned away from him and wiped herself off. She tossed the box over to Donnie.

"Wow you thought of everything," He said.

She tied her robe and walked to the sleeping bag. "This was supposed to happen closer to your birthday. It took me a lot longer to gather up everything I needed."

"Why's that?"

"Well baby wipes and candles are no big deal," she said. "My mom would have freaked out if I put lingerie into the shopping cart at the store."

"Yeah I guess so."

"Can I leave it here at the fort?"

"Sure," He said and picked it up and put it in a cardboard box in the corner.

"Thanks, I don't want to have to explain it to my parents if they found it."

"What time do you have to be home?"

"No later than ten, but nine would be better."

"Do you think your parents would let you go camping?"

"I don't know, I'd have to ask."

"Ask them. I'm going to ask Jimmy and Brenda if they want to go one of these weekends."

"Sounds fun, I'll ask my parents tonight."

"I'll be right back. I'm going to walk up to the house and get the truck. I'll bring some soda back too."

"Good that's one thing I forgot. I'm thirsty."

"I'll be back in a flash," Donnie said and headed out the door. He came back with the truck and a couple cans of Mountain Dew. They drank the soda and talked a little then Donnie drove her home. He drove back to his house happy. He went upstairs and went right to bed.

Chapter Six

The next day Jimmy showed up at the fort. "You're already here," he said, noticing Donnie inside. "I was gonna walk to your house but decided to check here first."

"I just got here. I figured I'd clean the place up a bit."

"Well?"

"Well what?"

"What the hell do you mean well what?" Jimmy yelled. "Did you guys do it or what?"

"Do what?"

"Oh my God are you kidding me?"

Donnie started laughing and pulled the lingerie out of the box holding it up to his chest and said, "What do you think?"

"I think you'd look better in red," Jimmy said with a smirk.

"Okay, okay I deserve it. Your turn to act stupid, I get it," Donnie said as he dropped the garment back into the cardboard box. "Yes we did it."

"Well how was it?"

"It was okay."

"Oh man, here we go."

"What?"

"I already know what you're going to say."

"Oh yeah, what am I going say than smart guy? What?"

"She was alright but not as good as Tracy," Jimmy said in a whiny voice. "Tracy Tracy Tracy..blah blah blah."

"I wasn't going to say that at all."

"Sure you weren't"

"I wasn't," Donnie said firmly. "I was gonna say it was kinda weird because she was a virgin."

"Did she scream?"

"No, I don't know, kinda."

"Brenda screamed like I was killing her the first time."

"She did?"

"She said it hurt like hell and didn't let me do it again for two whole weeks."

"Man, two weeks."

"Yeah, but after that we were like a couple of rabbits for a while."

"I know, I remember," Donnie said rolling his eyes.

"Well congratulations buddy," Jimmy said as he slapped Donnie on his back.

"Thanks," Donnie said. "Do you think you can borrow your Dad's truck? I mean if I can't borrow my Dad's."

"Nope."

"Why not? Won't you at least ask?"

"I don't have to ask anymore."

"You don't?"

"That's what I was coming over here to tell you. My Dad is buying a new truck today."

"He won't let you borrow the new truck?"

"He's giving me the old truck, numbskull. That's why I don't have to ask anymore. It's my truck after today I can use it whenever I want."

"No way!"

"Yes way, we're going to the dealership here in a little while. I can't wait."

"Man you're lucky."

"I know. I can't believe it."

"Is the old truck worn out or something? Why is your dad getting a new one?"

"No the old truck runs good. It's a little beat up from all the years of working the farm but that's just looks other than that it's in good shape. You know you've driven in it. My Dad just said the truck fund is full and he wants to use the money to get another truck."

"Truck fund? What the hell is a truck fund?"

"My Dad likes to put his small bills away. Whenever he breaks a twenty or a ten he puts the change away and saves it."

"Puts it away where?"

"I don't know, Jimmy said shrugging his shoulders. "He puts it in a coffee can or something I guess. Whenever the truck has a problem like a flat or the battery dies he dips into the truck fund to fix it."

"That's a good idea, I guess."

"It's like a game of his," Jimmy said. "The truck hasn't had any problems in a long while so the money kept piling up. I guess it built up enough for a new truck or at least a good down payment on a new truck."

"Man, your very own wheels, wow."

"I know. What did you want me to borrow the truck for anyway?"

"I had an idea. I thought maybe we could all go camping."

Jimmy's eyes lit up. "That's a great idea. Spend the whole night with the girls, man you are a genius!"

"You think Brenda's folks will let her?"

"I don't know, maybe."

"Gina is going to ask her parents tonight. Run it by Brenda tell her to ask her parents too so we can figure it all out."

"I will. Camping, why didn't I think of that? Well I'm gonna get home and see if my dad's ready to go truck shopping yet."

"Okay stop by tomorrow."

"I will."

The next day the boys met up at the fort. Donnie was already there when he heard an engine outside. He stepped out of the fort and instead of the old pickup there was a shiny new Chevy Silverado.

"Wow, that's nice!" Donnie said giving Jimmy a thumbs up.

"Brand spanking new."

"I'm surprised your dad let you drive it over here."

"Let me drive it?" Jimmy said in a shocked tone. "He gave me this one and kept the old Ford."

"No friggin' way!"

Jimmy started to laugh. "I'm just pulling your leg," He said between chuckles. "You should have seen the look on your face. Man that was priceless."

"Let's go show the girls."

"No can do."

"Why not?"

"I had a hard enough time talking him into letting me drive it over here to show you."

"How's she drive?"

"Oh man it's sweet, all power and fast."

"Let's go for a ride somewhere."

"Hop in, you can go with me to get gas and I got to take it back. I told the old man I'd be back in 15 minutes."

Donnie got in the truck. It was nice maroon interior matching the maroon paint. The boys drove to the closest gas station and Jimmy filled it up. They drove back to Jimmy's farm and parked. The boys climbed out of the cab and noticed Jimmy's Dad was sitting on the porch smoking a cigarette.

"Nice truck Mr. Davidson," Donnie said.

"Thanks Donald," he said eye-balling the pick-up seemingly looking for damage.

Donnie just looked at Jimmy. Jimmy looked back and just rolled his eyes. "You want to go over to Brenda's house with me? I want to see what her parents said about the camping trip."

"Yeah let's go."

The boys hopped in the old Ford and took off in a cloud of dust. Donnie looked at Jimmy and said, "Your Dad is kind of weird, huh?"

"I guess he is. I don't know he's no weirder than most parents."

"Well how does it feel?"

"How does what feel?"

"Having your own wheels? Not having to ask permission anymore."

"I don't know. I guess it hasn't really sunk in yet. It feels like I'm still just borrowing it."

The boys pulled up to Brenda's house and hopped out of the cab. They walked up the path and knocked on the door. Brenda opened the door and smiled. "Hey boyfriend," she said.

"Hey," Jimmy said and kissed her on the cheek.

"What's going on Donnie?" she asked.

"Oh nothing, just riding around in my buddy's new truck."

Jimmy punched Donnie in the arm.

"Ow, what was that for?"

"I wanted to tell her."

"Sorry, I thought she already knew."

"What? This is yours now?" Brenda asked full of excitement.

"Yep, my dad bought a new one and said this one is all mine."

"That is so cool," Brenda squealed with excitement.

"Did you ask your parents about going camping?"

"Yeah I asked. My dad said no."

"Aw man."

"He didn't only say no, but hell no you're not spending the night with a teenage boy out in the middle of nowhere," she said in a mocking tone.

"That sucks."

"Gina's parents said pretty much the same thing. I talked to her earlier. No camping for us."

"Wow, I thought your parents would let you for sure."

"I didn't, not my dad anyway."

"What are you doing today?"

"I'm helping my mom clean the house, as a matter of fact I better get back in there."

"Okay," Jimmy said and kissed her on the cheek.

"Sorry," she said and turned to go inside. "See ya Donnie," she added before disappearing into the front door.

The boys got back in the truck and headed home. "That's a drag," Jimmy said.

"We can still go."

"Do you want to?"

"Yeah we can do some fishing and hang out for a day or two."

"Let's do it," Jimmy said. "It would have been a lot more fun with the girls though."

"We would have never left the tents," Donnie said laughing.

"Yeah, I guess you're right."

Jimmy dropped Donnie off at his house. Donnie told his dad he wanted to go fishing with Jimmy for a day or two. His dad drew him a crude map to their old fishing spot and told him to have fun. Donnie didn't waste any time gathering up his camping gear, tackle box and fishing pole. He borrowed the truck and hauled it all out to the fort. When he got there he was surprised to see Jimmy's truck there. He walked into the fort to find Jimmy taking an inventory of his fishing gear.

"Hey, I didn't expect to find you here," Donnie said.

"I figured I better go through this stuff and decide what I should take."

"Did you ask your dad if you could go?"

"Yeah, he's cool with it."

"When should we go?"

"Well we should tell the girls and I got a few things to take care of, so how about tomorrow right after dinner?

"Alright we'll eat and meet up here right afterwards," Donnie said.

The next day they met up at the fort like they had planned. They loaded up Jimmy's truck with all the camping and fishing gear they thought they needed. Once they had it all secure they headed out. They followed the map Donnie's dad drew up for them. They were surprised how accurate it actually was. They reached the spot and set up camp.

"Check this out," Jimmy said as he pulled a cooler out of the back of the truck. He put the cooler on the ground and opened the lid. He shined his flashlight inside revealing a bunch of cans of beer surrounded in ice.

"Where did you get those?" Donnie asked clearly surprised.

"Bobby happened to be at Brenda's when I stopped by to tell her about the trip."

"Good old Bobby I haven't seen him in a while. What is he up to?"

"He told me he dropped out of school and got a job."

"Well no wonder I haven't seen him."

"Yeah, well he overheard me telling Brenda about the trip and he gave me a twelve pack."

"Way to go Bobby!" Donnie yelled happily.

"Yeah, I couldn't believe it," Jimmy said with a smile. "He told me you can't go fishing without beer and walked to his car, pulled out this twelve pack and just gave it to me."

"Does he just drive around with beer in his car all the time?"

"I asked him the same thing. He said he just bought it to test a fake ID card he just got from someone he works with."

"Well I guess it works," Donnie said with a laugh.

"Lucky for us it did."

The boys each cracked open a cold can of beer and walked around the area checking it out. "Jimmy come here and look at this," Donnie called out. Jimmy walked over to take a look. Donnie shined his flashlight on the ground in front of him. "Me and my dad put this here years ago," Donnie said. On the ground were about a couple dozen large rocks in a circle overgrown with weeds.

"Let's get some wood and make a fire," Jimmy said.

The boys split up and went searching for dead branches to burn. After a while they met back up at the ring of rocks and piled the wood they had found in the center. Jimmy walked over to the truck and grabbed a backpack from the cab. He came back, put the pack on the ground and unzipped it. He started digging around inside. "Here it is," He said as he pulled out a can of charcoal lighter fluid from the bag. He dug around a little more producing a box of strike anywhere matches.

"You remembered everything," Donnie said. "I forgot all about matches."

"You gotta be prepared," Jimmy said as he tossed a match into the pile of wood igniting the lighter fluid with a woof.

The fire roared to life. The boys sat around the fire shooting the breeze. They talked about the girls until they got buzzed and fell asleep. They woke the next morning with headaches.

"I'm starving let's go see if we can catch some fish," Donnie said holding his head.

"Okay let's go."

The boys grabbed their fishing rods and headed down to the river. Beers in hand they cast their lines. After about an hour went buy Jimmy yelled, "I got one!" He started reeling in his line as fast as he could. The fish popped out of the water a few times as it fought.

"Man, that fish is huge!" Donnie yelled.

Jimmy pulled and reeled and pulled and reeled. Finally the fish was right at his feet. He reached down and grabbed it, throwing his rod to the side as he did. "Got it," he yelled as he picked the fish up and pulled the hook from his mouth. He looked at Donnie with a big grin and said, "Let's eat". He no longer got the words out of his mouth and the fish squirmed vigorously. Donnie watched as Jimmy's mouth dropped open as the fish flew into the air. Jimmy's hands flailed like a juggler. With a splash the fish fell into the river and swam away like a bat out of hell. "Son of a bitch," Jimmy yelled. Donnie started to laugh uncontrollably. "Rrrr," Jimmy growled and picked up a baseball sized rock and threw it into the river.

"The one that got away," Donnie said in between laughs.

"Real funny," Jimmy said. "Come on, let's go get some wood."

"Why? We don't have a fish to cook."

"Just help me find some wood."

"Okay." Donnie said still chuckling a bit.

Jimmy just glared at him and stormed off to go hunt down some firewood. The boys met at the ring of rocks with arms full of dead branches. They dropped them on the ground. Donnie started making a fire as Jimmy walked over to the cooler and started digging around in it. He banged around the cans floating in what used to be ice but was mostly water now. He pulled out a can of soda then put his hand back in and started feeling around some more. He walked back to where Donnie had a fire going and produced a pack of hot dogs.

"Man, you really did think of everything," Donnie said.

"I told you, you got to be prepared."

"You should've been prepared with a net for that fish," Donnie said laughing. "Maybe a club to knock it out at least."

"Yeah, yeah I'm gonna get a club and knock you out."

Donnie burst out laughing again. Jimmy couldn't help himself he started to laugh too. They got some sticks and cooked their dogs on the fire and ate. All out of beer they had to settle for root beer. They cooked and ate the whole package of hot dogs in no time.

"I'm still hungry." Donnie said.

"Yeah, me too."

"I'm bored with this camping trip, how about you?"

"You read my mind."

"Let's pack up and get out of here."

"Good idea."

The boys started taking down the tent and packing up the fishing gear. Jimmy took the few remaining sodas out of the cooler and dumped the icy water onto the fire. With a hiss and a puff of smoke the fire was out. Donnie walked down to the river to make sure they didn't forget anything. Jimmy finished packing the truck.

"I think we got it all." Donnie said.

"Good, let's get going."

The boys climbed into the cab of the truck. Jimmy put the key in the ignition and turned it only to hear a click.

"What's wrong?"

"I don't know," Jimmy said turning the key again, click.

"Great we're stuck out here."

"Don't panic, let's give it a minute and try it again."

The boys waited about five minutes and Jimmy turned the key again, click.

"Let's push start it," Donnie said all excited like he had the idea of the century.

"It's an automatic, dummy."

"So what."

"It needs to be a stick shift to push start it you gotta pop the clutch."

"Are you sure?"

"Don't you know anything about cars? Anything at all?"

"Not really," Donnie said in a depressed tone. "Don't you?"

"Yeah, I know a little. I don't know how to charge a battery in the middle of the woods though," Jimmy said as he got out of the truck and slammed the door. Donnie got out and walked to the back of the truck. He found Jimmy sitting on the tailgate thinking.

"What should we do?" Donnie asked as he hopped on the tailgate next to him.

"I don't know. I guess we're going to have to hike to the nearest road and hope we can flag someone down and get a ride."

"Man, this sucks," Donnie said as the boys sat in silence for a moment.

"Well we may as well start walking now," Jimmy said as he hopped off the tailgate.

"Hang on a second. Open the hood," Donnie said.

"You're not a mechanic. You don't even know you can't push start an automatic," Jimmy said sarcastically.

"Just do it. I just remembered being with my dad once and our truck making that same click." Donnie said.

"Alright, but I doubt you can fix it," Jimmy said. He walked around and popped the hood of the truck and raised it up.

"I think I know what it is." Donnie said looking under the hood.

"Get the hell out of here."

"I'm serious, do you have any tools?"

"Of course I have tools. There is a toolbox behind the seat."

"Go get it, will ya?"

"Alright but we're wasting time if you ask me," Jimmy said as he stormed off to get the toolbox. "Here you go Mr. Mechanic. Work your magic. This I gotta see," Jimmy said as he sat the toolbox on the ground by Donnie's feet with a clank.

"Give me a Crescent wrench," Donnie said holding his hand out like a surgeon asking for a scalpel.

Jimmy just rolled his eyes but dug around the box and handed him an adjustable Crescent wrench. "Here you go," he said with a smirk. Donnie grabbed the wrench and started loosening the battery terminal. He took it off the battery post. He reached in his pocket and pulled out his pocketknife. He opened the blade and started scraping the inside of the battery terminal and scrapped the post. White stuff flaked off as he scraped. "Do you think that's it?" Jimmy asked kind of amazed.

"Get in and give it a try," Donnie said as he tightened down the terminal.

Jimmy got in the truck and turned the key, Vroom it started. "Man I could kiss you," he yelled out the window.

"Do it and you'll still be hiking down the road and flagging down a ride," Donnie yelled back. They both laughed. Donnie opened the door of the truck, plopped the toolbox on the floor and climbed up in the seat. "Let's get out of here," he said and slammed the door shut.

"I'll never doubt you again buddy," Jimmy said as he pulled the shifter putting the truck in drive.

"Just shut up and drive."

They drove slowly down the winding dirt road in the woods. They drove and drove. "Man this would have been one hell of a hike," Donnie yelled over the screeches of the branches scrapping down the side of the truck on the narrow road. Finally they reached a paved road. Jimmy gave it some gas and they were cruising along. Something in the rearview mirror caught his eye.

"Shit," Jimmy yelled and stopped the truck.

"What's the matter?"

"We forgot to shut the damn tailgate."

Donnie turned and looked out the back window and could see the tent flapping in the road. He looked farther down the road and could see objects scattered here and there. "What next?" He said.

"Let's gather this crap up and get home." Jimmy said frustrated. "And do me a favor."

"What's that?"

"Don't ever ask me to go camping or fishing ever again."

"It was all worth it just to see the look on your face when that fish wiggled out of your hands."

"Yeah, yeah."

The boys gathered up all their stuff and drove to the fort. They just unloaded everything inside it.

"We'll put this stuff away later," Jimmy said. "I got to go get something to eat, I'm starving."

"Me too," Donnie said looking around the fort he thought something looked strange but was too hungry to care. He plopped everything just inside the fort and headed to the house to get something to eat. He found some leftovers in the fridge and gobbled them up. Then he went upstairs and went to sleep.

Chapter Seven

The next day Donnie went to the fort to go through the camping gear. He wanted to store it back in the barn to get it out of the way. When he entered the fort he noticed a tablecloth on the table. He looked around and noticed a comforter where the sleeping bag used to be. He also noticed a couple of big, comfy looking pillows. He separated his and Jimmy's gear and loaded his into his dad's pick-up. He drove it all to the barn and unloaded it and packed it neatly back in the barn. He then drove to Gina's house to tell her he was back and ask about the new décor in the fort. He knocked on the door.

"Hey sweetie you're back all ready?" Gina asked as she answered the door.

"Yeah, it was boring without you there."

"Awe, you missed me?"

"I did."

"Did you catch any fish?"

Donnie started to laugh and told her the story of Jimmy's fish getting away. Gina laughed, then he told her about the truck not starting and the tailgate ordeal.

"Wow, it sounds like you guys had some adventure," She said with a big smile.

"Yeah, nothing went as planned."

She leaned in and whispered in his ear," Do you wanna go to the fort and mess around?"

"Heck yeah!" He said a little louder than he intended.

"Shhhh," She said with her finger to her lips. "Let me go tell my Mom I'm leaving for a bit."

"Okay."

Gina went into the house to tell her mom and Donnie danced a little jig on the front porch and giggled like a little kid. She came back out and said," Let's go I told my Mom I'd be back in a couple hours."

"After you," He said bowing a bit and motioning his arm towards the truck. He opened the truck door for her.

"Awe, what a gentleman," She said and kissed him on the cheek before climbing into the cab. He shut her door and walked around the front of the truck. He pulled his keys out of his pocket and climbed in.

"We're off," He said as he slammed the door and started up the truck.

"Thirsty?" She asked as she pulled a can of soda out of her bag.

"I'll wait 'til we get there."

"Okay," she said smiling. She just stared at him as he drove.

"What?"

"Nothing, I just like looking at you is all."

Donnie blushed a little bit and kept on driving. They reached the fort and went inside.

"What's all this?" She asked.

"That's Jimmy's fishing gear and tent."

"He's not going to keep it here, is he?"

"Nah, I just had to separate it. He'll take it back to his house later," He said. Just then he thought to himself, What if my Dad needs the truck? "I'll be right back," He said. He got in the truck and drove it back to the house. He hung the keys on the hook where they go and walked back to the fort. He was excited so it was more of a jog than a walk. When he entered the fort Gina was laying on the comforter leaning against the two big pillows. Donnie's eye got wide. All she had on was her bra and panties.

"How do you like the new bed?" She asked rubbing her hand along the soft fabric of the comforter.

"It's nice," He said. "Not nearly as nice as what's on it."

Gina giggled and blushed a little. "I got some new bedding so I brought my old stuff over here."

"Cool," Donnie said staring at her practically naked body.

"Bobby drove me and Brenda over here when you guys were gone," She said. "Hope you don't mind."

"No, not at all," He said still staring mesmerized by her body.

"Well, come over here and kiss me."

Donnie snapped out of it a little and walked towards her. He peeled his shirt off and dropped down next to her. He started kissing

55

her. "Ow!" He yelled. Once again he felt like his boner was going to rip through his pants.

"What's the matter?"

"I gotta take these pants off," he said. He stood up, kicked his shoes off and unbuttoned his pants. He pulled his pant off and his boxers looked like a tent.

"Looks like you're ready." She said with a little giggle.

"Oh, I'm ready," he said doing a little dance as he pulled his sox off trying not to fall over. He pulled his boxers off and Gina just stared at his erection.

"Oh hold on, I almost forgot," she said fumbling around in her bag on the ground next to her. "Here they are," she said as she pulled out a box of condoms. She ripped the box open all the while not taking her eyes off his penis. She pulled one out and ripped it open with her teeth. "Come closer," she said.

He took a step closer and she put the condom on and rolled it down. "There," she said. "Now you're ready." Donnie dropped down and started kissing her. He reached around her back and fumbled with the clasp on her bra. To his surprise he got it open quite easy. He pulled the bra away, cast it to the side and kissed her some more. She reached down, arched her back and pulled her panties off. They kissed some more as he climbed on top of her. She gasped as he inserted his penis inside her.

"Am I hurting you?" He asked with concern in his voice.

"No. Don't stop it feels good," she whispered into his ear sending tingles down his spine. They both moaned quietly as he pushed in and pulled out faster and faster.

"Ahhh," Donnie moaned and collapsed on top of her. She squeezed him tightly wrapping her legs around him.

"That was good," She said and kissed his ear. They both just lay there a moment, breathing heavy.

"It was?"

"Much better," she said smiling.

"Good." He said as he got up and put his boxers on. He discarded the condom in a trash can by the door. They both got their clothes back on. Gina grabbed the box of condoms. "Where did you get those?" Donnie asked.

"I snuck away while my Mom was grocery shopping and bought them," she said as she grabbed a Tupperware container at the end of the makeshift bed. She pulled the lid off and dropped the ripped box of condoms inside and snapped the lid back on. He noticed the white lingerie in the Tupperware as she did so. He looked around the room. His heart started to race as his eyes darted all around the fort.

"What happened to the box I put the lingerie in?" He asked with a nervousness in his voice.

"I used it for trash when I cleaned up in here."

"You what!?" Donnie yelled.

"I used it for...."

"How could you do that? I had stuff in there my own personal stuff," He screamed. His face was red and full of anger.

"You don't need that stuff anymore, I'm your girlfriend now," Gina said and started to cry.

"I know you're my girlfriend now, but you can't just go throwing my stuff away," he yelled. "It's mine!"

"Take me home," Gina said sobbing.

"I can't believe you..."

"Take me home now!" Gina yelled interrupting him in mid-sentence. She grabbed her bag and stormed out of the fort. She slammed the door behind her.

"Son of a bitch," Donnie muttered to himself under his breath as he bent down to tie his shoes. He walked out the fort door and saw Gina squatting down leaning her back on the fort wall crying. "I'll be right back with the truck," He said as he walked by her on the way to the house. She just stayed there and continued to cry. He came back with the truck and drove her home. Neither of them said a word the whole way there.

Donnie pulled up to the front of the house. He tried to talk to her. "Gina, I don't want to..." he started to say but before he could finish she got out and slammed the door behind her. "Well fuck you then," He muttered under his breath as he threw the truck in drive and peeled out down the street. He went home and worked on the farm the rest of the day, pissed off the whole time.

Two days later Jimmy knocked on Donnie's door. Donnie opened the door and stepped out on the porch. "What's up man?" Jimmy asked. "Are you alright?"

"Yeah, me and Gina got into an argument the other day."

"I know she told Brenda."

"She threw all Tracy's letters away."

"When did she do that?"

"When we were camping," he said angrily. "Not only the letters the whole damn box."

"The box from the fort?"

"Yeah, it had her picture in it, all her letters she wrote me and her panties," He said slapping his hand on his forehead. "I forgot all about the panties."

"Man, that's messed up."

"No shit it's messed up." Donnie said clearly still angry.

"Well Brenda asked me to come over and talk to you."

"About what?"

"I guess Gina feels real bad and want to talk to you. She wants to tell you she's sorry," Jimmy said looking at him out of the corner of his eye. "What do you say?"

"I'll think about it," he said staring at the ground. "Tell her I'll think about it."

"Alright," Jimmy said. "You gonna be alright?"

"Yeah, I'll be fine."

"Alright buddy, I have to go back to work, meet me at the fort later."

"Maybe."

"Okay, well I'll be there," Jimmy said and got in the truck and drove off. Later that night Jimmy drove to the fort. He packed up all his fishing gear and his tent and cleaned up the fort. Once he was done and decided Donnie wasn't coming he drove home, unpacked the truck and went in to call it a night.

"A few days had passed and no one seen or heard from Donnie. Finally Jimmy drove over to Donnie's house and knocked on the door. Donnie opened the door and stepped out on the porch. Jimmy just looked at him.

"Hey Jimmy, how are you?"

"I'm good, what are you doing right now?"

"Nothing."

"You're not busy?"

"No, I'm just kicking back right now."

"Good, get in the truck."

"Where are we going?"

"The fort."

"I don't really feel like…"

"Get in the truck." Jimmy interrupted with an assertive tone in his voice.

"Alright, alright but I'm telling you I'm not in the mood to play any games."

"I don't want to play a game."

"Then what's going on?"

"We need to talk," Jimmy said as he turned the key starting up the truck.

"What do we need to talk about?"

"What do you think?"

"Gina?"

"Yeah, Gina," Jimmy said as he pulled the truck up in front of the fort. "Brenda has been driving me crazy. She's been driving me crazy because Gina has been calling her crying driving her crazy." Jimmy turned the truck off and popped his door open. Donnie opened his door and got out of the truck. He walked to the fort and opened the door. The whole time he had been talking to Jimmy, but he failed to realize Jimmy had never got out of the truck. Donnie stepped into the fort and heard the truck door slam, the truck start up and drive away.

"Donnie, I'm sorry!" Gina said as she wrapped her arms around him, crying her eyes out. She stood there a moment holding him tightly and crying into his shoulder. "You are right, I never should have touched your things," she said in between sobs. "I was wrong, please forgive me," she said as she pulled away from him wiping away tears from her eyes. "Will you forgive me Donnie?"

"Yes, I forgive you."

"Thank you," she said as she tackled him, knocking him down on the makeshift bed, kissing him. They rolled around on the bed, kissing and undressing each other. They had sex, Donnie thought it was the best sex they had, had together. He almost felt it was worth losing the letters over but changed his mind. Then he thought of something.

"Ut oh," he said looking at Gina.

"What's the matter?"

"We forgot to use a condom."

"Oh my God we did!" She said in a panic. "Did you?..." Donnie shook his head yes. "Inside me?" Donnie continued to shake his head. That's all it took. The tears started to roll down her cheeks again and she started crying loudly all over again.

"Don't worry," Donnie said and wrapped his arms around her holding her tight. "It'll be alright."

"I hope so," she said still sobbing. "God, I hope so,"

The next two weeks Gina was worried. They went to the fort a lot and more often than not they had sex. They never forgot to use a condom again. Donnie had to go buy another box. He wasn't stressed at all. He was loving it. One day at the fort, when they had finished Gina said," I'm worried Donnie."

"Worried about what?"

"I should have started my period three days ago is what."

"I guess I shouldn't have wasted the money on those condoms," Donnie said and started to laugh a little.

"That's not funny!" She yelled slapping him on his chest.

"Stop worrying," He said and pulled her close to him. "Worrying isn't going to change anything."

"I guess you're right," she said and gave him a kiss. She knew in her heart she was not going to stop worrying though.

The next day Donnie drove to Gina's house. He knocked on the door. Gina answered stepping out on the porch. He gave her a kiss on the cheek and said, "Hey baby, want to go to the fort?"

"No, not today," she said.

"Well you wanna go swimming?" Donnie asked. "We can see if Jimmy and Brenda want to come over for a while."

"I can't," she said and smiled.

"Why not?"

"I started my period,"

"See I told you, you were worried about nothing."

"Yeah, you were right," she said as she wrapped her arms around him hugging him tightly.

"What do you want to do?"

"I think I'm just going to hang out and watch T.V. or take a nap if you don't mind," she said. "I don't feel so good."

"That's fine, you rest up and I hope you feel better," he said and gave her a kiss. "I'm going to take off, maybe see what Jimmy is up to."

"Okay, bye."

60

Donnie was relieved. He had no idea how his parents would react if he had gotten someone pregnant at his age and he wasn't real eager to find out. Between sex at the fort and swimming at Gina's the rest of the summer flew by and the school year started back up in its usual fashion and regular routine.

Chapter Eight

Donnie showed up for school in his new shoes and clothes. He was immediately blinded by all the bright white sneakers on everybody's feet as they marched through the parking lot to school. It was the same every year kids all got new clothes and shoes for school so everything was bright. He waited in the parking lot by where he always met up with Jimmy and the girls. He saw the old pickup pull into the parking lot and park. Donnie walked over towards the truck. Jimmy stuck his head out the window and asked, "Why didn't you walk to my house and get a ride to school?"

"I felt like walking today."

"I waited a while but figured you weren't coming so I took off."

"I wanted to break in these shoes," he said stomping his feet in the parking lot. "I hate new shoes they are always so stiff and uncomfortable."

"Yeah but they look nice," Brenda said from inside the cab.

"Yeah, I guess," Donnie said looking down at his shoes. "Where is Gina?" He asked.

"I don't know," Jimmy and Brenda said at the same time.

"You guys didn't go to her house and pick her up?"

"I didn't know we were supposed to," Jimmy said looking at Brenda.

"She didn't say anything to me about it," Brenda said shrugging her shoulders.

Just then Gina's mom's car pulled into the parking lot. The car stopped behind the pickup. The passenger side door opened and Gina stepped out. "Thanks Mom," she yelled as she slammed the door shut.

"Hi honey," Gina said and wrapped her arms around Donnie as her Mom sped off through the parking lot.

"Good morning," Donnie said and kissed her on the cheek.

Jimmy and Brenda got out of the truck and they all walked to the school building together. The first day was always kind of a pain in the neck. First you had to wait in a line to get your schedule of classes. Then you had to wait in lines to get the books you needed for the classes. It was a headache and Donnie hated it.

"I hate the first day of school," Donnie said as he got in line for his schedule.

"I like it," Gina said excitedly. "Everybody's all dressed to impress in new clothes and happy to see each other."

"Yeah, it's like a fashion show," Brenda chimed in.

Donnie and Jimmy just looked at each other and rolled their eyes. "I hate all the waiting in line," Jimmy said.

"Yeah, it takes forever," Donnie agreed.

"It's not that bad," Brenda said. "Besides you got us here to keep you company," she said as she gave Jimmy a squeeze.

"Yeah, I guess," Jimmy said not very enthused.

"You're a jerk," Brenda said and smacked him on the chest.

"I didn't mean it like that… I just meant it sucks waiting in all the lines."

They all got their schedules and compared them. They hardly had any of the same classes together. Donnie and Jimmy had one class together, beginning guitar. Neither of the two had ever played an instrument but had talked about it one night at the fort and decided they'd give guitar a try. Now that they had their schedules it was time for them to split up and get their books. They all agreed to meet up at the library when they were finished so they could all go to lunch together. With their rendezvous point mapped out they all went their separate ways to the various book lines.

Donnie walked and looked up at a banner that read 'Math Books', he let out a sigh and stepped in line behind a couple chatty girls. A moment later a kid he had never seen before got in line behind him. He looked young he had short hair parted to one side and was very slender. "Excuse me," the young man said. Donnie turned around to talk to him. "Is this line only for Math books?"

"Yes, only Math," Donnie said.

"Wow, they didn't do it like this at my old school."

"Where did you go before?"

"It was in California."

"How did they do it there?"

"You just handed a worker your schedule and they went down the isles picking out all the books you needed and handed them to you all at once."

"That makes a lot more sense than this."

"Yeah you only had one line to wait in. It was a lot longer but it was only one line."

"What's your name?" Donnie asked extending his hand to shake.

"John, John Campbell."

"Donnie McKay," Donnie said shaking the boy's hand.

"Nice to meet you," John said.

"Same here."

"I'm just glad I won't have to wear a school uniform anymore."

"A uniform, were you in a catholic school or something?"

"No it was a regular public school."

"Why did you have to wear a uniform?"

"Well it wasn't like a military uniform or anything like that, it was just a white collared shirt and grey slacks."

"Everybody wore that?"

"Yep, well the girls had grey skirts that they wore."

"Were your school colors grey and white or something?"

"No, they just had a dress code so people couldn't wear gang colors and stuff."

"Man, that would suck to not be able to dress like you want."

"Yeah, it did."

Chatting in line made it go by fast. Donnie got his book and headed to the next line. He didn't find anybody to talk to in line so it seemed to take forever. By the time he got his last book it was time to meet up with the others for lunch. When he showed up at the designated point everyone else was already there.

"Well it's about time, slow poke," Jimmy said.

"How long have you been done?"

"About an hour."

"How the heck did you get done so fast?"

"He's full of crap baby, he showed up about two minutes before you did," Gina said giving Donnie a hug.

"Damn it Gina you ruined it," Jimmy said disappointedly. Gina just stuck her tongue out at him not saying a word.

"Hey, I heard there is going to be a fight after school," Jimmy said excited.

"Who is supposed to fight?" Brenda asked.

"He's just making another joke," Gina said giving him the evil eye.

"No, it's true. What's that kid's name, he always had headphones on?"

"Billy, I think," Donnie said.

"Yeah, Billy Braum. I overheard someone in line saying he was going to clobber some guy after school today."

"Why?" Donnie asked.

"What's that girl's name that he used to go out with?"

"Cindy," Donnie said.

"Yeah, Cindy something or other... "Jimmy said drifting off starring into the sky apparently trying to remember her name.

"Well, what about her?" Gina asked impatiently.

"I guess they broke up over the summer and she started seeing someone else and he's mad."

"How romantic," Gina said.

"It is," Brenda agreed.

"Would you fight for me baby?" Gina asked.

"Heck yeah, I'd fight King Kong for you," Donnie said throwing some air punches and giving Jimmy a wink. Gina grinned from ear to ear and pecked him on the cheek.

"Would you fight for me?" Brenda asked.

"No," Jimmy said point blank.

"You're such a jerk," Brenda said and punched him in the arm.

"Well not if we were broke up..." He said trying to back talk and explain his way out of it.

"You're still a jerk," Brenda said crossing her arms.

Donnie just shook his head looking at Jimmy. He was by no means an expert at women but he knew enough from movies and his Dad that sometimes you had to tell them what they want to hear. They all went to lunch. By the time they were done eating Jimmy had kissed ass enough to be back in Brenda's good graces.

The first day of school was easy. Once you got all your books you just went to your classes and got a little speech from your new teachers and that was it. Today was a little different. Everywhere was talk of the fight after school. As the day progressed the rumor grew and grew. The more the rumors grew the more ridiculous they became. By the time the day was over they were having a knife fight

65

to the death in the parking lot. Donnie was surprised he hadn't heard they were going to shoot it out with dueling pistols.

Three O' Clock finally rolled around and there was a crowd gathering in the parking lot. Cindy's new beau was waiting in the parking lot with Cindy on his arm. She was all giddy, no doubt feeling important due to all the fuss and gossip. Billy made his way through the crowd and stepped into the parking lot. He walked by where Cindy and her new boyfriend were standing just as cool and calm as could be.

"Hey, do you have a problem with me seeing Cindy?" The boy yelled as Billy walked by.

"I don't give a rats ass you can have her," Billy responded not even breaking his stride or bothering to take off his headphones.

"Are you kidding me?" Brenda yelled looking at Jimmy. Jimmy just shrugged his shoulders and started to laugh.

"How romantic," Donnie said in a mocking tone, imitating the girls earlier.

"It is," Jimmy replied and they both started laughing uncontrollably.

"Screw you!" Brenda yelled.

"Yeah you guys suck!" Gina added.

"Aw c'mon we were just kidding," Jimmy said trying to sound sincere, but he couldn't keep a straight face or hold in his laughter.

"Come on Brenda we'll walk home," Gina said grabbing Brenda by the hand and disappearing into the dispersing crowd.

"Boy, you sure do know how to put your foot in your mouth when it comes to women," Donnie said.

"Hey, you were right along with me this time."

"Yeah, I guess."

"C'mon let's go get the truck."

"What about the girls?"

"I know which way they'll walk, we'll pick 'em up on the way home."

"Okay."

The boys hung out a minute and talked to a couple people from the crowd. They got in the truck and drove looking for the girls. "There they are," Donnie said pointing at the girls walking on the side of the road. Jimmy just drove right past them like he didn't even see them. 'What are you doing?" Donnie asked.

"Were gonna have a little fun."

"Man, you never learn."

"Aw c'mon quit being a chicken."

"What are you gonna do?"

"You'll see," Jimmy said and pulled off the road and parked the truck behind some bushes. "C'mon we'll go hang out in those bushes by the side of the road."

"Alright, but this is all your idea. Remember I said that," Donnie said not feeling too good about having anything to do with Jimmy's plans. The boys waited hunched down behind some bushes. "Man, this is stupid," Donnie said and started to stand up.

"Wait, I think I hear them," Jimmy said as he pulled him back down.

"I can't believe they just drove right by us like that. They didn't even try to get us to come with them," Brenda said faintly in the distance.

"Shhh," Jimmy held his finger to his lips. "They're coming."

Brenda's voice got louder and louder, the closer they got. She rambled on about the boys.

"Hey little girl do you want some candy?" Jimmy said disguising his voice. The girls just looked at each other and picked up their pace. "Maybe you could help me find my lost puppy," Jimmy yelled in the deep voice. He started to shake the bushes and the girls took off running. The boys stood up and started laughing loudly.

"You're an asshole!" Brenda yelled. Gina couldn't help herself and started to laugh. Brenda gave in and started to laugh as well. They all walked to the truck piled in and drove to their houses. All was well again.

Chapter Nine

Donnie was not a good guitar player. He just couldn't seem to get it. Jimmy on the other hand was learning fast. He had an old guitar that had been passed down in his family over the years. He'd bring that old guitar to school to play in class and played it at the fort sometimes on weekends. He and the other kids in class would teach each other songs they figured out by listening to the radio or learned from song books. One day in class Jimmy was playing 'Smoke on the water' as Donnie watched.

"How do you do that?" Donnie asked.

"It's easy everyone knows how to play that song."

"Not me."

"Let me show you," Jimmy said. "Pick up that guitar and just do what I do."

Donnie picked up a guitar and tried to copy what Jimmy was doing but the notes were not clear.

"You need to push down harder with your fingers," Jimmy said.

"I'm trying," Donnie said frustrated. Jimmy tried and tried helping him position his fingers and gave him advice but Donnie just couldn't get it.

"You're hopeless," Jimmy finally said.

"I know."

"Maybe you could be a drummer."

"We don't even have a drum set. This is guitar class."

"I know I'm just saying maybe you'd have better luck on another instrument."

"Whatever." Donnie said and put the guitar down.

The school year was moving along at a good pace. One day Gina didn't show up for school. The next day she came but was late. Her mom had dropped her off after everyone was already in class. Donnie didn't know she was at school until he saw her a little before lunch. He walked up to her and she looked him in the eye and started to cry.

"What's the matter?" He asked. She didn't answer she just hugged him and cried harder into his shoulder. "What's wrong?" He asked again.

"Arabaca." She managed to say between cries and sniffles.

"What?"

"Arabaca."

"What the hell does that mean?" He asked looking at her puzzled. "Is that some kind of disease?"

"It's a mine, my dad got a job there."

"So what's wrong with that?"

"It's by Tucson." She said and started crying again.

"Where the hell is Tucson?"

"Arizona."

Donnie's eyes got wide. He couldn't believe it. He almost blurted out that Tracy moved to Arizona but caught himself. She didn't see his reaction cause her head was buried in his shoulder. He held her and thought to himself, what are the odds. He held her a bit then asked, "How did this happen?"

She pulled back from him, wiping away tears from her cheeks. "About a month ago, I guess he got a letter asking if he'd like to work at the Arabaca mine."

"Maybe it won't happen."

"Oh, it's going to happen," she said. That was all it took and her head was buried in his shoulder again. She was crying uncontrollably again.

The bell rang signaling for them to head to class. He hugged her and said, "It will be alright." He gave her a quick kiss and they went their separate ways. Donnie was in shock on his way to guitar class. He entered the classroom and sat down next to Jimmy, already playing his guitar. "You're not going to believe this."

"What, you learned a song?"

"No, smart ass."

"What then?"

"Gina is moving away."

"Get out of here."

"I'm serious. I bet you'll never guess where she's moving."

"I don't know, Alaska?"

"Arizona."

69

"Holy crap! Does every chick you have sex with run off to Arizona?"

"It looks that way."

"What are the odds?" Jimmy said staring off into space.

"That's what I said. It's crazy."

"Well maybe it won't happen."

"That's what I told her, but she seemed pretty confident it was a sure thing."

"When?"

"We didn't talk about that yet. She was crying so much and then the bell rang. We didn't have a chance to talk much at all."

"I bet it falls through." Jimmy said and started playing his guitar. They went about their day. At lunch they all met up as usual. Brenda showed up last. Gina had her head buried crying into Donnie.

"What's wrong with Gina?" Brenda asked.

"Her Dad got a new job and they're moving away to Arizona." Jimmy said.

"Hey isn't that where..." Before she could finish her sentence a notebook hit her in the arm. She looked at Donnie. He was holding Gina to his chest with one arm and holding his finger to his lips with the other. Brenda looked at the notebook on the ground and then at Donnie shaking his head no and understood. " ...where the Grand Canyon is?" She tried to finish her sentence without sounding obvious.

"I believe it is." Jimmy said smiling.

"Who cares about the stupid Grand Canyon." Gina said muffled by Donnie's shirt.

Everyone just stood there quietly for a moment, not knowing what to say. Gina just sobbed. They all ate lunch, well except for Gina. She didn't eat a bite. They all sat quietly not knowing what to say. Finally the bell rang and broke the uncomfortable silence between them. Donnie hugged Gina and said," I'll see you after school."

"Okay," she said with a sniffle and they went their separate ways once again.

After school they all met up at Jimmy's truck in the parking lot. They all piled in the pickup and Jimmy drove out of the parking lot. Gina had finally stopped crying but didn't say a word. Nobody did. Jimmy dropped the girls off one at a time. The boys got out and kissed their girlfriends goodbye at each stop. Finally, the boys were alone in the truck.

"She's a wreck." Jimmy said.

"I know."

"How about you are you okay?"

"I'll be fine," Donnie said staring out the window.

"Aren't you gonna miss her?"

"Yeah, of course I will."

"It doesn't seem to bother you much at all."

"She's not gone yet."

"You don't even think she's going , do you?"

"I don't know, but I'm not going to get all upset about something that might not even happen."

"That makes sense."

"If we could only get Gina to understand it."

"Yeah, girls are crazy."

Jimmy turned on to Donnie's farm. "You want off at your house or the fort?"

"House."

"Okay man, I'll pick you up tomorrow."

"Alright Jimmy, see ya," Donnie said and got out of the truck. Jimmy turned around and drove off in a cloud of dust. Donnie just stood there for a minute shaking his head. "What a day," he muttered to himself out loud as he walked up the porch steps and went inside.

Chapter Ten

The next day Gina didn't show up for school. Donnie figured he'd let her be. When she didn't show up the next day he thought he better check on her. When Jimmy dropped him off at home, he borrowed his dad's truck and drove to her house. He knocked on her door. She answered the door. "Hey," she said, not sounding very enthused or happy.

"What's up Gina, why haven't you been at school?"

"Why bother?"

"What do you mean? You still want to graduate on time don't you?"

"I guess," She said shrugging her shoulders.

"Well if you get dropped that's going to follow you to your next school."

"Yeah, I guess it will."

"C'mon Gina snap out of it," Donnie said as he grabbed her by her shoulders and looked her in the eye.

"I will, I've just been sad but I'm getting better."

At least she wasn't crying anymore, Donnie thought to himself. "Is this a for sure thing or is it up in the air still?"

They were sitting on the swing on her porch. She raised her right arm and pointed to the front yard. Donnie's eyes followed the direction she was pointing. He saw a sign in the front yard with a little sign hanging from it at the bottom which read 'For Sale'. He was surprised he didn't notice it when he pulled up. He looked back at her and asked, "How long?"

"One month, maybe two."

He leaned in and gave her a hug. "Well you shouldn't be locking yourself up in your room the whole time. We should be spending as much time as we can together. You know make the most of it."

"I guess you're right," She said and actually managed to smile.

"I know I'm right, so let's not sit around being sad, let's enjoy the time we have left together."

"Okay," she said and gave him a kiss. "Thanks for coming over Donnie."

"No problem, you're my girl."

"I am."

"So I'll see you at school tomorrow?"

"I'll be there."

"Okay, I gotta get the truck back and do some chores for my dad."

"Thanks again Donnie," She said and kissed him deeply.

"See you tomorrow," He said and walked down the path to the truck. He got in started it up, waved goodbye and drove away.

From that day forward Gina and Donnie spent a lot of time together. They went to the movies, hung out at the fort. Gina would even come over and help him with his chores sometimes. The thing they seemed to do the most though was have sex. Donnie couldn't believe how much sex they had when he thought about it. The time seemed to fly by.

One day Gina didn't show up at school. Donnie drove to her house after Jimmy dropped him off at his own. Donnie turned onto Gina's street and the first thing he noticed was the big moving truck in the driveway. He looked at the sign in the yard and noticed another little sign had been added. 'Sold' the sign read in red letters with a white background. He parked in front of the house and walked up the path to the front door. Before he could even knock Gina opened the door with tears in her eyes. "We are leaving tonight," She said as tears streamed down her face. Donnie wrapped his arms around her, he was speechless.

Donnie stayed over and helped them load the big orange and silver truck. He didn't stay to help load everything. He mostly just helped with the big furniture. He was only there for an hour or two. "I better get going," He said to Gina.

"Do you have to?"

"Yeah."

"Hold on a minute." Gina wiped some tears from her cheek and walked down the hallway disappearing into her room. She came back out carrying a big box wrapped with a bow on it.

"A present for me?"

"Yeah, it's nothing you'll see."

"I'm just going to go check in with my dad and let him know what's going on and I'll come back."

"Well don't open it 'til I'm gone."

"I won't."

"You promise?"

"I promise," Donnie said holding his hand over his heart smiling.

73

She snatched the box out of Donnie's hands and said," I'll give it to you when you come back. I didn't trust that smile on your face." She marched back down the hall and put the box back in her room. When she returned he just stared at her.

"There now you have to come back,"She said.

"What if my dad won't let me come back?"

"He will."

"What if he needs the truck?"

"Have him drop you off."

"What if he won't?"

"I'll tell you what. If we leave before you get back I'll leave it on the front porch. If you can't come back you can pick it up on the way to school."

"Okay," Donnie said and gave her a kiss and went on his way.

Donnie drove home and explained to his dad that Gina was moving for good tonight. His dad let him use the truck for the rest of the night. He ate supper and headed back to Gina's. Gina's parents were very grateful for all Donnie's help. They tried to feed him. He explained he already ate. In the end Gina's dad insisted on giving him twenty dollars for helping. Gina's parents gave them ten minutes to say goodbye.

"I'll write you as soon as we get there," Gina said once again in tears.

"Okay."

"Here you go," She said handing over the wrapped box.

"You really shouldn't have."

"Yes I should, you'll see when you open it." She grabbed him and gave him a big kiss. "I love you Donnie, I'll never forget you."

"Oh Gina I'm going to miss you so much," He said and they kissed some more.

"I gotta go."

"I know."

They kissed once more and he walked her out to the truck. He said goodbye to her parents and they started the big truck. They all waved to Donnie as they drove away with Gina's mom's car in tow. Donnie kept waving as they got further and further down the road. He looked at the box next to him. He picked it up and shook it by his ear. He thought about opening it right then. He decided he could wait. He put the box in the truck and drove home. He carried the box up to his room, he was tired. He got ready for bed and laid down. He couldn't sleep. He decided he should open the box.

He sat on his bed with the box on his lap. He ripped off the wrapping paper. Inside was just a plain cardboard box. He peeled the tape back and opened the flaps. He found an envelope with his name on it sitting on top of something in a green garbage bag. He opened the envelope and found a short note.

Donnie,

    Sorry I was so immature. I hope you forgive me.

    Love, Gina

He pulled the garbage bag out of the box and ripped it open. Inside was the box from the fort with all Tracy's letters and pictures in it. He fumbled through the box laughing to himself. "I thought these were long gone," He said out loud to himself. He felt around and there they were under all the envelopes, Tracy's panties. He started to laugh. He stayed up late looking at the pictures and reading the letters and cards. He finally went to sleep he was so happy to have his box of Tracy memories back.

The next day Jimmy picked up Donnie for school. Jimmy honked his horn outside. Donnie came out sprinting down the porch steps and climbed in the cab. "Gina's gone," he blurted out as his butt hit the seat.

"Gone as in moved?"

"Yep, I helped them pack up the U-Haul yesterday and watched them drive away."

"Wow, there was no warning."

"No not at all, well unless you count the last two months or so." Donnie said sarcastically.

"You know what I mean."

"I know I'm just messing with you."

"You alright?"

"Yeah I'm cool, a little sad ya know."

"Yeah, that's understandable," Jimmy said as he pulled up to Brenda's house and honked the horn.

"You'll never guess what she gave me."

"What?"

"The box with all Tracy's stuff in it, the one I had in the fort."

"No way, she said she threw it out," Jimmy said honking the horn again impatiently.

"She had it the whole time."

"Chicks are crazy," Jimmy said as he was just about to honk again. Brenda came out the front door. Donnie got out so Brenda could slide in the middle. He got back in and shut the door.

"You only have to honk once, I'm not deaf," Brenda said angrily.

"Well you didn't come out."

"I was coming."

"Good morning," Donnie interrupted them to stop the argument.

"Good morning Donnie," Brenda said. "And good morning to you horn blower," She said and kissed Jimmy on the cheek as he drove down her street.

"Gina left last night," Jimmy said staring straight ahead at the road.

"She did?" Brenda said surprised. "She didn't even have a chance to say goodbye."

"I think the people who bought the house wanted to move in right away," Donnie said.

"Well that sucks. I would have liked to talk to her before she left, she should have called me."

"Her phone was disconnected last week. She said her dad didn't want to pay the bill since they were moving."

They got to school and went their separate ways. It seemed weird at first not having Gina around. Life went on and Donnie got used to the fact she was gone. Weeks went by and he got a letter from Gina. She said she missed him but she was meeting new friends. She said she moved to a small town right outside of Tucson called Sahurita.

Donnie read Gina's letter a few times. Every time he tried to write her back he could never think of anything to say. He would start it out telling her he missed her and that was it. After a while he'd just give up and do something else. Once a month had gone by he decided not to write her back. He figured he'd never see her again so why bother.

Chapter Eleven

The school year was going by and before Donnie knew it, it was his birthday again. Jimmy had gotten a hold of some beer somehow and they met at the fort to drink it. Technically Donnie's birthday wasn't until Monday but the boys celebrated it on Saturday.

"Happy Birthday Donnie," Jimmy said as he ripped open a twelve pack of Budweiser. He pulled out a can and handed it to Donnie. He took another one out for himself and dumped the remaining cans into the ice chest. He grabbed the bag of ice and tore it open then dumped it over the cans in the ice chest.

"Thanks Jimmy," Donnie said as he popped open his beer.

"It's the least I could do on your birthday," Jimmy said opening his own can.

"Summer is on the way."

"I'm gonna miss swimming at Gina's house," Jimmy said and took a big swig of beer.

"Yeah, it's going to be different, that's for sure."

"We're gonna have to find you a new girl."

"I'm not in any hurry."

"Do you like anyone at school?"

"Nah, not really. I haven't really thought about it."

The boys played games and drank beer in the fort all night. They were pretty drunk by the time they fell asleep. The next day they woke up with headaches. They woke up groaning and moaning. They both went home and ate and slept off their hangovers.

Monday morning Donnie woke up to a huge breakfast. His parents wished him happy birthday. They instructed him to come right home after school. He knew the drill, his mom would bake him a cake while he was at school. They would eat an early supper and have the cake for dessert, same as last year. It was nice to have regularity in your life, things that you could count on not changing.

Jimmy showed up to pick Donnie up for school. Donnie made it out of the house before Jimmy had time to honk. Donnie got in the truck and said, "Hey Jimmy, feeling better?"

"Yeah I was better after I had something to eat and got a little sleep."

"Yeah, same here."

"Happy birthday, officially."

"Thanks Jimmy."

"You want to do something after school today?"

"I can't, I told my folks I'd come straight home after school, its kinda tradition."

"Oh, okay just thought I'd ask."

The boys picked up Brenda and went to school. It was a typical school day other than once in a while Donnie would get a Happy Birthday from someone in class. The school day ended and Jimmy drove Donnie home as usual. When Donnie walked in the house he could smell the food. He thought how different it was without Gina and thought again how nice it was that some things stayed the same.

Donnie ate pork chops, mashed potatoes and corn on the cob with his parents. When they were finished eating his mother disappeared into the kitchen. A few moments later she came back in carrying a cake with candles burning on top. She and Donnie's father sang Happy Birthday as she sat the cake down in front of him. "Make a wish," his mother said.

Donnie blew the seventeen candles out with one deep breath. He made his wish. He wished for the same thing he'd been wishing for, Tracy to return. This year he added, or at least write, to his wish. When he opened his eyes there were a couple of wrapped presents on the table. There was also an envelope which Donnie could only assume was a Birthday card. "Open your presents," His mother said. "Then you can cut the cake and we'll eat."

Donnie grabbed one of the presents off the table and tore it open. It was a package of underwear. He sat them down and picked up the other present. He squeezed it as he picked it up. He already knew what it was going to be. He tore off the paper and to no surprise unveiled a package of sox. "Thanks Mom and Dad," he said placing the sox down next to the underwear.

"Don't forget your card," his mother said excitedly.

Donnie picked up the envelope off the table and ran his finger across the back flap. He pulled the card from the envelope and read the front of it out loud. "Happy Birthday, Son." He opened the card and a bill fell out.

It flipped as it floated down to the floor. It finally came to a rest at Donnie's left foot. His eyes zoomed in on the bill. He saw right away it was Benjamin Franklin and smiled. "Hope you have a wonderful day with many more throughout the year," He said reading the inside of the card out loud. He reached down and picked up the hundred dollar bill. "Thank you," Donnie said happily.

"You're welcome son," his parents said in unison.

"Now let's cut that cake," his mom said as she handed him a knife. "My mouth is watering," she added.

"Okay," Donnie said. He cut the cake into even pieces. He put a piece on each of the three plates already on the table. He ran his finger down the side of the knife and licked the frosting of his finger. "Mmmm, that's good, chocolate is my favorite," he said with a smile. They ate cake and drank some milk and that was it. Donnie's birthday was done in his eyes.

Chapter Twelve

The last day of school came and went. Summer was here, but it wasn't the same. Gina was gone so there was no hanky-panky at the fort. Without Gina there was no pool. Swimming took up a lot of groups' time in the previous summers. They never knew how much they liked that pool until it was gone. Without anything to kill the time the summer seemed to crawl. Jimmy stopped by from time to time to see if Donnie wanted to hang out at the fort. Sometimes he would go and play games with Jimmy, but more often than not he stayed home.

Donnie couldn't remember ever wanting a summer to end so much in his life. All he did to occupy his time was work and sleep. Sometimes he would read one of Tracy's letters in hopes he would have dreams of her. He never did. A few times he started a letter to Gina but always ended up crumbling it up and throwing it away. He had never been so bored in his whole life.

Finally the school year started. Donnie was excited to go back to school. He was excited knowing it was his last year. The excitement was short lived when he showed up to school to the mundane ritual of getting books and classes. After that he felt relief. Relief that this was the last year he'd have to wait in those stupid lines, the last year of homework, tests and teachers. Donnie had no plans of going to college. He was going to be a farmer like his father before him and his father before him. This was it, finish this school year and he was free from school for the rest of his life.

The school year was moving along. Donnie was still bored. He missed Gina and it showed. He still ate lunch with Jimmy and Brenda everyday but it wasn't the usual girls against boy's banter they had before. He felt like a third wheel. He never went to the fort anymore. It was like the summer only now it was school, work and sleep instead of the last two. That was his routine. The thing about having a routine is time seems to go by fast. It seems when you do the same thing, day in and day out, the days tend to blur together. Before you realize it months have gone by.

One day Donnie's mother had given him a calendar she'd gotten from the bank. It was then that he realized it was already April. He hung the calendar on the inside of his bedroom door with a thumbtack. He taped a pen to a string and hung it with another thumbtack next to the calendar. Now every day when he got up he would cross off the day on his calendar. This became part of his routine.

Donnie woke up, got out of bed and rubbed his eyes a minute. He walked over to the door and grabbed the pen. He put an X through the box with the twelve in the corner. It was April twelfth 1993. He went down the hall to the bathroom and started washing up for school. Once he was ready he ate and sat on the porch steps to wait for Jimmy. It wasn't long and Jimmy came rolling up in a cloud of dust. Donnie got in the truck.

"Good morning Donnie. You were already waiting for me."

"Good morning. Yeah I seem to be getting up a little early lately."

"I was talking to Brenda and she mentioned that she has a friend she's been hanging out with. She was thinking she should introduce you two and see what happens."

"Who?"

"Shelly."

"Shelly Peterson?"

"I guess. That might be her name."

"That chick is ugly."

"I've seen her, she's not that ugly."

"Did you hear what you just said? The fact that you said not that ugly proves she's ugly."

Jimmy started to laugh. "Brenda just wanted me to see what you thought about it."

"She's fat too."

"Okay, okay, I'll tell Brenda to just forget it," Jimmy said trying not to laugh as he pulled up to pick up Brenda. She was also already outside waiting as Jimmy drove up. She came sprinting across the lawn towards the truck. Donnie got out so Brenda could get in the middle.

"Good morning Donnie," she said as she stepped by him to get in the truck.

"You can forget about it," Donnie said as she was sliding across the seat.

She gave Jimmy a kiss and asked, "What is he talking about?"

"Shelly," Jimmy said.

"Awe, she's sweet Donnie. I bet you would like her if you got to know her."

"Forget it," Donnie said as he got in and shut the door.

Jimmy put the truck in drive and headed for school. He was staying out of this one. Nobody said a word the rest of the way to school. When Jimmy parked Donnie got out and headed for class.

"What's his problem?" Brenda asked.

"I don't know."

"She's real nice."

"I'm sure she is," Jimmy said as he gave her a kiss. The bell rang and they went their separate ways.

The group all met for lunch as usual. To Donnie's surprise nobody mentioned Shelly. They just made small talk as they ate. The bell rang and they dispersed. They met in the parking lot after school. Jimmy dropped Brenda off first as always. Once she shut the door of the house Donnie finally spoke. "Thank God," he said.

"Why"

"We made it all the way through lunch and to her house without hearing about Shelly."

"But she's a real nice girl, you'll like her Donnie," Jimmy said in a high pitched voice mocking Brenda.

"Shut up," Donnie said. Jimmy just laughed.

"Don't worry she'll bring it back up. Just give her some time," Jimmy said with a smirk.

"I'm sure she will."

Jimmy turned in to Donnie's farm drove up to Donnie's porch and stopped. "I'll see you tomorrow, buddy."

Donnie opened the door as he said, "Alright Jimmy have a good night,"

"You too," Jimmy said as Donnie shut the truck door. Jimmy drove off in his usual cloud of dust.

Donnie went up to his room and changed clothes. He went and did his various chores around the farm, just as he always did. When he was finished he went in and took a shower. When he was finished it was time for supper. He sat down and ate with his parents. He was clearing the dishes for his mother when he thought he heard a truck outside. He put the last of the dishes in the sink and went to the front door. When he opened the door Jimmy was standing there with his fist in the air, just about to knock.

"Hey Jimmy what's up?"

"Are you busy?"

"Not really, I just got done eating."

"C'mon let's go to the fort."

"I'm not in the mood for games tonight I'm tired."

"Just for a little while."

"I'm too tired."

"Trust me. You want to go to the fort with me right now."

Donnie looked at Jimmy with a bit of distrust. He could only think Brenda and Shelly were out there at the fort. He stood there for a second then said, "Hold on, let me go tell my folks I'm going. I'll be right back."

Jimmy walked around and got in the truck. He sat inside and giggled to himself. Once he heard the door open he stopped and regained his composer. Donnie opened the truck door and got in. "This better be good," He said as he shut the door.

"You'll thank me later," Jimmy said and started the truck. They drove to the fort and Jimmy turned the truck off. He got out first and went into the fort. Donnie walked in right behind him. When Donnie stepped in the fort his eyes opened wide and his jaw dropped open.

"Hey stranger," Tracy said opening her arms for a hug. Donnie's eyes filled with tears as he ran to her and wrapped his arms around her. Tears ran down his cheeks.

"I told ya," Jimmy said with a huge smile.

"I can't believe you're here," Donnie said hugging her tight.

"I'm here," She said squeezing him back.

"I told you, you'd want to come to the fort," Jimmy said again. He may as well have not even been in the room. They were paying no attention to him. Donnie started kissing Tracy. "Alright I'm outta here," Jimmy said standing there waiting for a response. He just threw his arms up in the air and walked out of the fort. He got in his truck and drove home without Donnie even noticing. He was so excited Tracy was here that she was all he seen and heard. Donnie kissed Tracy some more as they made their way to the sleeping bag. He took his shirt off and looked around a bit.

"Where's Jimmy?" he asked.

"He left," Tracy said. Donnie started kissing her again. He pulled her shirt up over her head between kisses. They undressed each other and had sex. Afterwards they laid there holding each other.

"I missed you so much Tracy."

"I missed you too."

"Why did you stop writing?"

"I moved away for a while, I kept getting in trouble with my parents. It's a long story. I'd rather not get into it."

"Okay. How did you get here?" He asked as he pulled her closer and rubbed her back.

"My parents got mad at me and told me they were sending me to the farm for the summer. At first I told them you can't make me do anything I'm eighteen years old. Then I thought about you and how I could come see you and they'd pay for it. So I told them go ahead and send me, I don't care, so they did." She started to laugh.

"They sent you how?"

"They bought me a bus ticket. They even stayed to make sure I got on and waited for it to drive off."

"So you'll be here all summer?"

"I don't know what I'm gonna do yet. I don't know how long I can stand all the work Uncle James will have for me." She grabbed Donnie's arm and looked at his watch. "Oh shit, I better get back."

"I better get home too, I got school tomorrow."

"Oh yeah, school is still in session," She said as she got dressed. "What time do you get out?"

"About 3 O' Clock, but after that I got farm work to do."

"Can you meet me here after?"

"Yeah, I'll come to the fort after supper tomorrow."

"Okay. I really got to go," She said and kissed him on the cheek and hurried out the door.

Donnie just laid there for a while smiling. He stared at the plywood ceiling and whispered, "Thank you," out loud.

Chapter Thirteen

The next day Jimmy picked up Donnie for school as usual. Donnie was already waiting on the porch. When Jimmy pulled up Donnie climbed into the truck. He was grinning from ear to ear. "Happy day?" Jimmy asked as he put the truck into drive and started heading down the dirt driveway.

"It's a very happy day."

"I really thought you would never see her again."

"I told you I would."

"I know and you were right. I still can't believe it but you were right."

"Your dad didn't tell you she was coming?"

"You know my dad never tells me anything, unless he needs me to do something."

"He must have known."

"Of course he knew, he drove to the city to pick her up from the bus station."

"I don't care it was a nice surprise."

"Of course you don't care. She's here what difference does it make how she got here, or if you knew she was coming or not. None of that matters." Jimmy said as he pulled up to Brenda's house and honked the horn. He just honked the horn a second time as the door of the house was opening.

"Shut up!" Brenda yelled as she pulled the door closed. "I'm coming." She walked towards the truck carrying an arm full of books, shaking her head. Donnie had already gotten out of the truck for her, so she hopped onto the bench seat and slid over to Jimmy. "I'm going to disconnect that damn horn. I swear to God I am," She said as she rested the books on her lap.

"Good morning to you too," Jimmy said sarcastically.

"You're going to get it," She said as Donnie got in and shut the door.

"Come here and give it to me then," Jimmy said puckering his lips for a kiss. Reluctantly she leaned over and gave him a peck as he put the truck into drive.

"Good morning Donnie," She said.

"Good morning," Donnie replied.

"I talked to Shelly last night on the phone and told her all about you."

"Forget it Brenda. I already have a girlfriend."

"A long distance girlfriend maybe, but Shelly just lives…"

"Tell her Jimmy," Donnie interrupted.

"The love of Donnie's life has returned," Jimmy said in his best announcer voice.

"What? Gina? Is she back?"

"Not Gina baby doll, my cousin Tracy."

"Really, when did this happen?" She asked surprised.

"She showed up yesterday. I was as surprised as he was when I got home and she was there," Jimmy said. He was actually being serious for once. "I had no idea she was coming."

"I guess it was a good thing Gina left when she did. That could have been a real mess."

"I never thought of that," Donnie said. He knew he would have dumped Gina in a heartbeat to be with Tracy. It really would have been a mess though.

"Everything happens for a reason," Jimmy said as he parked the truck in the school lot.

"That's a fact," Brenda agreed.

They all got out of the truck and headed for class. All year long time had been flying by. Donnie couldn't believe how slow the day was going now that he wanted it to go by fast. It didn't help matters that he was looking up at the clock every five minutes. He tried to not look at the clock. He decided he'll just stay focused on his desk, but his eyes just wandered to his watch. "Errr," he moaned under his breath.

Finally the final bell rang. Donnie hurried to the truck. Jimmy and Brenda came walking up a couple minutes later. "Man, today went by fast," Jimmy said unlocking the truck door.

"Are you kidding me? I thought it was never going to end," Donnie said.

Jimmy dropped off Brenda. He and Donnie headed for his house. "When you get home tell Tracy to meet me at the fort at 6 O' Clock, would you?" Donnie asked.

"Six, I thought you'd be meeting her right now?"

"I can't. I gotta get my chores done first. Then I gotta eat supper. The last thing I want to do is piss my dad off and get grounded. Not while Tracy is here."

"Yeah, I guess you're right."

Jimmy dropped off Donnie and went home. Tracy was sitting on the couch watching TV. He delivered the message to her as Donnie had asked.

Donnie did his chores as fast as he could. He couldn't remember ever getting them done that fast. He had to double check and make sure he didn't forget anything. He didn't. He went upstairs and took a shower and put on some clean clothes. He was in his room pacing back and forth, looking at his watch every two minutes again. Finally he heard his mom yell for him to wash up dinner was ready. He hurried downstairs and sat at the table.

"Wow, that was fast," His mother said. "You must be hungry."

"Yeah, I'm starving." He didn't want to tell his parents Tracy was back just yet. All he cared about was getting to the fort and meeting with her. He was eating fast.

"Slow down, I don't want to have to give you that Hymlick thingy, whatever it's called. You know CPR, when you're choking."

"Heimlich maneuver," His dad chimed in correcting her.

"Yeah that's it. You really were hungry."

"I was but I'm full now," Donnie said with a smile and patted his belly. "May I be excused? I have to go out to the fort for a while."

"Who's going to help me clear the dishes?"

"Oh, I'm sorry mom I can wait."

"I'm only kidding honey run along. I think I can handle three plates and glasses." She gave him a wink and shooed him away.

"Thanks mom," he said with a little laugh. She had gotten him with that one. He went upstairs and grabbed his backpack. He went to the kitchen and grabbed some sodas. He thought about it and added a few snacks to the bag in case they got hungry. Once he felt he had everything he needed he started his hike out to the fort.

He made it to the fort and to his surprise Tracy was already there. She blew out a big plume of smoke. She patted the sleeping bag next to her and said," Come here baby love, I got something I want you to try." Donnie took his backpack off and set it on the floor. He sat next to her on the sleeping bag. "First things first," She said and gave him a big kiss. "How was your day?" She asked with a smile and a bat of her eyelashes.

She looked so good. She was wearing cut off shorts with a pink half-shirt which exposed her mid-drift. She obviously wasn't wearing a bra the way her nipples were poking out.

"My day's a lot better, now that I'm with you."

"Oh, how sweet, you always say the nicest things to me. I missed you so much," She said and gave him another big tongue kiss. She held out her hand with her palm up. Between her first finger and thumb she held what looked like what looked like a small dumbbell that was missing a ball on one end. It was made of glass and looked like it had a white coating on the inside. "Have you ever smoked this?" She asked with that dazzling smile.

"What is it?"

"It's speed, you know meth."

"What's meth?"

"I didn't think you'd know about it. Here put this in your mouth," She said and started feeling around behind her. "Here it is," She said revealing a purple lighter. "Now I'm going to light this and when I tell you to breathe in through the pipe real slow." She lit the lighter and held it under the ball at the end of the pipe. Donnie noticed there was a hole on the top of the ball. "Let your breath out through your nose," She said. Donnie obeyed. "Okay here it goes breathe in slow," she said. Occasionally she pulled the lighter away and put it back under the ball. Donnie noticed a little smoke escaping from the hole in the top once he couldn't breathe in anymore. She pulled the pipe away from his lips. "Blow it out. It's not like weed. You don't need to hold it in."

Donnie exhaled through his mouth and couldn't believe how much smoke came out. "Wow the whole inside of my skull is tingling."

"Feels good, huh?" Tracy asked with a huge smile.

"Hell yeah it does."

Tracy pushed him back on his back on the sleeping bag and straddled his shins. "Here hit it again slow like I showed you." Donnie grabbed the lighter and lit the pipe again as he leaned back against the fort wall with his shoulders. "I know what else will make you feel good," Tracy said as she popped the buttons on his Levi's. Donnie took another hit off the pipe. Tracy pulled out Donnie's penis and put her mouth on it. Donnie gasped and another huge cloud of smoke came out his mouth. Tracy lifted her head up and said, "Smoke some more and relax and enjoy this. Donnie took another pull from the pipe as Tracy performed oral sex on him. The two of them stayed up all night talking, having sex and smoking meth.

Donnie went outside to pee. It was only then that he realized the sun was up. He came back inside and looked at his watch. "Holy shit!" He yelled and jumped to his feet again.

"What's the matter?"

"I gotta cut off Jimmy before he drives over to my house and starts honking the horn," He said pulling his pants on. "I should be able to catch him on the road if I hurry." Donnie pulled his shoes on and ran out the door. He ran down the tree line towards the road. He finally reached the road and bent over holding his knees huffing and puffing. A few moments later he spotted Jimmy's truck coming towards him. He waved his hands and flagged him down.

"You look like hell. What's going on are you okay?" Jimmy asked with concern in his voice.

"I'm alright, but I need a favor," Donnie said still a bit out of breath.

"What?"

"I'm not going to school today but I don't want my folks to know. I need you to drive over to my house and act like you picked me up. You know just park a second and drive off like you always do. Will you?"

"Alright, but if your dad comes out and starts asking me a bunch of questions I'm not getting in any trouble over this."

"Fair enough if he comes out just drive to the fort but he won't he never sees me leave for school you'll be okay. Stop by the fort after school too if you can."

"Okay I'll be there."

"Thanks Jimmy."

Jimmy showed up at the fort after school as promised. When he went inside he found Donnie and Tracy in there fast asleep. He almost yanked the sleeping bag off them and yelled for them to wake up. But after noticing all the clothes on the floor he decided not to. He knew they'd be naked as jaybirds under there. He decided his best course of action was to bang on the table. "Wake up!" He yelled banging on the wooden spool table.

"I'm up," Donnie said startled from his sleep, he sat straight up. Tracy just moaned a little and rolled over.

"Have you guys been sleeping all day?"

"No, we barely fell asleep," Donnie said looking at his watch.

"What the hell have you been doing all day? Never mind don't answer that."

"How was school?" Donnie asked as he put his clothes on.

"Not as fun as you had. Don't worry you didn't miss anything," Jimmy said with a smirk.

Donnie gathered up Tracy's clothes and put them under the covers next to her. "Wake up," He whispered in her ear and gave it a little kiss.

"Mmmm, I'm tired," Tracy said groggily.

"Jimmy's here."

"So."

"I'm going to have him drive me to my house so it looks like I went to school today."

"Okay," she said still half asleep.

"Don't you want to come with us and go back home with Jimmy?"

"I think you should. There is nothing to eat or drink out here."

"My dad was pretty upset this morning when you weren't at breakfast. I can just hear him now," Jimmy chimed in.

"Okay, okay," She said not very happy and started to get dressed.

Jimmy drove Donnie to the house as if they had stopped by the fort on the way home from school. His parents were none the wiser.

Chapter Fourteen

The next day Donnie went to the fort. He and Tracy had agreed to meet there when Jimmy dropped him off at the house the day before. When Donnie showed up at the fort she was nowhere to be found. He waited at the fort awhile but she didn't show. He walked back to the house and ate dinner with his parents. He walked back to the fort but Tracy still was not there. He was tempted to walk to Jimmy's and see what was going on but decided against it. He figured if she was in trouble he'd only make it worse asking for her at the door.

Jimmy picked Donnie up for school the next day. He told Donnie that Tracy and his dad got in a huge argument. He also said he wouldn't expect her to be able to leave the house for a while. Jimmy handed Donnie a note from Tracy. The piece of paper it was written on was all folded up and had about four or five staples through it. Donnie assumed it was so Jimmy couldn't read it so he just put it in his pocket.

"Aren't you going to read it?"

"I'll read it later."

"Why?"

"I got a test today and I don't want anything to distract me from the answers I memorized last night"

"Oh, yeah I guess that makes sense," Jimmy said as he honked for Brenda to come out.

Donnie was lying. He didn't have a test but he knew if he read it in the truck Jimmy would ask all kinds of questions. He knew those staples meant it was private. He knew Jimmy would bug him until he knew what the letter said. He was dying to know what the note said but he had to wait.

They got to school and spilt up to their different classes. As soon as Jimmy and Brenda were out of sight Donnie tore into the note. It was short and to the point it simply said meet me at the fort tonight-8PM love Tracy. Donnie tore the note up, threw it away and went to class thinking how unnecessary all those staples were.

The school day dragged on, they always did now that Tracy was back. When the final bell finally rang Donnie was the first one at the truck. He always was these days. He didn't have to wait long though. Jimmy and Brenda soon followed. They dropped Brenda off and as soon as she was out of the truck Jimmy asked, "So, what the note say?"

"Nothing much really, just that she was grounded and won't be able to see me for a while. Basically what you said," Donnie lied.

"Don't worry as long as she works around the house in the daytime my dad won't care what she does in the evenings. She just needs to be helpful for a few days and she can come out."

"I'm sure she will."

"I don't know she's pretty stubborn."

"Well, I hope she will."

"We'll see."

Jimmy stopped at Donnie's house. "Thanks Jimmy," Donnie said as he shut the truck door.

"See you tomorrow," Jimmy replied and drove off.

Donnie got to work on his chores. Farm work was hard but Donnie was used to it. Today he was actually grateful to have something to kill the time. Once he was done he went upstairs and took a shower. He ate supper and helped his mom with the dishes. He got his backpack ready as he usually did for a trip to the fort. Once he felt he had enough supplies to spend the night, if it came to that, he headed to the fort.

It was a nice night for a walk. He took his time walking to the fort, taking in the cool April air. He gazed up at the sky as he walked it was a crystal clear night. He was in awe of all the stars out bright as could be. He got to the fort and lit some candles. He unpacked the backpack and looked at his watch. He was pleasantly surprised to see it was already past seven thirty. He grabbed the broom and started sweeping and tidying the place up a bit.

Donnie had just finished cleaning when he heard footsteps outside. Tracy came through the plywood door, a bit out of breath. "Hey, baby love," She said and gave him a kiss.

"Hi, sit down and catch your breath."

"Okay."

Donnie went to the table and got her a soda. "Drink this," He said handing her a can of Mountain Dew.

"Thanks," She said and popped the top and took a long drink. "I needed that."

"Why are you so out of breath? Did you run all the way here or something?"

"I jogged most of the way. I had to sneak out and was worried someone would look out the window and see me."

"So you're still grounded?'

"Nope, not anymore," She said as she slipped the straps of her own backpack off her shoulders.

"Why'd you have to sneak out then?"

"Because I'm leaving and I'm not going back."

"What do you mean?"

"Just what I said, I'm not going back. There is nothing they can do about it either. I'm an adult in the eyes of the law. Eighteen years old and can come and go as I please."

"I don't understand. Why didn't you just tell them you're leaving, you didn't have to sneak out. Just tell them like you just told me right now."

"Because of this," She said and pulled a handful of money out of her backpack."

"What the hell! Where did all that come from?"

"The last time I was here I got grounded, remember?"

"Yeah, I remember."

"Well I got bored, being cooped up in that house all day so I snooped around. One day I got up on the counter and was looking through the top cupboards. When I opened one up, I found this old cookie jar. I thought it was cool. It was big and it looked real old and was shaped like a teddy bear. Anyway I slid it to the front of the shelf and opened it. When I reached in I expected it to be empty but it wasn't it was full of money."

"The truck fund," Donnie whispered half out loud and half to himself.

"The what?"

"Nothing, how much money was in it?"

"A little over two thousand dollars, can you believe it?"

"Holy crap!"

"That's nothing, the last time I was here there was a lot more. You could tell some of it was counted though. There were stacks of bills with rubber bands around them. I guess when it got filled up someone would count it and rubber band it in stacks of a hundred to make more room for loose money." She pulled out a rubber banded stack showing him. "See, like this one."

"They're going to notice it gone."

"I know, that's why I can't go back."

"Where are you gonna go?"

"I'm going back to Arizona."

"When?"

"Tonight, I'm leaving tonight."

"I don't want you to go."

"Well, I was kinda hoping ya know, you'd come with me."

"Come with you to Arizona?"

"Yeah, why not?"

"I got school. I'm going to graduate in a couple of months."

"Shit, I keep forgetting about that."

"Can't you wait two months?"

"No way, I can't risk getting caught putting this money back. Plus this is all I got left. I got to get back to Arizona and get some more," She said holding up a little Ziplock of meth showing him. "I'm sick of this bullshit farm work too. I can't stay here a day longer, forget it."

"You just got here I can't stand the thought of you leaving again."

"I want you to come with me."

"You really do?"

"Of course I do. I could have just left. Gave you a goodbye note instead of the one I did."

"I want to go with you but…"

"I understand."

"I think you should tough it out for a bit longer."

"Not happening, I can't take it anymore."

"What are you going to do?"

"I'm going back to Arizona. I told you."

"I know that. How are you going to get there?"

"Well, I have money I'll buy a bus ticket. Hell, I could fly."

"What if Jimmy's dad notices the money missing sooner rather than later? He'll call the cops I'd imagine. I don't think a bus or a plane is a good idea. If he calls the cops I'm sure they'll check the bus stations and airports first."

"You're right, I didn't think of that. What should I do, any ideas?"

"Maybe, I got to go back to my house. I'll be right back. Stay here, I won't be long."

Donnie ran all the way to his house. The whole time he couldn't help but think if she leaves again he's really never going to see her again. When he reached the porch he bent over and grabbed his knees. He was out of breath. He didn't want to wake his parents so he took a moment to calm down. Once he got his breathing under control he went inside and up to his room. He dug around in his nightstand drawer. Finally he found what he was looking for. He pulled out a little brown address book and headed downstairs. He flipped through the pages then picked up the phone and dialed a number. He tried to be as quiet as possible. The phone rang once, twice and halfway through the third ring someone picked up.

"Hello?"

"Is Bobby there?"

"This is Bobby, who's this?"

"This is Donnie, Jimmy's neighbor, remember me?"

"Of course I remember you, why are you whispering?"

"My parents are asleep, so I gotta be quiet. I was wondering if you still have your car."

"Yeah, I'll never get rid of that car, why?"

"Do you think if I gave you a hundred bucks and filled up your gas tank you could give my girl a ride somewhere tonight? I mean if you're not busy."

"A hundred bucks, hell yeah I'll give her a ride, you bet."

"Do you remember where I live?"

"Yes, I remember."

"Don't drive to the house go to the fort, remember the fort?"

"Yep."

"Try to be quiet by the house and turn your lights off when you pull in the driveway, can you do that?"

"Yeah, no problem."

"When can you get here?"

"Give me an hour, maybe less and I'll be there."

"Perfect, I'll see you then."

"Okay, bye."

"Bye," Donnie said and hung up the phone. He crept back upstairs and sat on his bed thinking. "Screw it," He said quietly to himself. He got his big duffle bag out of the closet and filled it with clothes.He snuck back downstairs as quietly as possible. Once he was out on the porch he put his head through the handles of the duffle bag so they were like a sash across his chest. He positioned the bag on his back and started jogging toward the fort. He only made it about halfway before he ran out of breath and had to walk. He made it to the fort dropped the duffle on the floor and cracked open a can of soda from the table. "Someone is coming to give us a ride," He said and took a huge drink.

"Us?"

"Yeah, I'm coming with you," He said and pointed to the bag.

"What about school?"

"I'll make it up later."

"What about your parents? Will they call the police?"

"I got an idea for that," He said and pulled some envelopes and paper out from his duffle bag. I'm going to leave them a note." He sat down at the table and wrote a note to his parents. He kept it short and to the point. He told them not to worry about him and he'd be back soon. Once he finished that note he started on one to Jimmy. He asked Jimmy to give the note to his parents for him and said he was running away with Tracy but he'd be back. He wrote Jimmy on one envelope and sealed it. Then he wrote Mom and Dad on the other and sealed that one.

"Who's coming to get us?" Tracy asked.

"My friend, Bobby."

"He has a car?"

"No, he's coming on horseback."

"Smart ass," She said and they both started to laugh.

"I told him we'd give him a hundred dollars and fill his tank, I hope that's okay with you."

"That's fine we just got to be out of here before they wake up."

"Don't worry we will be. Don't mention anything to Bobby about the money. I think the less he knows the better it is for everyone."

"Mums the word," She said and kissed him on the cheek. "I'm so glad you're coming with me."

"This is crazy, isn't it?"

"Yeah but it's exciting too. Do you want to do the rest of this speed?" She asked him and batted her eyelashes.

"Maybe we should save it in case we get tired later."

"That's a good idea," She said and hugged him tightly.

Chapter Fifteen

Donnie heard the faint blub, blub, blub of the glass packs on an eight cylinder motor outside. He poked his head out the plywood door. He saw the familiar Chevelle approaching slowly with its headlights off. It came to a stop in front of the fort and Bobby killed the motor. Bobby got out and Donnie opened the door and invited him in. "Did you see any lights come on at the house?" Donnie asked.

"No, all the windows stayed dark."

"Good, have a seat and a soda if you want."

Tracy was sitting on the sleeping bag Indian style. She looked up at Bobby and smiled. "Hi, I'm Tracy," she said and extended her hand to shake.

"Bobby," He replied shaking her hand. "So what's the big emergency? Where do you guys need to go?" He asked turning in Donnie's direction.

"Well, it's kind of complicated," Donnie said.

"I'm going back to Arizona. I don't want my Uncle knowing I left until I'm long gone," Tracy said.

"So you're running away?"

"Yeah, but not really, I am eighteen years old so I'm an adult," She said.

"So what do you need me to drive you to the bus depot or something?"

"No, I'm going too and I'm not eighteen yet so I think a bus is a bad idea. I don't know if my parents are going to freak out and call the cops when they read my note or not. I would think they'd contact the bus stations and have them looking out for me."

"Yeah, I'd imagine they would and the airport too," Bobby said and sat down looking to be in deep thought.

"Besides two bus tickets to Arizona might be more then we can afford. I don't know how much they are but were not rich," Tracy said and gave Donnie a wink.

"The bus is pretty cheap I think. Well I mean compared to flying it is. They'll make you show some I.D. though and... wait I got an idea. I know this truck stop off the interstate where you guys could maybe hitch

97

a ride and at least get out of the state. Then you could catch a bus no problem I'd imagine. What do you guys think?" Bobby asked.

Donnie thought about it. He wondered how long they had until Jimmy's dad broke a bill and discovered the missing truck fund. He knew it wouldn't be long and if Jimmy's dad called the cops he didn't want to leave a trail of bus tickets for them to follow. "That might work. Hopefully we can get a ride all the way to Arizona."

"Trucks are going everywhere in those places especially to California and I-10 goes right through so you should be able to find a ride easy. They stay open 24 hours so just drink some coffee and hit up drivers until you find one going your way," Bobby said.

"I think that is a great idea," Tracy said.

"I'd offer a driver some money for gas if you can. I bet one will jump at it since they are heading that way anyway. I know I would. I don't know what you guys are working with but I bet fifty bucks would do it," Bobby added.

"I like it, great idea Bobby," Donnie said.

The three of them gathered the bags and put them in the trunk. Donnie went back in the fort and got the two envelopes from the table. "I almost forgot these," He said holding up the envelopes like playing card as he got in the car. "We just need to make one quick stop on the way," He added and shut the car door.

Bobby fired up the hot rod, turned around and headed down the dirt road with his lights out. Once he passed the house he turned the lights on. When he reached the asphalt he hit the gas and they were in front of Jimmy's farm in seconds. "Pull over here for a sec, I'll be right back," Donnie said and got out of the car on the side of the road. He jogged the dirt driveway to Jimmy's house. When he reached Jimmy's truck he could hear a dog barking. "Shut up," He muttered under his breath as he tucked the two envelopes under the windshield wipers. He jogged back to the idling car. "Okay, let's go," He managed to get out between labored breaths as he got in and shut the door.

Bobby put the car in drive and hit the gas. The tires spun on the dirt shoulder kicking up a cloud of dust. The tires made a little chirp as they hit the pavement. They quickly found traction and the car zoomed down the road. "Man, this car is fast. I feel like my head is glued to the headrest." Donnie said.

"Yeah, it's got some balls that's for sure," Bobby said with a grin.

They made their way through the Kentucky roads. Both sides of the road were farmland with trees between them. Kentucky was beautiful, real green, of course at this hour most of the green was hidden in darkness. The air smelled so clean and fresh pouring in the partially open window as the car sped along the back roads.

They reached interstate 65 and headed south toward Tennessee. Not long after they crossed the border Bobby pointed toward an exit ramp. "Here we go," He said as he exited the freeway. He pulled into a parking lot with diesel trucks coming and going. Rows of big rigs lined one side of the parking lot. "This place looks good, it's booming," he said.

"We're bound to find a ride here," Tracy said excitedly.

Bobby parked the car in front of what looked like an old fashioned diner. They got out and took the bags from the trunk. "Do you guys think you'll be okay from here?" Bobby asked.

"Yeah, this place is busy, we should be fine," Donnie said looking around the parking lot.

Tracy put her backpack on the sidewalk. She squatted down and unzipped it. She reached inside and took a rubber band off one of the bundles. She was careful to keep her hand in the bag as she counted out twenty dollars. She pulled out the twenty and one of the rubber banded bundles. "Is twenty enough for gas?" She asked as she zipped up the backpack and got to her feet.

"Yeah, that's plenty," Bobby said.

Tracy handed him the money and gave him a hug. "Thank you so much," she said.

"Yeah, you really came through for us," Donnie said shaking Bobby's hand.

"No thank you guys I really needed this money. If you two are stuck and can't find a ride give me a call and we'll figure something out."

"We will. Remember you never saw us," Donnie said shouldering his duffle bag.

"Don't worry, I won't tell anyone," He said as he climbed in the driver's seat and started the car.

"Bye and thanks again," Tracy said. She and Donnie both wave as he drove out of the parking lot.

They entered the diner through swinging glass doors. It was loud inside with typical restaurant noise. Dishes clattered and customers chatted back and forth. It was a lot bigger inside than it looked from the parking lot. Booths went all the way around the windowed walls in a U

99

shape. There were tables in the middle with four chairs each. They walked to the back where there was a long counter. Along the bar style counter were stationary bar stools on poles from the floor.

Donnie put his bag in between two stools and sat down. Tracy took off her backpack and sat down next to him. She put her backpack on her lap and reached for a menu. "What do you feel like eating?" She asked flipping through the menu.

"I don't know," He said. Then he noticed the pies on the other side of the counter. "That looks good," he said pointing over the counter at the pies.

Tracy looked at the row of pies down the inner counter. They were covered with glass lids with handles on top. On the front of each lid there was a sticker with the flavor of the pie written in marker. She worked her way down the row of pies reading all the flavors to herself. She noticed a sign on the cash register at the end of the pies. "Look," She said and pointed the sign out to Donnie.

Donnie looked toward the register, squinted his eyes and read the note taped to the register out loud. "I need ones and fives," He recited.

Just then the waitress passed them carrying two plates of food. "I'll be right with you," She said as she hurried by in front of them. She had an accent. She sounded a lot like Flo from the old sit com 'Alice'. She even resembled her a little except her hair was dark brown instead of red.

"No hurry," Tracy replied to the waitress. "What kind of pie do you want?" She asked looking at Donnie.

"Apple with whipped cream and a glass of cold milk," Donnie answered.

"I'm going to have some pie too."

A few moments later the waitress returned, pen and pad in hand. "Y'all ready to order?"

"Yes we'd like pie. He'd like a slice of apple and I'll have cherry. Both with whipped cream please."

"Alright, what would like to drink with that?"

"Two milks."

"Okay, anything else?" She asked scribbling on her pad.

"That's all. I noticed your sign. I have a lot of ones and fives too." Tracy reached in and pulled a stack of one's out of her backpack and showed her.

"Look at all those ones," The waitress said delighted. "You must be one of those dancers from the bar down the interstate."

"Guilty," Tracy said with a smile.

"Oh, it's nothing to be ashamed of honey. If I had your looks I wouldn't be working in this dive. How much do you have?"

"How much do you need?"

"Well I have two one hundred dollar bills and then about a hundred more in twenties in the register and I have a fifty, so three fifty all total."

"No problem."

"Sweetie, I could kiss you. Just about everyone who comes through that door orders about seven dollars' worth of food and wants to pay with a twenty dollar bill. There's no way any of these jimmy jammers is going to give me a thirteen dollar tip. Let me go get your pie and I'll be right back."

"Looks like you made a friend," Donnie said as the waitress walked away.

"It's better than making enemies. I bet she'll help us with our ride situation."

"Think so?"

"We'll see right now."

The waitress returned with the milk and pie skillfully balanced. "Here you go," She said with a smile setting down the plates and glasses. "I'll be right back. I'm going to get the money from the register." She came back with three hundred dollars no fifty. Tracy pulled out three stacks of money and placed them on the counter.

"These should be a hundred each, but you should count them to be sure."

"No problem after doing this for twenty years I've gotten good at counting fast," She said and reached for a bundle and un-banded it. She started counting to herself and made it through the three bundles fast. She separated the fives as she counted the ones. She counted the fives at the end. "Three hundred on the nose," she said placing the two hundreds and five twenties on the counter in front of Tracy. She tucked the small bills into a pocket in the front of her apron.

"I have a question," Tracy said.

"Shoot, honey."

"Me and my boyfriend here are relocating to Arizona and we were hoping we could find a trucker headed there and catch a ride with him. We'd be willing to give them a hundred bucks for gas and the inconvenience. Would you know anybody who might be headed West?"

101

"Normally I have a rule about people hitching rides in here, but you really saved my bacon, so I'll make an exception," She took one of the hundred dollar bills from the counter and held it in the air. She put her middle finger and thumb together and put them in her mouth and whistled. "Listen up everybody. I got a young couple here headed to Arizona. They have a hundred for gas. If any y'all is interested let me know." She placed the bill back on the counter. "That's the best I can do. Now you two eat up before your milk gets warm," She said. She gave them a wink and trotted off the stock the register.

Tracy and Donnie ate their pie. Just as they were finishing up the waitress came over. "I think I may have found you two a ride," She said with a smile as she stacked their plates and wiped the counter. "Once he's done eating I'll walk him over here. I guess he has some questions for you two."

"Thank you so much," Tracy said glancing at her name tag. It read Donna.

"One good deed deserves another, honey."

About ten minutes later Donna came walking up behind them. Following her was a man who looked to be in his mid-forties. He walked with a slight limp and had a beer belly. He had dark curly hair down to his shoulders and a burly beard to match. He wore a baseball cap with a picture of that mud flap girl on it. He had a red and black flannel with blue jeans and work boots. Donnie thought he looked like a lumber jack.

"Here's the couple I told you about," Donna said and went about her business.

"Nice to meet you my name is Dale," The man said extending his right hand to shake.

"I'm Donnie and this is my girl Tracy," Donnie said shaking the truckers hand firmly. Dale shook Tracy's hand as well.

"So you two are going to Arizona?"

"Yes, I'm from there and I came down to talk my boyfriend into moving with me," Tracy said.

"You two ain't in any trouble with the law or nothing like that are ya?"

"No sir, we're just trying to get to Arizona as inexpensive as possible," Donnie said,

"Where in Arizona are ya headed?"

"North Phoenix," Tracy said.

"Well you two are in luck," He said as he pulled a piece of paper from his back pocket and unfolded it. "I have to be at 4720 West Van Buren by

Friday morning. I'm hauling a container of toys to a warehouse there. I just slept so I'm planning on driving straight through."

"We sure would appreciate it mister," Donnie said. Tracy nodded in agreement.

"I'm going to use the can. I suggest you two do the same. We'll shove off here in about ten minutes, sound good?"

"Sounds great," Donnie said.

Dale headed off to the restroom. "He seems nice," Tracy said.

"Yeah, he seems nice enough. I just can't believe how easy that was."

"I know, this was a good idea," Tracy said as she picked up the ticket on the counter. She turned it over and laughed a little. The pie was two fifty a slice and milk was a dollar a glass. She remembered Donna saying everyone orders seven dollars' worth of food. She dug in her bag and found a pen. She pulled a napkin from the dispenser on the counter and scribbled out a short note. The note read: Donna, thanks for everything here's your thirteen dollar tip. She placed four five dollar bills and the note under the ticket and headed to the ladies room. Donnie went to the men's room.

Donnie and Tracy exited the diner. Dale was standing just outside the door smoking a cigarette. "Ready?" He asked as he dropped the butt to the ground and stepped on it.

"We're ready," Tracy said.

The three of them walked through the parking lot. "This is me, I'll unlock the passenger side for you when I get in," He said and walked around the other side of the truck. It was a beautiful truck with dark maroon paint and lots of chrome. As Tracy and Donnie stood there admiring the truck the passenger door popped open. They climbed up into the cab. "Are you two tired at all?" Dale asked.

"I am, I've been up since four in the morning," Donnie said.

"I'm tired too,"

"I just changed the sheets on the bed in the sleeper. If you want you can crash out for a while."

"That sounds like a plan," Donnie said and the two of them climbed between the seats into the sleeper of the truck. They were surprised how big it was. They kicked off their shoes and laid down on the bed. They heard the rumble of the Diesel motor come to life. Donnie reached his arm around Tracy. He slid his hand up her shirt and cupped one of her breasts.

"Don't even think about it," She said as she pushed his hand away.

"I can't believe we're going," Donnie said.

"Go to sleep," Tracy said and pulled his hand up to her mouth and gave it a little kiss. They fell asleep.

Chapter Sixteen

Donnie woke up, it took him a minute to realize where he was. Tracy remained sleeping as Donnie pulled the curtain separating the cab from the sleeper. To his surprise he saw sunlight shining through the windshield. He climbed into the passenger seat.

"Mornin'," Dale said.

"Good Morning."

"Boy you two must have been tired. You've been sleeping for ten hours."

"Where are we?"

"Oklahoma. Oklahoma City to be exact. We're making good time too. You got up at a good time. I was just planning to pull over for some go-go juice and a bite to eat."

"Good, I'm starving and need a bathroom break."

"Well, why don't you wake up your gal. This is our exit coming up."

Donnie climbed back to the sleeper. By the time he got Tracy upright and coherent the truck came to a stop.

"Where are we?" Tracy asked groggily.

"We're at another truck stop."

"What time is it?"

"I don't know, six maybe seven."

"I gotta go to the restroom."

"Me too, let's go," Donnie said as he climbed back through the seats again. Tracy followed. The two exited the passenger side of the truck.

"Welcome to Oklahoma," Dale shouted as he banged on a tire at the back of the trailer. "You two head inside. I'll catch up when I'm done inspecting the truck."

Donnie just gave him a thumbs up and they headed into the diner. They split up and each hurried to their gender restroom. Donnie was done first and sat at a booth with a view of the ladies room. Shortly after Tracy emerged and he waved her over. They sat on the same side of the booth reading menus.

"Would you like some coffee to start out?" A waitress holding a steaming glass pot of coffee asked.

"Okay," Donnie said and turned over a coffee cup already on the table and slid it toward her. Tracy did the same.

"Are you ready to order?" She asked with a smile. She was a short woman about five one. She was chubby with blonde hair and a round pleasant face. The blonde clearly came from a bottle judging by her roots and she wore way too much make-up.

"Not yet our friend will be in, in a minute we'll order then." Tracy said.

"Okey Dokey," She said with her winning smile and trotted off filling other coffee cups.

Tracy and Donnie sipped coffee and chatted for a bit. Dale entered the diner and they waved him over. He sat across from them and laid a leather binder and sat a thermos down on the table. "Were all gassed up," He said and flipped over one of the two remaining coffee cups on the table. He took a menu from the holder. He scanned it for a quick second and put it back. "I'm going to the can. If the waitress comes by order me a number three and have her fill up my coffee cup would you?"

"Will do," Donnie said and pointed. "The men's room is on the other side of that juke box."

Dale nodded and marched to the restroom. The waitress appeared as if on cue. She freshened up their coffee. "Need another minute?" She asked.

"No we're ready. Our friend would like coffee and a number three. The waitress filled Dale's cup. She put the pot down and pulled an order pad and pen from her apron pocket.

"I think I'll have a number three also." Donnie said.

"Number six for me," Tracy said.

"Alright, two number three's and a six," The waitress said scribbling on the pad. "Your order will be right up." She picked up the coffee pot and was off.

Dale returned from the restroom wiping his face with a bandana. He stuffed the bandana in his front jean pocket and sat down. "Alright, Coffee," He said and took a drink of the black coffee. "I got to fudge my log here a bit," He said and opened the leather folder and started writing.

"How long you think 'til we reach Phoenix?" Tracy asked.

"Well I feel pretty good right now, but I might need some rest in a few hours. We're about halfway there. I'd say we should be there by nine PM tomorrow." He said and took another drink of coffee.

The waitress returned with the food. Donnie's eyes got big. It looked good and smelled even better. Donnie and Dale had scrambled eggs with sausage and bacon and hash browns on the side. Tracy had a stack of pancakes with scrambled eggs and bacon on the side. They all dug in. "I'll be right back to freshen up your coffee."

After the waitress topped off the coffee cups and left to make her rounds Tracy shook a couple sugar packets and dumped them in her coffee. "It must be hard to stay awake for long periods of time," She said as she poured some creamer in her coffee.

"It can be. I drink a lot of coffee," Dale said and shoveled a fork full of eggs in his mouth.

"Do you ever take anything else?" Tracy asked.

"You mean drugs? I guess most long haul truckers have dabbled in speed here and there. Me included," Dale said before taking another bite.

"Do you want some?"

"What do you got?" Dale asked curiously.

Tracy leaned forward and spoke softly. "I have some good speed from Arizona. One line of this and you'll be up for a good day or two."

"I'll try some, sure."

Tracy dug around in her backpack. "Here she said and passed him the little baggie wrapped up in a napkin. "Go to the men's room and snort about half of this. Make sure you crush it up real good. Keep the rest for later."

"Thanks," he said tucking the napkin into his front shirt pocket. He finished eating and went to the restroom. He came back a few moments later. "Man did that ever burn. You weren't kidding, I can feel it already," He said as he took a seat back at the table.

"Give it about ten minutes. You'll want to take a crap before we get back on the road," Tracy said.

"Is everything alright? Can I get you anything else?" The waitress asked with a smile.

"Could I get this filled up?" Dale asked handing her the thermos.

"Sure thing hon, I'll be right back."

Dale stood up and took out his wallet. He pulled out a ten dollar bill and laid it on the table. "This ought to cover my share. Just put the change toward a tip. You're right again little lady. I'm gonna hit the can. You two settle up the bill and we'll hit the road soon as I get back."

"Got it," Donnie said.

Dale hurried off to the men's room again. Tracy and Donnie looked at each other and giggled a little. "I bet we get there eight hours earlier now that he won't need a sleep break," Tracy said with a grin.

"That was good thinking."

"I wanted to offer it to him earlier, but I didn't want to scare off our ride."

"You did right," Donnie said and pecked her cheek.

"Thanks," Tracy said blushing a bit.

The waitress came back with the full thermos and the check. She put the thermos on the table and ripped the bill from her order pad and placed it face down on the table. "You all have a good day now, ya hear?"

"Thank you, you too," Tracy replied.

"You can pay the cashier on your way out," She said pointing to the counter by the door. "You sure there's nothing else I can get you?"

"We're fine, everything was very good."

"Glad you enjoyed it," She said with her final smile and trotted off.

Tracy pulled some money from her backpack. She laid a five dollar bill on the table for a tip. She handed the money to Donnie along with the check. "Will you go pay this sweetie? I got to use the little girl's room before we shove off."

"Okay," Donnie said. He went and paid the cashier and headed to the restroom himself. He passed Dale on the way. He handed him his thermos and log and said, "Bill's paid, we'll be out in a minute."

"I'll be outside having a smoke," Dale said.

Donnie finished up in the restroom. As he exited he saw Tracy had just finished as well. "Ready?" He asked.

"Good to go."

"Dale's already outside, Arizona here we come," Donnie said grabbing Tracy's hand leading her out the diner.

Dale was just snubbing out his cigarette as the two came out the glass doors. "Good timing, I just finished, ready to roll?" he said.

"Yessir," Donnie replied.

The three walked to the waiting truck and scaled the metal monster. It wasn't long and they were back on the interstate. Tracy was sitting on Donnie's lap in the passenger seat of the cab. The speed really had Dale going. He was rambling on about trucking and how nobody's log ever matches the actual hours they were driving. Tracy seemed to be listening. She asked a question here and there. Donnie just blocked all the talking out. He was lost in his thoughts. He wondered how his parents took the note. Surely they'd read it by now. He wondered if Jimmy's dad discovered the truck fund was missing yet. He wondered if Jimmy would be pissed at him when he found out the money was gone. His thoughts raced as he stared out the window at the lines in the freeway zipping by as country music played faintly in the background.

Chapter Seventeen

Donnie must have dozed off. He woke to the sound of laughter. Tracy was still on his lap asleep with her head on his shoulder. Still half asleep he heard another burst of laughter. He rubbed his eyes and realized it was Dale having a conversation with someone on the C.B. radio. He shook Tracy and woke her up. "Let's go lay down in the back. My neck hurts and my legs are asleep," He said rubbing the back of his neck.

"Okay," She said groggily.

They climbed back into the sleeper and Tracy fell back asleep right away. Donnie just laid there and held her. He listened to Dale chatter back and forth on the C. B. 'til he fell back asleep. He woke up again a little while later. He could hear Dale singing along with the radio. 'The Devil went down to Georgia' by Charlie Daniels was playing and Dale was murdering it. Donnie opened the curtain and climbed into the passenger seat.

"Have a good nap?"

"Yeah, was I asleep long?"

"A few hours I'd say, including when you fell asleep up here."

"Where are we?"

"We just crossed the Texas border. There's a rest stop coming up, you need a restroom break?"

"Yes, I could use one. I'll go wake up Tracy."

They pulled into the rest area and got out of the truck. They all walked to the brick building where the restrooms were. Dale and Donnie went to the right and Tracy to the left. It felt good to walk and stretch their legs a bit. Donnie went pee and washed his hands. He wiped his hands on his pants. When he did he felt change in his pocket. He remembered he put the change from the diner in his right front pocket. He reached in and pulled out a dollar bill. There were vending machines on the wall between the restrooms. He put the dollar in a machine and pushed a button. A can came thumping down. He reached through the metal cage and grabbed it. It was ice cold. He popped the top and took a drink. Man, did it ever taste good. It was his favorite, Mountain Dew. Tracy came out of the ladies room. "Want a drink?" He asked.

"Oh yeah," She said and took the can. She took a big drink. "Wow, that's cold!"

"Let's get some for the road."

"Okay," She said and sat her backpack down. That backpack never left her sight. She squatted down and got a couple of one dollar bills out. She bought four cans and put them in the backpack. Donnie got the two quarters from the change return. He was just inserting the second quarter in the machine when Dale came out of the men's room.

"What's your poison?" Donnie asked pointing to the machine.

"Root beer."

Donnie pushed the button and clunk, clunk the can dropped down. He pulled it out and handed it to Dale. "Here you go, nice and cold."

"Thanks, you kids are alright."

They piled in the truck and got on the road again. They drove and drove making the occasional rest stop. They finally crossed the Arizona border and Tracy let out a cheer.

"We'll stop in Flagstaff and get something to eat." Dale said.

They made it to Flagstaff and just picked up some burgers and fries to go at the local McDonalds. "It won't be long now," Dale said as he shifted the semi on the entrance ramp.

"How long do you think?" Donnie asked in between bites.

"Hour and a half, two tops."

"I don't know how you do it."

"What do you mean?"

"You're cooped up in this truck all the time, day in and day out. I think I'd go crazy."

"Ahh, you get used to it. At least I'm my own boss. I drive when I want, sleep when I want and eat when I want."

"I could do it," Tracy chimed in.

Donnie just looked at her and smiled as he chewed his food. Two hours later they were in Phoenix.

"Here's our exit," Dale said as he flipped on his turn signal. They got off the freeway at 59th Avenue.

"Are you going to the Circle K truck stop?" Tracy asked.

"I guess you know Phoenix," Dale said.

"I know Phoenix like the back of my hand. I was born and raised here. I was born not too far from here at Maryvale Hospital."

111

"I stop in Phoenix quite a bit myself," Dale said turning the big rig into a parking lot flanked with trucks. He parked the truck and before he even asked Tracy had his money in her hand.

"What would you prefer, a hundred dollar bill or small bills?" Tracy asked.

"Small bills," Dale said. "Sometimes it's hard to break a hundred."

"Here you go," She said handing him a rubber banded stack of bills. It should be a hundred, you might want to count it."

"I trust you," Dale said as he folded the stack and shoved it into his left shirt pocket. "How are you two gonna get where you're going?"

"We'll take the bus. We'll be fine," Tracy said.

"Thanks again Dale, it was nice meeting you," Donnie said shaking Dale's hand.

"Same here, you kids stay out of trouble now ya hear?"

"We will," Donnie said as he opened the door and climbed down.

"Bye Dale," Tracy said and followed Donnie down. Donnie shouldered his bag. Tracy shut the truck door and put on her backpack. They walked through the parking lot to the sidewalk. "Do you have any change on you?"

"I have a little," Donnie said and dug some coins out of his right front pocket.

"Perfect, we'll need exact change for the bus."

"How much is it?"

"A dollar twenty five each."

"They made their way to the nearest bus stop and sat down on a bench. Ten minutes later a bus pulled up. Tracy got on first and fed two fifty into the meter.

"Transfer?" The driver asked.

"Two please."

The driver ripped two pieces of yellow paper from his pad and handed them to Tracy. They walked down the aisle and sat at the back of the bus. "Here," Tracy said and handed Donnie one of the yellow slips of paper. It was thin like newspaper with times printed down the side.

"What is this for?"

"When we change buses just show it to the driver and you won't have to pay again."

They sat at the back of the bus watching people get on and off. After five miles Tracy stood up and pulled a cord that ran down the inside of the bus over the side windows. Ding, the sign above the rearview mirror lit up reading 'Stop Requested'. "This is our stop," Tracy said.

They started walking toward a crosswalk at a three-way intersection. "What's that? Donnie asked as they crossed the street.

"That's the State Fair Grounds. Every year before Halloween the fair comes to town. They have rides and games and all kinds of food. See that?" She pointed to a big oval building with a weird wavy roof. "That's the Coliseum, they have concerts there all the time. Oh shit! Here comes our bus." She grabbed Donnie's hand and they ran across the crosswalk. The bus stopped at the bus stop. They were in luck, there were three people getting on the bus which gave them time to catch it.

They got on the bus and flashed the driver their transfers. He gave them a nod as they took some seats by the front this time. This bus was more crowded than the last one. "How far to the next bus?" Donnie asked.

"This one is our last bus we'll walk after this one. "We got about..." She started counting on her fingers. "Seven more miles and we'll get off."

As people got off the bus Donnie and Tracy changed seats. They made it all the way to the back. "I like to sit in the back," Tracy said.

"Why?"

"I don't know. I guess I like to be able to see everybody and know no one can see me."

The bus traveled on. The driver would announce the street names as he approached every traffic light. People got on and off at just about every stop. This went on a while. The driver's voice came across the speaker, "Dunlap," he said.

"We're almost there," Tracy said excitedly. The bus made a couple more stops and Tracy pulled the cord. They got off the bus and started walking back the way they came. They turned down the street they had just passed.

"Hatcher," Donnie read the sign out loud.

"Welcome to Sunnyslope baby," Tracy said. This is my neighborhood. They kept walking East down Hatcher. On the other side of the road there was a guy riding a bicycle in the opposite direction. "Billy!" Tracy yelled to him. "Have you seen Skeeter?"

"Yeah, he's headed to Circle K!" The guy yelled back.

"C'mon," Tracy said as she took Donnie by the hand and picked up the pace. They passed a little store. Then they passed a bar that was connected to another little store. They cut through the little parking lot of store connected to the back of the bar. Across a small side street was another little parking lot and a Circle K convenience store. They crossed the side street as a young skinny kid was walking out the swinging glass doors. He was sucking on a straw coming from a cup that was almost as big as his head. "Skeeter!" Tracy yelled as she let go of Donnie's hand and ran to the kid. She gave him a big hug.

"What are you doing here? I thought you went to Mississippi?" Skeeter said and took another big pull from the straw.

"It was Kentucky, you knucklehead. Let me have a drink of that," She said snatching the cup from his hand.

"Don't drink it all," Skeeter said.

Donnie walked up to them. Tracy held out the cup. "Want a drink? It's Dr. Pepper."

"No thanks," Donnie said after catching Skeeter's glare at her.

"This is Donnie. He's my boyfriend from Kentucky I told you about. This is my best buddy Skeeter," Tracy said introducing the two.

"My real name is Jimmy but everyone calls me Skeeter,"

"I'm gonna call you Jimmy then," Donnie said with a smile shaking Jimmy's hand. Jimmy smiled back. "Why do they call you Skeeter?"

"Have you ever heard of the band Primus?"

"No."

"Well anyway they are my favorite band. I used to wear a shirt of theirs with a mosquito on it. He's kind of like the bands mascot or something. Here I'll show you," He said and handed Tracy his soft drink and pulled up his right sleeve. On his arm was a tattoo of a cartoon mosquito.

"He wore that shirt every day until it fell apart," Tracy said with a laugh.

"Yeah, I miss that shirt," Skeeter said quickly grabbing back the soda from Tracy. "People started calling me Skeeter and it just stuck."

"Have you noticed any apartments for rent around here? You know cheap ones." Tracy asked.

"I saw they put a for rent sign in the window of one of those apartments on North Lane and Eleventh," He said and went right back to his straw. He gulped down some more soda and let out a belch.

"Man, you really like that Dr. Pepper don't you?" Donnie said.

"Primus and Dr. Pepper that's all this kid cares about," Tracy said messing up his hair.

"And a bowl, do you have a bowl Tracy?"

"Not right now but I will," Tracy said squatting down putting the backpack between her knees and unzipped it. "Do me a favor take Donnie and show him that apartment."

"Okay."

Tracy stood back up and handed Donnie a five dollar bill. "Here's some money so you can get something to drink. Get him a refill, he's gonna need it. I'll meet up with you guys in Duck Park in a bit." She crossed the street and headed into the neighborhood. The boys went into Circle K and Donnie got a drink while Skeeter got his refill. They walked into the parking lot.

"So how long have you known Tracy?" Donnie asked before taking a drink.

"A couple of years I guess."

"How old are you?"

"I'm sixteen and a half. C'mon we got to cross the street and walk down Eleventh." The boys hurried across Hatcher in between cars. They walked down the street. Donnie was looking around in amazement. Some girl rode by on a long skateboard with headphones blasting. A tall guy on a bike came riding toward them. His bike had a trailer on it with a bunch of bike frames and wheels and an old laundry basket full of aluminum cans.

"What's up Dave?" Skeeter said to the man.

"Hey Skeeter," The man replied in passing.

"Wow, is this place always so....active?" Donnie asked.

"Pretty much, you're in the heart of the Slope," Skeeter said with a big smile. "Check it out, see the sign?" Skeeter pointed, "The apartment on the left," He added.

Donnie looked down the street a little ways. He saw a big red sign in a picture window. It had big white letters reading 'FOR RENT' and a white strip with a phone number written in it in magic marker. "Yeah, I see it," Donnie said. They walked across a side street. They walked through the gravel front yard making crunching noises with each step. They peered inside the window on the side the sign wasn't taped on with cupped their hands on the glass. "It looks pretty small," Donnie said.

"I've been in this apartment before. On the other side of that dividing wall is the kitchen. If you go down that little hall on the right there's a bathroom. Right across from the bathroom is a bedroom. It's a lot bigger than you think. "Do you have a pen on you?"

"I think so," Donnie said putting down his duffle bag and digging through it. "Here's one," He handed it to Skeeter. He looked at the number and scribbled it on his left wrist.

"Come on," Skeeter said and led Donnie into the carport. "You got storage right there," He said pointing to a door at the end of the carport. He tapped on the door on the right. "This side door goes into the kitchen. This is the bedroom window," Skeeter said sounding like a real estate agent. "Those other windows are to the apartment next door."

"I guess it is bigger than I thought."

"Well we got the number let's go to the park," Skeeter said and started walking toward the next door apartment. They cut through a dirt driveway and got back on Eleventh Ave. They walked to the end of the street and Donnie looked up and read the name of the street making a T with Eleventh Ave. Peoria he said to himself. They turned right on Peoria. "I hope Tracy scored some shit, I want to get high," Skeeter said as they walked East on Peoria.

They passed a school and reached the end of the road which curved to the right and became Seventh Avenue. To the right was the school yard and then some houses or apartments. To the left was the park. It was huge. They made their way to the park's parking lot. By the parking lot there was a brick building with a small playground next to it. "Thank God we made it. My bladder is about to explode," Skeeter said.

"Mine too," Donnie said as the boys entered the men's room. Donnie took his duffle bag off. "Man I'm tired of carrying this thing," He said putting it down by the sink. They finished up in the restroom and went outside taking a seat at a picnic table by the playground. "I expected a pond with some ducks at a park called Duck Park," Donnie said.

"It's actually called Mountain View Park. Duck Park is just a nick name."

"Why?"

"There used to be a big statue of a duck over there. I remember climbing on that duck when I was little. There used to be these cement slides with water running down them they used to tear up my shorts real bad. I didn't live far from here."

"Do you still live around here?"

"My folks died in a fire when I was twelve."

"Holy shit, I'm sorry I didn't know."

"It's alright. I know it sucks. They put me in this foster home. I was there for about a year then I ran away and came back here. I've been on the streets ever since."

Donnie was lost for words. The boys just sat there in silence for a while. The sun started to go down. "Here comes Tracy," Skeeter said pointing to her as she stepped into the park.

Tracy walked through the grass. Donnie waved his hands. She waved back letting him know she saw them. She reached the picnic table took off her backpack and sat in on the table. She grabbed one of the cups off the table. "Whew, I need a drink," She said and drank some soda.

"It's probly watered down," Donnie said.

"I don't care as long as it's wet."

"Any luck?" Skeeter asked.

Tracy unzipped her backpack. She reached in and pulled out a zip lock bag and held it up. The baggie was full across the bottom about an inch deep.

"Damn Tracy, how much did you get?" Skeeter asked with his eyes bulging.

"I got a quarter ounce. But don't get too excited, I'm going to need you to help me sell a lot of this."

"No problem."

"Do you have a pipe?"

"Think I don't?" Skeeter said producing a glass pipe from his right front jean pocket.

"Load it up," Tracy said handing him the bag. Skeeter took it with a big smile.

"Are we going to smoke this right here?" Donnie asked nervously.

"Why not?" Tracy asked. There were some kids playing Frisbee on the other side of the park but they were far away. Other than that the park was deserted.

"C'mon," Skeeter said and zipped the bag of meth up and put it in Tracy's backpack. "I got a little camp up by the mountain. We can smoke up there if it makes you feel better." He took a lighter out of his left front pocket. "Let me melt this so it doesn't spill," He said and heated the bottom of the pipe with the flame. He blew into the end of the pipe and smoke came out the top hole. He eyed the bottom of the pipe watching the drugs harden. Once they were he put the pipe back in his right front pocket. He picked up Donnie's duffle bag and threw it over his shoulder. "Follow me," He said and started walking to the mountains.

117

The back of the park had a line of bushes and small trees growing wild. There was a bit of an incline. There were huge mountains beyond the bushes. Skeeter navigated them through the bushes a little ways. They came to a chain link fence with 'No Trespassing' signs and 'Federal Mountain Preserve' every ten feet or so. Under a small tree hidden from the park was a sleeping bag. There was a plastic grocery bag full of empty Dr. Pepper cans and a twelve pack box full of food wrappers and various other trash.

"Do you sleep here?" Donnie asked.

"Sometimes," Skeeter said as he untied the string around the sleeping bag. He spread it out on the ground. "Pretty soon it will be too hot to camp out doors but it's still nice right now."

"Well you can crash out at our place whenever you want. Did you guys check out that apartment?" Tracy asked as they all sat down on the sleeping bag.

"Yeah, I got the number right here," Skeeter said pointing to his wrist as he handed her the pipe.

"Good, after we smoke this I'm going to try to call the landlord."

They finished smoking and went back to the picnic table. Donnie left his duffle at Skeeter's camp after he assured him it would be safe there.

"I'm going to a pay phone, you guys wanna come?" Tracy asked.

"There's a payphone right there. Across the street," Skeeter said pointing. "See it at that little apartment complex."

"I see it. I'll be right back okay?" She grabbed Skeeter's arm and read the number to herself.

"Do you want to write it down?" Donnie asked.

"I'll remember it," She said and started walking toward the phone.

She returned about ten minutes later. "I'm going to meet the lady there at 8 O' Clock in the morning. She sounds nice."

"What are we going to do 'til then?" Donnie asked.

"Well we don't want to be in this park after ten. The cops come through here making sure there are no homeless people sleeping in here. I've avoided the police this long. I ain't going back to no home" Skeeter said defiantly.

"That's why your camp is hidden from view," Donnie said with a now I get it tone.

"Yeah, I've known more than one dude who was just sleeping in the park and ended up in jail cause they had something on them or a warrant or something."

"Well take us around the neighborhood. You got to know somebody who wants to buy some of this," Tracy said.

"I'm sure I do." Skeeter said.

The three of them roamed around the neighborhood the rest of the night. They bounced from apartment to apartment selling twenty here and forty there. Then one time they were leaving a house and were surprised to see the Sun was coming up. "Let's get some breakfast," Tracy said.

"Good idea, I'm starving," Skeeter said.

They walked to Circle K and bought a box of cereal and a half gallon of milk. "Do you have any courtesy cups back there?" Skeeter asked the clerk.

"Yeah," The clerk answered.

"Can we get three of them," Skeeter asked as he grabbed three plastic spoons from a cup by the microwave.

"Sure," The clerk said. He was about thirty years old. He had dark hair and about three days of stubble on his face. He looked tired like he'd been there all night.

"What time is it?" Tracy asked as she paid for the cereal and milk.

"Six-eighteen," The clerk said with a quick glance of his watch. He handed her, her change and the courtesy cups and said, "Have a good day."

"Thanks, you too."

They sat at the bus stop and ate Frosted Flakes from Circle K cups. "I don't want you guys around when I meet the landlady," Tracy said.

"Why?" Donnie asked before shoveling a spoonful of cereal into his mouth.

"Cause it is bad enough I'm only eighteen. I don't need her seeing a couple of minors with me."

"Okay." Donnie said.

"I wonder if she's going to ask me if I have a job."

"As long as you have a month's rent and enough for a deposit, she ain't going to give a shit," Skeeter said with a mouthful of cereal.

"You're probably right. I really don't want to pay her with a bunch of ones and fives. It might look a little strange to her."

"That's no problem, look," Donnie said pointing to the Circle K window. There was a yellow sign which read 'MONEY ORDERS 25 CENTS'.

119

"You're so smart," Tracy said and kissed him on the cheek. "I'll be right back." She went into the store and returned a bit later. "They only go up to three hundred dollars so I got three of them."

"That should be enough," Donnie said. Skeeter nodded in agreement chomping on cereal with milk running down his chin.

Chapter Eighteen

Later that morning Tracy met with the landlady at the apartment. She pulled into the driveway and saw Tracy was already waiting by the front door. She opened her car door and exited with a slight grunt. She was a chunky lady about five foot five with curly red hair down to her shoulders. She was dressed casual in a pair of blue jeans and a Phoenix Suns tee shirt. She had a chain with reading glasses hanging from it around her neck. She put the glasses on as she walked toward Tracy reading a post-it note stuck to the front of a folder. "Hi, you must be Tracy," She said extending her right hand to shake. "I'm glad you are here already. My name is Mary. Have you been waiting long?" She asked as they shook hands.

"No, maybe five minutes."

"Good I don't like to keep people waiting. Let's go inside shall we?" Mary asked digging keys from her jean pocket. Tracy just nodded and Mary unlocked the dead bolt on the front door. "Well this is the living room," Mary said with a smile. The back wall of the living room had an opening on each side to walk through. Mary led Tracy through the right side. "Here's the kitchen, as you see it has a refrigerator and stove both electric. Here is the bathroom and directly across is the one bedroom." Mary opened the door revealing a decent size room.

"Wow, this is bigger than I expected," Tracy said.

"Apartment two is bigger. It has two bedrooms the tenants there have a little one so I'm not sure about their noise level but I had no complaints from the previous tenants. You share a wall with apartment three in the bedroom but it is vacant right now."

"How much is the rent?"

"It is four hundred a month. The water is included but you will have to get the electricity turned on and you'll be responsible for that bill. I do require one month rent for a security deposit as well as the first month's rent prior to move-in. So it would be eight hundred total. Is it just you who will live here?"

"My boyfriend is moving from Kentucky. He will be living here with me."

"Would you want his name on the rental agreement if you decide to rent it?"

"No, it's not important."

"You look kind of young are you sure you'll be able to handle the rent?"

"It won't be a problem, my boyfriend works construction and I care for an elderly lady who pays me well," Tracy lied.

"Well I rent on a month to month basis so I don't do a credit check. The rental agreement is basically just a contract stating you agree to pay four hundred by the fifteenth of each month. It will also state you've paid me a four hundred dollar deposit. The deposit is refundable when you move after an inspection of the apartment for damage. The deposit will be forfeited in the event you are evicted for non-payment of rent or there is damage found when a move out inspection is conducted. Now, I am flex-able I understand paychecks are late from time to time and things happen. I have no problem working with you as long as you call me and explain your situation. How does it sound?"

"I like it," Tracy said

"You want to rent it?"

"I do and I have three money orders adding up to nine hundred dollars for you right now."

"Great, I can bring change back for you once I type up the rental agreement if you'd like. I could also just apply it to the next month's rent along with the pro-rated amount owed to you for this month, it's up to you."

"You can just put it toward next month."

"Okay, do you have any questions?"

"How much will it be to turn on the electricity?"

"Have you had a bill in your name with A.P.S.?"

"Never."

"Good, then you can't have any prior balance. It shouldn't be more than two hundred dollars."

"What do I do if something breaks like the stove or something?"

"Just give me a call and I'll fix it or replace it. This will also be covered in your rental agreement. You'll get your copy before I leave. Let me just get your I.D. I'll start filling it out and we'll sign it and that's it. I'll type it up so it's neater later and we'll re-sign"

Tracy handed Mary her I.D.

"Wow, eighteen years old, wish I was again. Is this your first apartment?"

"Yes."

"Good for you, I bet you're excited."

"I'm thrilled to death."

"I've had a lot of luck with first time renters don't let me down."

"I won't."

"Okay, here's my card. I've written the number for A.P.S. on the back. The water is already on but I put the City of Phoenix number on there too just in case you need it. Let me write you a receipt for the nine hundred," Mary said as she pulled a small receipt book from her folder. She signed the receipt and the lease. She tore the stubs off the money orders and handed it all to Tracy. She removed the key from her key ring and gave it to Tracy. "Here you go, congratulations," Mary said.

"Thank you," Tracy said grinning from ear to ear.

"No problem, thank you dear," Mary said and walked to the front door. Mary got in her car and waved as she backed down the driveway.

Tracy stood in the front doorway as Mary's car disappeared down the street. Once the car was out of sight she pumped her fist in the air and let out a little cheer. She was so excited. She took a few dollars from her backpack and put it in her pocket. She put the backpack in the bedroom and went out the front door locking the dead bolt behind her. She walked to the park.

Donnie and Skeeter were sitting at the same picnic table by the playground. They were watching some kids playing and laughing back and forth as Tracy approached. Donnie noticed her coming and noticed something was missing. "Where's your backpack?" He asked concerned.

"It's in our apartment," She said dangling the key from her finger.

"You got it?!" Skeeter yelled.

"Alright!" Donnie yelled and gave her a kiss. They walked to Skeeter's make shift camp and retrieved their belongings and headed toward the apartment. "I can't wait to take a shower," Donnie said.

"The water is on but the electricity is off. You're going to have to take a cold shower," Tracy said

"In the dark," Skeeter added.

"It will be better than stinking," Donnie said.

The three of them made it to the apartment. Donnie put his duffle bag in the bedroom. Skeeter laid his sleeping bag on the floor in the living room against the wall. He sat down on it and leaned back. "You guys need some furniture," He said.

"Yeah we need everything," Tracy said. "Let's go to the store and get some shampoo and soap and a couple towels at least."

"Okay," Donnie said.

They went to the store and bought various hygiene items. They returned to the apartment and took showers. Donnie had a couple of sheets and a thin blanket in his duffle bag. He laid them out making a bed on the bedroom floor. He could hear Tracy and Skeeter talking and laughing in the living room. He laid on his make shift bed and thought how just about a week ago Tracy came to Kentucky. He laid there thinking how much had transpired. He ran away, hitched a ride halfway across the country and was living with Tracy. He couldn't believe it. A lot can happen in a week he thought. He wanted to call his parents but couldn't think of what to say. He knew he wasn't about to leave Tracy and go back home, not yet anyway.

Chapter Nineteen

Life was a party. All Donnie did was smoke meth, drink beer and have sex. He felt like a rock star without a care in the world. Life was good. Skeeter knew everybody in the neighborhood and there was nothing he couldn't get. He just put the word out and the shoplifters would steal it and trade it for meth. He furnished the whole apartment dirt cheap with his wheeling and dealing.

Donnie's eighteenth birthday rolled around and Tracy got him a cake. He loved her. He knew he was probably never going back to Kentucky now. He did write his mother a letter, but he never got a stamp and put it in the mail box. He missed his parents but getting high and drinking was a major distraction.

When June arrived the inevitable happened. They barely made the rent with the three smoking as much meth as they were selling. That's when things started going bad. Tracy and Donnie started to argue a lot. Sometimes Tracy would just leave and not show up for a day or two. She'd come back and they would make-up until the next fight and she'd take off again.

"I don't know what I'm going to do Jimmy," Donnie said clearly upset with his head in his hands.

"Every time you guys fight it over money," Skeeter said.

"I know."

"Well let's go out and make some money."

"How?"

"How do you think I survived all these years on the streets?"

"I don't know. I never really gave it much thought."

"There's all kinds of money to be made. I go around and collect cans. I comb all the alleys and while I'm doing it I look for vacant houses. At night I would go and strip the copper out of the house and scrap it for cash."

"You can't get that much from scrap metal."

"You'd be surprised how it adds up. Plus I'd go to the mall and break into cars. You wouldn't believe what some people leave in their cars."

"You never got caught?"

"I've had some close calls but never been caught. Knock on wood." Skeeter knocked on the end table.

"How much could we make?"

"You never know. I've gone weeks eating Top Ramen cause I've only had cans. One time I found four one hundred dollar bills in a car. I couldn't believe it. It was right in the ashtray."

"Man, four hundred bucks just like that."

"That only happened once. What do you say you wanna go hit some cars?"

"Okay, I'll go with you."

That's how it started. Donnie and Skeeter started breaking into cars. Skeeter was right you never knew what you'd find. One thing you almost always found was change. You could easily get ten to twenty dollars out of an ashtray full of spare change. Skeeter would steal stereos. He was good at it. He could get a stereo out of a car in twenty seconds flat. The hard part was selling them. Nobody wanted car stereos and if they did they'd only trade drugs for them.

The boys had a little system. They would wait in the parking lot until someone parked. They'd watch them get out and listen for an alarm. If there was no alarm one of the boys would follow them into the mall. After fifteen minutes or so they know the car had been gone through and meet back up in the parking lot. If the person was coming out too soon they would signal each other to get out of the car. They didn't always do this. They were usually in and out of a car so fast it was un-necessary. Some cars were harder to get into than others. That's when they'd follow the mark.

Cars were a risky endeavor. You always had to keep an eye out for a security guard or a good samaritan in the lot. You never wanted to stay in an area too long or go to the same spot too often. Most of the time they just got change, but from time to time they'd find cash. A twenty here a five there it added up. One time Skleeter found a gun. On the bus ride home Skeeter opened his backpack so Donnie could look inside. Donnie saw a .22 caliber revolver lying on a bunch of loose change.

"What do you think Jimmy? Worth about fifty maybe a hundred bucks?"

"Fifty tops," Skeeter said zipping his bag. "I think I'm going to keep it."

They got off the bus and started walking back to the apartment. Donnie noticed a canvas bag on the front seat of a car parked on the street. "Jimmy did you see that bag on the front seat? I think the door is unlocked."

"Forget it."

"Why?"

"Cause we don't shit in our own backyard. Someone might see you and know the owner of the car. Besides, it's just bad luck."

"What about stripping houses?"

"That's different."

"How?"

"You're not ripping off people in the neighborhood. You're ripping off a slumlord with insurance."

Donnie didn't like stripping houses. It was too much work for the money. They'd be in a house for hours cutting pipes and pulling wire. Then they had to strip all the wire and cut all the pipes into small pieces. The only good thing was they did it at night. The Phoenix heat was brutal. Donnie was not used to it. But he'd rather spend an hour in the heat and make fifty bucks in change than go through the hassle of the copper for the same amount if you were lucky.

The boys weren't getting rich off their life of crime, not even close. By the time they paid bus fair and Skeeters Dr. Pepper fix they'd only have twenty bucks to show for it. Sometimes more it was hit and miss. They did manage to save up a couple hundred by the time July rent was due. A lot of time the risk hardly seemed worth the reward.

Tracy was happy the boys were pitching in on rent. The truck fund was long gone and they were barely staying afloat. The boys went out more often and took more chances. What it all came down to was a crap shoot. They were just hoping to get lucky one time and get ahead of the game. Donnie felt something was about to happen, but he never would have guessed what did.

It was early August when Donnie and Skeeter decided to hit Metro Center. Metro Center is a huge shopping mall in North Phoenix. The parking lot was always full and they hadn't been there in weeks. They made their way through the parking lot glancing into cars as they walked past. They got closer to the building and Donnie peeked into a Ford Taurus parked in the corner spot. "Jimmy, check it out," Donnie whispered.

Skeeter came over and looked around before cupping his hands to the glass and peeked inside. "Look under the seat," Donnie said.

"What is it?"

"I don't know, a briefcase maybe," Donnie said as he pulled a coat hanger out of Skeeters backpack. "We're gonna find out." Skeeter stepped back to be a look out. Donnie fished the coat hanger through the window frame.

"It's got power locks, just hit the button and it will unlock," Skeeter said quietly.

Donnie grunted in frustration as he wiggled the hanger back and forth.

"Here let me do it," Skeeter said walking up behind him grabbing the coat hanger sticking out the top of the window. Skeeter manipulated the wire bending it and twisting it over the button. He pushed on the hanger and click the door unlocked. "Got it," He said.

He no longer got the words out of his mouth and there was a bellowing voice behind them. "What are you doing?" The voice yelled. Skeeter and Donnie's heads jerked toward the voice. A security guard had walked around the corner and walked up behind them while they were distracted by the lock. He was a big guy about 6' 2", clean cut and in full uniform.

"Shit! Run!" Skeeter yelled and took off between cars.

Donnie stepped backwards from the car to turn and run in the other direction. He tripped on the curb and fell back right on his ass. Before he could get to his feet the security guard grabbed him. The guard jerked Donnie to his feet. "Breaking into cars huh? Not on my watch punk," The guard said and slapped some hand cuffs on him.

The security guard led Donnie down a back corridor to a security office and sat him down in a chair. He sat down at the desk next to him and picked up the phone. He dialed the phone and waited as it rang. "This is Metro Center security, I need an officer's assistance at the mall," He spoke into the phone. "Okay. I'll have a security guard waiting for him in the parking lot. Come in the South entrance off Dunlap and look for the cart. Okay, thank you very much." The security guard hung up the phone and pulled out his radio. "Five-nine to six-three."

"Six-three," came a response on his walkie talkie.

"Can you take the golf cart to the South entrance by the canal and keep an eye out for Phoenix P.D.?"

"Will do. Am I escorting them to your office?"

"Yes sir."

128

"Roger that."

Donnie and the security guard sat in silence. Donnie sat in a chair with his hands cuffed behind his back. The guard sat at his desk writing on what Donnie assumed was a log book. About forty-five minutes later another security guard walked into the office followed by a Phoenix Police Officer. The men introduced themselves and the guard ran down the events to the officer. The officer walked over to Donnie. "This is what's going to happen. I'm going to write you a citation for trespassing. You will be required to go to court on the date on the citation. You are hereby trespassed from the Metro Center mall. You are not to step foot on the mall property, understood?"

"Yes," Donnie said.

"Alright, stand up. I'm going to pat you down for weapons before removing those cuffs. You don't have anything sharp in your pockets that will poke me do you?"

"No."

Donnie stood up and turned around leaning forward, bracing himself with his forehead against a wall. The officer put on a pair of latex gloves. The officer began patting Donnie down. He felt something in his right front pocket. He pulled out a meth pipe and a small baggie of meth. "Change of plans, I'm placing you under arrest for possession of drugs and drug paraphernalia." Donnie's heart sunk in his chest.

The officer read Donnie his rights. He then put a second pair of cuffs on him. He got the security guards keys and removed the first pair of cuffs. He handed the keys and the cuffs to the guard. "Good job, this guy is in more trouble than we thought," The officer said and shook the guards hand.

The officer escorted Donnie to his police car. He put Donnie in the back. He got in front and started to drive. The officer tried talking to Donnie. He asked who he was with but Donnie just stared out the window in silence. He was scared and didn't know what to expect. The officer drove him to Madison Street Jail.

Chapter Twenty

The police car pulled up to some giant steel doors. The officer spoke into his radio and the huge doors parted. He pulled the squad car into a large parking garage. He parked the car and walked around and opened Donnie's door. "Watch your head," The officer said as he helped Donnie from the car. "This way," He said and led Donnie by the arm to a sliding door in the wall. The door opened to an empty room with another sliding door on the other side. "If I remove these cuffs are you going to behave?" The officer asked.

"Yes."

"Alright turn around," He said and fumbled with his keys a bit and unlocked the cuffs. He put the cuffs back in a pouch on his belt. He looked up at a camera over the second door and gave a thumbs up. The second door slid open. Inside there was a podium about three feet to the right of the doorway and about three feet from the wall. Along the wall was a bench that ran down the wall on his right. "Have a seat," the officer said, pointing to the bench. Donnie sat. He was the only one on the bench.

The officer walked over to the jail guard who was sitting on a bar stool type chair behind a camera. The officer started talking to the guard and handed him a plastic bag with Donnie's belt, wallet and keys in it. "Take your shoelaces out of your shoes," The guard commanded from behind the camera. Donnie obeyed. The two chatted back and forth as Donnie unlaced his shoes. The officer slipped through a sliding door out of sight. "Bring those laces over here," The guard instructed. He held open the plastic bag with Donnie's belongings in it. "Drop them inside and go stand behind the podium. Look up at the star on the wall over my head," The guard said. There was a click and a flash. "Have a seat on the bench." Donnie sat on the bench once again.

The guard began writing and stapling on a desk behind the camera. After a few minutes he looked up at Donnie and said," Take your shoes and socks off turning your socks inside out as you pull them off." Donnie did as he was told. "Shake your socks out and put them inside your shoes. Pick them up and follow me. The sliding door the police officer exited through opened. On the other side of the door was a long hallway lined with plexiglass windows and cell doors with windows in them also. To the immediate left was a room with no door and yellow arrows painted on the floor.

"Put your shoes on the floor and follow the arrows through the metal detector." The guard picked up Donnie's shoes and inspected them wearing latex gloves. Donnie followed the arrows in his bare feet on the cold concrete floor holding up his pants the whole way. Once Donnie circled through the metal detector he ended up back at the doorway. The guard handed him his shoes and said, "Follow me." He walked Donnie to one of the cells, unlocked and opened the door. "Step inside," he said. Donnie stepped into the cell shoes in hand as the door slammed shut behind him.

Donnie was in a twelve by twelve cinder block room. The walls were all painted white but there was graffiti scratched and written all over them. There were steel bunks resembling shelves protruding from two of the walls three high. In the corner was a stainless steel sink and toilet combo with a three foot privacy wall next to it. There was a concrete bench along the half plexiglass wall with the door. The concrete bench turned in the shape of an L to the privacy wall of the toilet. Above the bench on the wall to the left were three blue telephones.

Bodies were sprawled out on the floor and the mattress less bunks sticking out of the wall. Donnie carefully navigated his way across the room stepping over sleeping inmates to an empty space on the bench. He sat on the bench and put on his socks and slipped on his lace less shoes. The cell was filthy and stunk of body odor and bad breath from the fifteen or so unlucky criminals who had been arrested that day. Donnie just sat there in disbelief listening to the snores of his fellow inmates. He couldn't believe how these guys could sleep on the cold hard floor but they did. He leaned his head back against the wall and closed his eyes. He felt as if he was going to cry.

A detention officer (D.O.) came and unlocked the door holding a handful of papers. "Johnson!" He yelled. "Daryl Johnson...nobody?" He asked. Receiving no response he slammed the door behind him. Holy shit Donnie thought to himself, they don't even know where anybody is. About a half an hour passed and another guard came in, it was a woman this time.

"Everybody up!" She yelled. She clapped her hands loudly and yelled again. "Everybody up! Come on were moving to the cell next door." Everyone got up and headed to the cell door. They were all holding their pants up with one hand. Some of them held their shoes in their other hand. They all walked to the next cell. Before entering the next cell there was another detention officer handing them clear plastic lunch sacks. Donnie was the last to enter the cell. Slam! The door closed behind him with a thunderous bang. Some of the guys just used the sack as a pillow and went back to sleep. Most of them tore into the plastic bag and started making sandwiches. The sack consisted of: Four pieces of bread, A sack of what looked like bologna with a green tint, Two slices of individually wrapped cheese, A grenade shaped plastic bottle with some colored drink inside and a small pack of cheese crackers and one orange.

The cell was the same just reversed. Donnie found a spot on the bench again and opened his lunch. He went straight for the drink peeling back the tin foil lid. He took a drink. It tasted like Kool-Aid at first but then had a weird medicine like after taste. Donnie was so thirsty he drank it anyway. He ate the sandwich crackers. He picked up the bag of meat and smelled it. He didn't trust it so he sat it back down.

"You gonna eat that?" A voice next to him asked. It was a scruffy old man, homeless Donnie assumed by the look of him.

"It's all yours," Donnie said as he took the orange out and handed him the rest of the sack.

"Thanks," The old man said happily, like he won something.

Time crawled by. A guard came in from time to time and yelled names who didn't answer and slammed the door. There was only one time a D.O. came in and yelled a name that was actually in there. Donnie wondered if the guards did this just to torture the ones trying to sleep. Every so often they'd all get moved to a different cell. Once in a while they'd put someone new into the cell. There was always someone coming and going in the hall, yelling orders to inmates or yelling and laughing to each other. Donnie could not understand how anyone could sleep with all the noise. He knew he couldn't. He was wide awake anyway having smoked speed all morning.

Finally, a D.O. came in and called off a bunch of names. He called off about ten names and lined them up in the hall. He marched them down the hall barking orders the whole way until they disappeared through a doorway. A little later the same D.O. came back and called off more names. This time Donnie's name was included. They got marched down the hall into the same doorway. They were instructed to wash their hands with soap and water at the sink in the corner. One by one they were called and fingerprinted. They would wash their hands again after being printed and wait on a bench. They would be called one by one again handed a computer printed green and white card. It was thicker than computer paper more like construction paper torn in half on a perforated line. Once handed their paper they were lined up in the hall again and escorted to a nearby cell where they were reunited with the first ten people called.

Donnie got his booking sheet (I guess you'd call it) and sat on the bench and read it. Count 1: Possession of a dangerous drug felony class 3. Count 2 Possession of drug paraphernalia felony class 6. They had his name right but where the space was for his address is said "Transient". He didn't care he didn't want them knowing the address of the apartment. Hell, he didn't remember the address himself. He knew it was apartment one but that's all he remembered.

Time dragged on. After a while they were given another sack lunch. This time Donnie ate it all. He was hungry after waiting for God knows how long. They finished eating and a D.O. came and moved them to another cell. Donnie didn't understand all the moving but noticed they kept moving in the same direction. He overheard some guys talking calling it the 'horseshoe'. The other inmates just sat there bullshitting and joking like they'd been there many times before. They probably had.

A D.O. came and opened the cell door. He called out about twenty names. Donnie's name was called and he lined up in the hall with the rest. The D.O. called a few more names and slammed the door once everyone was in the hall. "Alright, you guys are going to court. You will be quiet and respectful to the Judge. If you are not I will pull you out and you can start all over again, understood? Okay, down the hall gentlemen."

They marched down the hall and were led into a big room with rows of benches almost like a church, but not nearly as nice. One by one a Judge called them to a podium with a microphone in front of his bench. Donnie was the fifth name called. He got up and approached the microphone.

"Please state your name for the record," The Judge said.

"Donald McKay Jr."

"Mr. McKay you are charged with one count of possession of a dangerous drug and one count of possession of drug paraphernalia. Count one is a class 3 felony under Arizona statue. Count two is a class 6 felony under Arizona statue. A plea of not guilty will be entered on your behalf. Your next court date will be in approximately thirty days from today. I see you have no address on your arrest record. Do you reside in Arizona?"

"No sir, I live in Kentucky," Donnie lied.

"In that case I'm ordering you to be held until your next court date. Your bond has been set at two thousand three hundred dollars. Thank you and good luck Mr. McKay. Please step to your right, the clerk has some paperwork for you to sign."

Donnie signed and got copies of his court papers as the Judge called the next person. Then he was instructed to have a seat in the back row with the other men who had already seen the judge. Donnie took a seat in the back of the court He sat next to an older guy with long hair and a beard. He wore jeans and a tee-shirt with a leather vest over it. He looked like a biker. "Damn kid haven't you ever been arrested before?"

"No, why?"

"You could have gave them any address and probably got O.R.ed"

"O.R. what's that?"

"Released on your own reconnaissance, the biker said pointing to the checked box on his own paperwork. I wish I knew back in the cell, I'd have told you what to say."

"Damn," Donnie said.

A D.O. escorted them back to another cell. Donnie sat reading the pink paperwork clearly upset. "Cheer up kid it's not the end of the world," The biker said and sat down next to him. "Let me see this," He said and picked up the green and white booking sheet. "Eighteen hundred on count one and five on count two. You could use a bondsman and bail out for Two hundred and thirty bucks if you have any collateral."

"I'm broke."

"You don't have any family or friends out here to help you?"

"Not anyone with money."

"I wish I could help you kid, Do you want me to call anyone when I get out?"

"No, I don't have a phone. Thanks though."

"Well you don't have any priors and these are just drug charges, your just gonna get probation."

"You think so?"

"I'd bet money on it."

They sat around in the cell for a while. It was hot and sticky from humidity. This place was horrible. Donnie wondered how the board of health didn't do anything about this place. He just sat on the bench resting his head back on the wall. He wished it was all over. For now he just closed his eyes and listened.

"Hey are you getting out?" He heard the biker ask someone.

"No, I'm going back to prison," The unseen man answered.

"Do me a favor keep an eye on this youngster. He's never been arrested before so he don't know shit."

"Okay."

Donnie opened his eyes to see who the biker was talking to. It was a guy about thirty. He had a scruffy red beard and a bald head. He wore blue jeans and a plain white tee-shirt. His arms were fully covered with tattoos. Donnie closed his eyes again. A detention officer came and unlocked the door. When the door swung open a nice rush of cool air came in. The D.O. began yelling out names. The biker got up and said, "Good luck kid, if you have any questions ask him. He's been around the block." The biker pointed to the guy with the red beard.

"Thanks," Donnie said.

The biker and about five other guys lined up in the hall. Slam! The D.O. shut the door. They were marched off and disappeared around a corner. "Lucky fuckers, I wish I was getting O.R'd," Said a voice behind Donnie. Donnie turned to see the guy with the red beard peering out the window. "Name's Mike," He said shaking Donnie's hand.

"Donnie," he said shaking back.

"First time in jail?"

"Yeah."

"Don't worry it only gets better from here."

"It does?"

"Yeah, once you get housed you'll get a mat and a blanket. I mean it still sucks but anything is a step up from this shit hole."

A D.O. once again came to move them to another cell. Four of them were instructed to stay against the wall in the hall. "Alright the rest of you inside," The D.O. shouted and swung the door open. It was a lot nicer in the hall. The air was cool and didn't stink of B.O. Slam! The door closed. The D.O. led the four men into a door across the hall.

"They're getting classified," Mike said.

"What's that?"

"You'll see they'll call us in and ask us a bunch of bullshit questions. Then they decide what custody level you are and where to put you."

About a half an hour passed and the D.O. returned. He opened the door and yelled out more names. Donnie and Mike were both called and escorted across the hall with two others. Inside there were three windows with metal stools bolted to the floor in front of each window. There was a partition on each side of the center stool. The plastic windows had a metal circle in the middle with holes in it to speak through. On the other side of the windows were mini blinds. Donnie sat on a stool with his back to the window. Mike sat on the floor with his back against the wall. The mini blind came up and the woman behind the window called Mike. He and Donnie switched places.

They were asked a series of questions. The woman or man (depending on what window you got) entered their answers into a computer. Once they were all done they sat around for a good half hour before the guard showed to march them to yet another cell. Donnie could hardly stand it anymore. Sitting on a cement bench waiting and waiting, just to be moved to another cell to wait some more. He couldn't stand it, but what could he do?

"Next they'll dress us out," Mike said.

"What do you mean?"

"They'll bag our clothes and give us our jail clothes."

Once again a D.O. came and marched them to a room. It reminded Donnie of a school locker room, without the lockers. Shower stalls lined the two sides and a long bench ran down the middle. In the center of the back wall was a split door with the top half opened. A D.O. stood behind the half door. The other D.O. exited locking the door behind him.

"Alright, everything off do not take a shower I repeat remove all your clothes do not shower. Once all your clothes are off line up at the door in single file." The D.O. yelled. They all started stripping off their clothes. There were about fifteen of them. They all lined up naked as jay birds holding their clothes. Donnie couldn't remember when he felt this uncomfortable, maybe never. "One at a time I want you to step up to the window and place your clothe in the bag," The D.O. shouted as he ruffled open a clear plastic bag. The first guy stepped forward and put his clothes in a bag. The D.O. twisted the bag shut and tagged it with the inmate's name. He asked what size the inmate wore then handed him a pair of socks, a pair of boxers and a blue or grey set of clothes. They were just like hospital scrubs except on the back of the shirt and down the right leg

'MCSO INMATE' was printed in white if grey in black if blue. Last the D.O. asked what shoe size and gave an orange pair of plastic sandals. "Next! The D.O. shouted as he ruffled open another plastic bag.

One by one they all got their clothes. Some of them had blue tops with grey bottoms. Only three of them had matching clothes. The D.O. called on his radio for an escort. Once again they were marched to another cell. Once inside some of the guys switched shirts so their tops matched their bottoms. Donnie didn't care. "Well this is it. We just got to wait to be housed. I can't wait to take a shower," Mike said.

"Yeah, this place is filthy," Donnie said.

"Disgusting," Mike agreed.

After a while a D.O. came and unlocked the door. "Listen up! When I call your name step up to the door and get you I.D." One by one he shouted out names and the guys got their I.D. cards. When Donnie's name was called he retrieved his. It was the size of a driver's license. It had a slit at the top with a plastic clip running through it. It was long from top to bottom instead of side to side like a license. In the middle was a color picture of Donnie with his name written underneath. The picture was bordered in green with the words minimum to the left in white and security on the right. Donnie sat down on the bunk next to Mike.

"You're going to Durango," Mike said.

"Durango?"

"Yeah you got a green card you go to Durango jail. See look at mine," Mike said pointing to his ID clipped to the pocket of his shirt. His had a pink border with maximum security printed down the sides. "I'm just going upstairs to the second or third floor. I haven't been to minimum for years."

"What's the difference?"

"Kids and cons," Mike said. Donnie looked confused. "Most of the guys upstairs have been to prison. A lot of them have dangerous crimes or are considered a threat to staff. The guys they send to Durango have less serious offenses. A lot of them are just young kids who got caught shoplifting or with drugs or something minor."

"So Durango is better?"

"Not to me. I'd rather be locked up with guys that have done some time. They know how to act and tend to be more respectful. You know what I mean?"

"I think so," Donnie said but he didn't quite understand. It showed on his face.

"Don't worry you'll get the hang of it. The best advice I have for you is don't be in a hurry for anything. If there is one thing you'll learn from being locked up it's how to be patient."

A D.O. came and yelled about four names. Mike was one of them.

"Okay, I'm outta here kid, good luck."

"Thanks Mike."

It must have been hours that went by. Over that time the D.O.s brought people adding to the cell population. People came but nobody left and it was getting crowded. Finally a couple of D.O.s showed up with a milk crate full of chains and cuffs. They opened the door and lined everyone up against the wall. They took a chain and looped it around Donnie's ankle and locked it with a pad lock. They had him raise his other leg and did the same. Once all the inmates were chained they handcuffed them together in twos. Once they were all cuffed they marched them out and loaded them all on a big brown bus with Sheriff written down the side in gold letters.

Chapter Twenty-One

The bus arrived at the jail. The inmates were all taken off and lined up in the parking lot. One by one their chains and cuffs were removed. They were placed in a couple of cramped holding cells. Little by little the cell began to clear out. Every twenty minutes or so a D.O. would call out about five names and take them out. Donnie was in the very last group called.

Donnie and the three other guys that were called with him were marched across a quad surrounded by buildings with a chain link pen in the center. The D.O. escorting them opened one of the building doors and instructed them to enter. Inside another D.O. was sitting on a metal table he had his feet on one of the four attached stools. He was eating an orange. He popped the last slice into his mouth and gave the other D.O. a nod. The other D.O. nodded back and exited the door they came in.

The D.O. stood up grabbed the orange peels off the table and threw them in a nearby garbage can. He walked back to the table and picked up a clipboard. "Alright when I call your name, grab a bed roll off the cart and go get a mat by the wall. Once you get your mat line up on this line," He said pointing to a line on the floor. "Donald McKay."

Donnie picked up a bed roll and tucked it under his left arm. He went to the wall and picked up a mat throwing it over his right shoulder and stood on the line. The D.O walked over to him and looked at his ID clipped to his pocket. He scribbled something on his clipboard and said," Follow me." The D.O led him to one of many doors. He unlocked it and said," You're in here, cell six." Donnie entered the L shaped room. To the right there were metal cell doors. To the left were more cell doors. In the middle on each side were rows of the same metal picnic style tables. The far two walls were covered with windows. All the cell doors were locked with the exception of two to the right. Donnie walked to an open door and looked over it seeing a 6.

Donnie entered the small cell. It was maybe ten feet by ten feet in size. The left and right walls had steel bunk beds on them with no mats. The cell was empty. He plopped his mat on one of the lower bunks. He

139

unrolled his bed roll. Inside the blanket was: a sheet, a towel, a roll of toilet paper, a three inch toothbrush wrapped in plastic, a clear tube of toothpaste and a small bottle of clear shampoo with a label reading 3 in 1.

Just as Donnie finished taking inventory of his bed roll one of the other guys he was called with entered the cell. He threw his mat on the other bottom bunk. "C'mon, I'll help you make your bed and you can help me with mine," He said. Donnie stacked his stuff on the top bunk. They each grabbed an end of Donnie's mat and carried it out to the tables with the sheet on top. The new guy spread out the sheet on the next table and they place the mat on top. "Now pull the corners together and tie them tight." Donnie tied the sheet and they carried the mat back to the cell. They did the same to the new guys.

"Okay now lock down. This pod is on lockdown until tomorrow," A voice said over the intercom.

"We just came from the horseshoe can we get showers?" The new guy asked.

"You got ten minutes," The voice answered.

The two of them hurried to grab their towels and shampoo. They rushed to the showers in the corner of the pod. Once they showered they hurried back to the cell and shut the door behind them. "What's up my name is Eddie," the new guy said shaking Donnie's hand. He was probably around twenty with short black hair and a starter mustache and some hairs on his chin.

"I'm Donnie, Have you been here before?"

"Yeah, a few times, I've never been to prison though. I'm pretty sure I'm going this time. I got a new charge while on probation."

"Man that sucks, are you looking at a lot of time?"

"Hopefully no more than five."

"Five years, holy shit what did you do!?"

"Stole a car, got busted red handed behind the wheel. I just hope I don't get a page two."

"What's a page two?"

"When they find something from your past and charge you with it. Like if they find my prints on another car they found abandoned and they run my prints through their data base and they match. They'll charge me with another count of theft of means."

"Are there other cars out there?"

"Oh yeah, lots of them, I'm pretty good at wiping them down though. A lot of them I sold or traded off so I'm not worried about those. "What are you looking at?"

Donnie pulled out his green and white booking slip and handed it to Eddie. Eddie read it and said," Oh shit this is nothing, first felony?"

"Yeah this is the only time I've been arrested?"

"I'm surprised you didn't get an O.R., I wouldn't worry you'll get probation."

"You think so?"

"I know you will. You're always probation eligible on your first offense. I wonder why the pod is locked down."

Donnie was happy Eddie was his celly. He seemed like a nice enough guy. He just wondered who else they were going to put in with them.

The next morning Donnie was awakened by the barking of a Detention Officer. "Chow! Everybody up! Chow's in the house!" He yelled He would unlock a few doors and yell it again. He worked his way around the pod unlocking and yelling. The inmates all lined up by the door where a cart of trays sat by another D.O. with a clipboard.

Donnie got up and got in line. He saw what Mike was talking about. With the exception of a few all the inmates looked young, most looked under twenty. There was a gray haired old man in front of Donnie in line. He was short maybe about sixty years old. He turned to Donnie and asked, "You came in yesterday?"

"Yeah."

"You smuggle in any tobacco with you?"

"No."

"How about your celly?"

"I don't think so."

"Damn, I'm dying for a smoke," The old man said as he stepped forward in line.

One by one they got a breakfast tray. There was not much to it. It had oatmeal, some eggs with some kind of greasy meat mixed in, two tortillas and a half pint of 2% milk. Donnie got his tray and started for the closest table. "Psst," The old man got Donnie's attention. "C'mon white boys sit over here," he said. Donnie followed the old man to another table. "This is our head," the old man said as he sat down.

"How you doing? Names Billy," the head said shaking Donnie's hand. He was about thirty with his head shaved bald. He was about six foot five and two hundred and fifty pounds Donnie guessed. He had a three day beard on his face.

"I'm Donnie."

"It's pretty simple in here if you have any problems with another race come and talk to me about it. What are you in for?"

"Drugs."

"What about you celly?"

"Stolen car," Donnie said as Eddie was coming to sit down.

"Yummy, just like mom used to make," Eddie said sarcastically. Billy introduced himself to Eddie. They ate then stacked their trays up by the doorway. When Donnie put his tray on the stack he noticed some books by the door. He went through them and picked one out. It was 'Cujo' a Stephen King novel. He went back to his cell and started reading. He was never much of a reader but there wasn't much else to do. A lot of the other inmates played cards and dominoes. Some just walked laps around the pod. That was all there was to do, very boring.

A few days had past. Donnie just stayed in the cell most of the time. He would try to judge what time it was by when the guard walked. Every half hour a D.O. would make his rounds. Even when he was reading he knew when the D.O. was walking. The sound of boots clumping and the jingle of keys gave it away every time. Donnie would make a line with his pencil on his book mark every walk.

Donnie was really into his book, it was a good escape. Every now and then the pod would get loud and distract him. Once there was a loud argument and two inmates headed to the bathroom to duke it out. Donnie could hear them fighting all the way in his cell. Everything echoed in the pod due to the concrete floor and brick walls. Once the fight was over Donnie went to use the bathroom. He couldn't believe all the blood. It looked like a murder scene in a horror movie. He assumed one of them got a bloody nose and kept fighting.

Donnie went back to his book. It wasn't long before he heard the boots and keys. Then came the sound of a whistle blowing and shouting. "Lock it down! Everyone inside! Lock it down now!" The D.O. yelled. All the inmates went to their cells.

"Did you see that fight?" Eddie asked as he came in the cell.

"No, I heard it though and saw all the blood."

"Yeah that dude's nose was bleeding like crazy."

"What were they fighting about?"

"A card game, I think."

"That's why I just read and keep to myself."

"You better find you another book. You know you can put in a library request."

"I can?"

"Yeah, you just got to catch a guard that has some tank orders on him. They usually put some out with toothbrushes and bar soap in the morning. I'm sure somebody has one. I'll ask around when we get off lock down."

"You think we'll be locked down long?"

"Nah, they'll come around and do knuckle/body checks and take those two to the hole and we'll be out."

Eddie was right. A couple of D.O.s went from cell to cell and looked at everyone's hands and made them lift up their shirts and spin around. They cuffed up the two brawlers and the pod was open again. Eddie found a tank order and a form that said I.L.S. at the top.

"What's this one?"

"It's for inmate legal services I thought you might want to find out when your court date is."

"Heck yeah I do. I'm glad you know all this stuff."

"Here I'll help you fill these out," Eddie said. He helped Donnie order some more Stephen King books and request his court date.

"Thanks man," Donnie said

"No problem," Eddie said and stuck the forms in the crack of the trap in the door. "When the guard walks he'll pick 'em up it's that easy."

"Cool."

The next morning the forms were gone. Breakfast was served and everyone's mundane activities began. Then it happened. When a D.O. came through on his walk he stopped at Donnie's cell. "Barns? Edward Barns?" The guard asked. Donnie glanced over his book and shook his head no.

"I'm over here," Eddie yelled walking toward the cell.

"Roll up, I'll pick you up on my next walk," The D.O. said and continued his walk.

"Page two?" Eddie asked nervously.

"Yep," The guard said walking away.

"Son of a bitch! I hope it's not a car," Eddie said.

"Damn, that's rough. What happens now?" Donnie asked.

"I gotta go back through the horseshoe again."

"Do you think you'll come back here?"

"Who knows, you can never figure this place out. They never do anything that makes any sense. Here you might as well keep this stuff," Eddie said handing Donnie a tube of toothpaste and a towel. "You can exchange it on towel exchange and have a spare. I'll get a new one in my bed roll."

"I hope you come back to this cell. I liked having you around."

"Yeah, I like you as a celly too," Eddie said as he rolled up his mat and placed it by the pod door. The D.O. came through on another walk. When he exited the pod Eddie followed. Donnie had the cell all to himself now. He laid down and opened his book. He marked a line on his paper bookmark with a golf pencil. He started to read.

The next day Eddie came back. He walked in the cell looking like hell. Donnie looked up from his book and smiled. "Alright you made it back," He said.

"Yep, I'm back. I need a shower," Eddie said unrolling his bed roll.

"Was it another car?"

"Yes, unfortunately it was," Eddie said and headed for the shower.

Another couple of days passed and Donnie finished his book. "Damn," he said.

"What's the matter?" Eddie asked.

"I finished my book. Now I have nothing to read."

"You'll find something."

"That was a good one though."

"I know I've seen the movie, a rabid Saint Bernard right?"

"Yeah," Donnie said and peeked out the cell door. He saw a couple of books by the door. He walked over to see what they were. One was a bible and the other was an A.A. book. "Damn it," He said and went back to the cell.

"No luck?"

"No."

"Let me go see what I can find. Let me have that book maybe I can trade it for something else." Eddie grabbed 'Cujo' and headed out into the pod. While he was gone a guard walked. He handed out mail and canteen forms as he made his way around. Donnie got a response to his I.L.S. form. He read it. It said his next court date was September 8th. He sighed it was only August 12th.

Eddie came back in the cell. He had a thin book in his hand. He tossed it to Donnie. Donnie caught it and read the title out loud. "The Stainless Steel Rat Saves the World." He looked at Eddie as if to say are you kidding me? "Hey it's better than nothing. It's science fiction. I thought you'd be into science fiction being a Star Wars baby and all."

"What the hell is a Star Wars baby?"

"I saw your ID you were born on May fourth."

"So, what does that mean?"

"May fourth is Star Wars day. You know May the fourth be with you."

"I have no idea what you're talking about."

"You've never seen Star Wars?"

"Nope."

"How is that even possible?"

"I didn't go to the movies much."

"Unbelievable," Eddie said shaking his head. "Well it's sci-fi or nothing for now."

Donnie picked up the book again. He studied the cover. The price was 75cents. He opened it and flipped a few pages. He read copyright 1972, by Harry Harrison. No wonder it was so cheap, this book was over twenty years old. He just tucked it under his mat and lay there thinking. He wondered what Tracy was doing. He missed her. He got up and walked some laps around the pod.

A couple of more days passed. Without reading time crawled by. Donnie was so bored. He walked laps until his legs were about to give out. He hated lying in the cell. Whenever he did he just thought about Tracy or his parents and it drove him crazy. He remembered the book. He pulled it out and started reading. He was surprised that he actually liked it. He decided he would only read fifty pages a day. The book was only one-hundred and sixty pages long and he wanted to stretch it as far as he could. Good thing he was a slow reader.

Donnie got lucky. On his third day of reading the sci-fi book, library came. He got three books, two Stephen King books and one by Dean Koontz. He was so happy he wouldn't have to ration his reading anymore.

"Hey, you got some books," Eddie said as he entered the cell.

"Yeah it's like Christmas around here."

"I don't know if I'd go that far," Eddie said laughing.

"What have you been doing?"

"I've been killing them at Dominoes. I got a hold of my Mom on the phone too. She's going to put a hundred bucks on my books next week."

"Wow, that's great."

Eddie went back to his game. Donnie finished his sci-fi book and started 'Skeleton Crew' by Stephen King. All was right in the world again. Donnie read his time away.

About a week later Donnie got called to a visit. He was escorted to a small room with a plastic divider in the middle. On the other side was a clean cut man in a suit. Donnie sat down on the steel stool bolted to the concrete floor.

"Hello my name is Dan Davis and I've been appointed to represent you in your current legal case," the lawyer said with a smile.

"I'm Donnie, Donnie McKay."

"Well Mr. McKay I've got good news for you. The state has offered a plea in your case. It's a good plea in my opinion. They've agreed to drop the F6-Paraphernalia charge if you agree to plead guilty to the F3-Possession charge. They are offering you two years' probation. How does that sound?" The lawyer asked sliding the plea agreement under the patrician.

"If I sign this I'll get out?"

"Yes, well not today. I'll request for the judge to sentence you on your September 8th court date which he will most likely do."

"I'll get out that day?"

"As long as the judge approves the plea, and I can't see why he wouldn't, you'll be released that day."

"Let's do it!"

"Just initial where the boxes are and sign on the second page where it says Defendant," The lawyer said passing Donnie a pen.

Donnie couldn't remember ever signing his name so fast. Now he was happy. Finally there was a light at the end of the tunnel.

"Okay Mr. McKay I'll see you on the 8th. Do you have any other questions for me?"

"Will I have to give the court an address in order to be released?"

"No, You'll be released and have 72 hours to report to your probation officer. He will want your address not the court, anything else?"

"What if I live in Kentucky?"

"There is such a thing called an interstate compact. You would have to apply and get accepted and there is a fee around two to three hundred dollars. Do your parents live in Kentucky?"

"Yes."

"I'll tell you what. Give me your parent's phone number and I will call them and see if we can at least get the paperwork started. I assume your parents have a phone and you know the number."

"Yes. I know the number," Donnie said and wrote it down for his lawyer.

"Do you have any other questions?"

"No."

"Alright, I'll let them know were done and see you in court on the 8th."

"Thanks."

The lawyer nodded and left through a door. A few moments later a D.O. came and escorted Donnie back to his pod. Donnie went back to his cell. Eddie was inside, "Legal visit?" He asked.

"Yeah."

"What happened?"

"I signed for two years probation."

"I told you you'd get probation. That's good celly I'm happy for you."

"Thanks," Donnie said and picked up his book.

Time really seemed to slow down the trick was not to think about it. Finally Donnie's court date arrived. They woke him up at four in the morning and packed him in a cell with everyone else who had court that day. Then they chained them all up and bused them all to the court building. When they arrived they were once again crammed in a cell together. A D.O. would come and call names. Donnie was relieved when his name was finally called.

Donnie and some others were cuffed and escorted into a courtroom. They were seated in the jury box of the otherwise empty court room. Donnie noticed his lawyer and another man enter the court. His lawyer placed his briefcase and a stack of folders on a table and approached Donnie. "Good morning Mr. McKay."

"Good Morning."

"I spoke with your father. He seems very upset with you. Something about you ripping off the neighbors, what is he talking about? On second thought I don't want to know. To make a long story short he said you are not welcome there so the interstate compact idea is dead in the water."

"What about the plea?"

"Everything is a go. You'll be sentenced today and released sometime before mid-night."

"Thank God."

The lawyer smiled and moved down the line to his other cases. After they all spoke to the judge they were herded back to the holding cell then bused back to Durango Jail and sent back to their pods. It was an exhausting day. By time Donnie got back to his cell it was three in the afternoon.

"How'd it go?" Eddie asked as Donnie entered the cell.

"Good, I'm out of here tonight."

"Good for you celly."

They didn't tell Donnie to roll up until 8 O' Clock that evening. Donnie said his goodbyes to Eddie and dragged his mat out of the pod. They put him in a small holding cell with about six other inmates. They waited. They were all called individually to the hallway. Once in the hallway they were each asked a series of questions. Then they had to sign forms put their thumb print on another. Once this was finished they were handed the plastic bag with their clothes in it. They were put in another cell where they were instructed to change. Once again they were called one by one given their property and put in the final cell.

"This is it, the last door," a man said.

It seemed like forever but eventually the door opened. The guys exited the building down a sidewalk by a brick wall and out a gate to the parking lot. There some of the guys got hugs from waiting family members. One guy took a waiting taxi. Donnie and the other remaining releases sat at a picnic table. "It's nice to breathe fresh air," An older man of about forty said to Donnie. He had dark hair with a short beard and mustache.

"Real nice," Donnie said.

"My name is Fred," The man said shaking Donnie's hand.

"Donnie."

"Were you in long?"

"A month, and you?"

"Only a week, I made bail my wife should be here any minute to pick me up. Who are you waiting on?"

"No one I'm trying to figure out how to get home."

"Where you headed?"

"Sunnyslope."

"Man that's a far walk. You can hitch a ride with me and the old lady."

"Yeah?"

"Sure we can take you to 19th Ave and Camelback, but you'll have to walk from there."

148

"That would be great. I'd really appreciate it."

"No problem."

Fred's wife showed up about fifteen minutes later. They dropped Donnie off at 19th Ave and Camelback. He walked North down 19th Ave. He had a good five mile walk to the apartment. He didn't care he was so excited to see Tracy and to be free he would have walked all the way from the jail.

Chapter Twenty-Two

Donnie was tired of walking but he marched on. He made it to the Circle K where he first met Skeeter. Fred and his wife were kind enough to give him some change when they dropped him off. He needed a drink. He bought a 32 Oz. Thirst Buster of Mountain Dew and headed down Eleventh Ave, his final stretch.

Before he even reached the apartment his heart sunk. Even in the dark he could already see the same red and white sign in the apartment window. He walked up to the apartment anyway. He sat in the carport leaning his back on the wall. He needed a break from walking and time to think. He sat there for a while resting his legs. The park he thought to himself, maybe they're at the park.

He let his legs rest a few more minutes then got up and walked to the park. The park was deserted, not a creature stirring. He climbed through the bushes to Jimmy's secret camping spot. There was a rolled up sleeping bag and a Dr. Pepper box of trash next to a bag of empty cans. He unrolled the sleeping bag and went to sleep. He was so tired from all the walking he slept like a baby.

The next morning he was awakened by Jimmy shaking him. "You're out," Skeeter said.

"What time is it?"

"Time to wake up, here," Skeeter said handing him a pipe and a lighter. Donnie took the pipe and started to smoke. "I was starting to think you were never getting out."

"Me too," Donnie said as he exhaled a cloud with his words. He handed the pipe back to Skeeter.

"Go ahead hit it again."

Donnie took another hit from the pipe releasing another cloud while he asked, "Where's Tracy?"

Skeeter's face lost his smile. "I don't know she's M.I.A."

"You don't have any idea?"

"I think she ran off with that dickhead that knocked her up."

"What? She's pregnant?"

"No he knocked her up a long time ago."

"What?"

"You didn't know Tracy was pregnant? She came back from Tennessee..."

"Kentucky." Donnie interrupted.

"Whatever, Kentucky and hooked up with this dude and he got her pregnant."

Donnie sat there stunned staring off into space. 'I got in trouble' he remembered Tracy's letter. "Holy shit," He said and hit the pipe again.

"Anyway what happened?"

Donnie pulled out his pink paperwork and handed them to Jimmy. "I got two years' probation."

"For what? We never even got in the car."

"A cop came and he found a pipe and a baggie of speed in my pocket when he searched me. I forgot it was even in there."

"Man that sucks. I'll show you where the probation office is it's right on Hatcher."

"How long has Tracy been gone?"

"I don't know maybe two weeks, no more than three."

"Damn it." Donnie said and dropped his head. He felt as if he was going to cry.

"She'll be back," Jimmy said and slapped Donnie on the back. "C'mon let's go to Circle K, you must be hungry."

They walked to the Circle K. Donnie bombarded Jimmy with questions the whole way. Most of them got I don't know for an answer. Jimmy explained how Tracy went to live with this couple while she was pregnant. How she said it was the only way she could stay clean for the baby. Once she had the baby the couple adopted it and Tracy moved back with her parents. He told him she fought with her parents all the time and they got sick of it and sent her off again.

Donnie wondered if she was pregnant with his baby. He wanted to ask Jimmy but how would he know? Besides, he could tell Jimmy was tired of answering all the questions by now. They walked back to the park and ate doughnuts Jimmy bought at Circle K. Donnie got a chocolate milk and Jimmy a Dr. Pepper of course. Donnie was depressed. He wanted to go back to Kentucky. He kept thinking about his lawyer telling him he wasn't welcome at his parent's house anymore. The more he thought about it the sadder he got and it showed in his face.

151

"Come on Donnie cheer up. You're out of jail you should at least be happy about that."

"Everything is a mess. Tracy is gone. I can't leave the state cause of probation. Even if I could leave my dad is pissed off at me and doesn't want me there."

"How do you know that? Did you talk to him?"

"My lawyer did. He called him to see if I could do my probation out there."

"Well you'll get through all this, you'll see."

"Where am I going to live? It's too hot out here."

"This is nothing you missed the worst of it when you were locked up. We went two weeks straight over 110 degrees it was crazy. Just stick with me you'll be okay."

Weeks went by and Donnie never did report to his probation officer. Tracy still didn't come back. Donnie and Jimmy slept in abandoned houses and stripped them of copper for money. Donnie refused to break in to any cars. He was a nervous wreck doing the houses as it was. Cars were way too risky in his opinion. He tried to save money but he just couldn't. Food and drinks along with a drug habit how could he?

The weather cooled down in October and Donnie was happy about that. The boys slept in the park now that the weather was nicer. They barely scraped by they ate dinner at the St. Vincent De Paul every night. That was all they served was one meal a day but it was free and it was good. The St. Vincent De Paul or 'Martha's' as the locals called it (because back in the day an old woman used to run it out of her house) handed out clothes also. People were good about donating clothes and food around the Holidays. Donnie got some jeans and some tee shirts and some much needed sweatshirts.

Thanksgiving rolled around and the boys went to eat at Martha's. It was a good meal and they were full. They were walking back to the park when something shined in the crack of the sidewalk catching Donnie's eye. "Did you see that?" Donnie asked.

"See what?"

Donnie hurried ahead a bit and kneeled down on the sidewalk. "Score!" He yelled as he got to his feet.

"What is it?"

"A diamond ring"

"Is it real?"

Donnie inspected it closer. "It's stamped 14k inside. What do you think its worth?"

"Not much, fifty bucks if you're lucky."

"Fifty bucks is fifty bucks."

"Fifty if you're lucky, most likely about twenty."

"I'd want at least thirty."

"I know who might buy it."

"Who?"

"Geezer, I always used to sell him jewelry I found in cars. I haven't seen him for a while but I'm sure he's around."

Skeeter asked around the neighborhood and found out Geezer was camping out by the Goodwill store at night. One night they walked to the Goodwill on 7th Street after it had closed to see if they could find Geezer. It was the first week in December so it was kind of cold outside at night. "I hope he buys this ring," Donnie said as they walked.

"He's more likely to trade you some speed."

"I'm cool with that. I just need to save up some money. If I could just get back to Kentucky and talk to my parents in person..."

"How are you going to do that? I bet you have a warrant by now. I wouldn't buy a bus ticket if I were you. I know if you rent a hotel room and have a warrant the hotel calls the cops. I'd imagine the bus station is not much different but I'm not sure. I wouldn't risk it."

"I'm going to do what me and Tracy did to get here, save up a hundred bucks and offer it to a trucker for gas who's headed that way."

"That might work."

"I know it will work. That's how me and Tracy got here. The only thing is I spend money as fast as I get it."

"Well you got to eat."

"I know."

"We'll figure something out."

They made it to the Goodwill parking lot. They could see a bike with a trailer on it parked on the sidewalk in front of the closed store. It looked as if a man was sitting on the ground leaning back on the store window. It was kind of hard to see in the dark, but there were lights all through the parking lot. Then they saw a lighter light in front of the shadowy figure.

"That's gotta be him," Skeeter said as they walked through the parking lot. They got about ten feet away and Skeeter yelled, "Geezer, is that you?"

"Who's askin'?"

"It's me Skeeter."

"Who's that with you?"

"This is my buddy Donnie from Kentucky."

"I haven't seen you in a while," Geezer said eyeing the two up and down. He was an older guy about fifty to fifty five years old. He had salt and pepper hair with a grey mustache and scruffy beard. "What have you been up too?"

"Same old, same old, we came to talk some business. My buddy here has a ring he's trying to sell. Do you still buy jewelry?"

"Yeah, I'm always interested in jewelry. Let's have a look."

Donnie pulled the ring from his pocket and handed it to Geezer. Geezer walked over to his bike trailer and started digging around in a duffle bag. He pulled out a jeweler's loop and held it up to his eye inspecting the ring. "Not bad," He said. "What are you trying to get for it?"

"Fifty bucks," Skeeter said.

"No way, that's too much."

"Make me an offer," Donnie said.

"I just got some pretty good shit. I'll give you a half gram for it."

Donnie looked at Skeeter. He just shrugged.

"C'mon, let's smoke a bowl of it and you can think about it," Geezer said walking back to his sleeping bag and sitting down.

"Right here?" Donnie asked.

"Yeah, I do it all the time."

"He's kind of paranoid cause he has a warrant."

Geezer got up and rolled his bike and trailer in front of the sleeping bag. He got back in the duffle and pulled out a sheet and draped it over the bike. How's that? He asked

"That's better," Donnie said.

The three of them sat down on the sleeping bag. The bike and sheet blocked Donnie and Skeeter from view from the street but Geezer was still exposed on the end. He didn't care. There was a good sixty feet of parking lot between them and Seventh Street. The cars passing by were going 45 miles per hour they weren't paying attention to what was going on at a closed store. That's probably why Geezer sat there, you could see anyone coming from far away.

Geezer pulled a pipe out of his pocket and handed it to Skeeter, who was sitting in the middle. Skeeter lit his lighter and took a hit. He released a cloud and passed it to Donnie who did the same. "What do you guys think? Pretty good huh?" Geezer asked.

They passed the pipe amongst themselves a few times. Skeeter noticed Geezer kept staring across the street.

"What do you keep looking at over there?" Skeeter finally asked.

"Do you guys want to make some money?" Geezer asked never moving his gaze from across the street.

"We were just talking on the walk over here how Donnie needs money to get back to Kentucky."

"I need some guys I can really trust." Geezer said making eye contact with Skeeter.

"You've known me a long time and I can vouch for Donnie here. He's a good dude."

"Well let's settle this ring business," Geezer said changing the subject. "Do you want the half gram?"

"Okay, I'll take a half gram."

Geezer got out a scale and weighed out the speed for Donnie. "Where are you guys staying at?" He asked

"We've been staying at the park."

"Which one?"

"Duck park."

"How about I meet you guys over there tomorrow at about noon and we'll talk. I've got a few things I have to take care of right now before it gets too late," Geezer said handing the speed to Donnie.

"Okay," Skeeter said.

Donnie and Skeeter started their walk back to the park. "I hate being out at night anymore," Donnie said.

"Relax," we'll be back at camp in no time.

"What do you think Geezer is talking about? To make money I mean."

"He probably wants us to sell for him. That's the only thing I can think of."

The next day Donnie and Skeeter were sitting at a picnic table in the park when they saw Geezer rolling up on his bike trailer in tow. "What's up guys?" He said as he dismounted his mountain bike.

"Not much, what's up with you?"

"Same shit, different toilet," Geezer said taking a seat at the table.

"So what's this money opportunity you have for us?" Skeeter asked.

Geezer looked over his shoulder and around the park to make sure no one was around. "You guys can't repeat this to anybody whether you're in or not."

"We won't."

"I mean not a soul."

"We won't, we promise you can trust us."

"Okay, I'm going to rob the bank across the street from Goodwill," Geezer said as serious as a heart attack.

Donnie and Skeeter just looked at him with wide eyes. "Are you crazy?" Skeeter blurted out.

"Yeah a little, but just hear me out. I've been casing that bank for six months. In the morning around 9 O' Clock is when it seems to be the least busy. I got a plan all figured out except one part. That's where you guys come in. I don't know what to do if some customer decides to play hero and comes after me."

"What are we supposed to do?" Skeeter asked.

I just need you to step in their way if they try to grab me or tackle me or something. I just need enough space to give me a head start if someone tries to chase me. Plus once I'm gone and the police come, you guys can fuck up my description a bit to throw them off. Nobody will know we know each other. Hell, most likely no one will know the bank was even robbed until I'm gone."

"I can't talk to the police I got a warrant out for my arrest," Donnie said.

"Just give them a fake name they're not going to ID you you're only a witness."

"What are you going to do stick a gun in the tellers face?" Skeeter asked.

"No need. I'm just going to show the teller a note. They are trained to just give up the money. You never want to give the teller a note. You don't want to leave any evidence behind they can get prints off of. I'm going to grow my beard out and dye all the grey out and my hair too. Then I'm going to shave it all off afterward and grow it back grey. You guys can describe me as a younger guy. Tell them you noticed a tattoo on my arm that I don't have, stuff like that. If you guys do this I'll give you each 25% of the take. I've read the average bank robbery gets four to five grand. What do you think?"

"Why not split it three ways?" Skeeter asked.

156

"Look I'm taking all the risk. You guys can't get caught. They'll just think you're customers. Giving you half to split is being too generous as it is."

"Plus it is his idea," Donnie added.

"Thank you very much," Geezer said smugly.

"Where are you going to go?"

"Don't worry about that I got a couple routes all mapped out up here," Geezer tapped his temple with his index finger. "I know this neighborhood like the back of my hand. I know what fences have dogs behind them and where alleys end up. I'm telling you I've been planning this."

"What if a cop just happens to be driving down 7th Street and sees you running out of the bank?"

"That's a chance I have to take. Hopefully I can just stroll out of the bank as long as no one chases me. I'll just have to run across the street and that would look normal."

"I have an idea," Donnie said excitedly. "You could wear a sweat suit, you know so you look like a jogger."

"See what I mean? If we put our heads together we can solve all these problems. A jogging suit, that's genius, why didn't I think of that? I could wear shorts and a tee-shirt underneath for a quick change it's perfect," Geezer said grinning from ear to ear.

"That just might work. A cop wouldn't think twice about someone running down the street in a jogging suit." Skeeter admitted.

"Of course it will work. It's brilliant!" Geezer said.

"What do you guys think? Are you with me?"

"I don't know, what do you think Donnie?"

"The only thing I don't like is talking to the cops."

"I'm telling you they ain't going to run your name for warrants. You're a witness to a crime, you did nothing wrong," Geezer said.

"He's right they're going to be too worried about catching the bank robber to think of anything like that," Skeeter agreed.

"Damn straight!"

"It would solve your money problem. Get you back home to Kentucky to straighten things out with your folks. What do you say Donnie? If you're in I'm in."

Donnie sat there a minute. "I am desperate for money," He said. He thought a little more. "Alright I'm in."

"Alright!" Geezer shouted.

"When do you want to do this?" Donnie asked.

"Not until after the holidays. The banks are too crowded during the holidays and the streets are too. It's better to wait until after New Year's. Plus we need time to prepare."

They met in the park every day for the next few weeks. They tried to think of every scenario they could that could mess them up. Then they'd figure out what they could do about it. Geezer let his hair and beard grow. They decided Skeeter would bring a ten dollar bill to the bank every week and get a roll of quarters. Geezer got the boys a couple of cheap BMX bikes. Donnie would stand by the glass door like he was keeping an eye on the bikes and Skeeter would wait in line and get the quarters. It would seem routine like they were just regular customers to the tellers.

Over the last three weeks Donnie and Skeeter made four trips to the bank. They also made several trips to different stores and bought what they needed. They got Geezer a jogging suit, a sweat band for his head, some dark hair dye and a fanny pack. Skeeter had been stashing the items at his camp behind the park. He figured Geezer had invested about forty bucks if you included the speed he traded for the bikes.

On New Year's Day Geezer met them in the park. Skeeter showed him the jogging suit he bought for him. It was red with white stripes running down the sleeves and pant legs.

"Holy shit, I'm going to look like the bionic man for god's sakes."

Donnie and Skeeter just looked at each other. They had no idea who the bionic man was. It was way before their time. "It's no good?" Skeeter asked confused.

"It will be fine it's just a bit loud is all."

"I got you these too," Skeeter said showing him a red sweat band and some amber lens sun glasses.

"The sweat band is a nice touch. I like the glasses too big lenses and not too dark so I can see in the bank."

"There's more," Skeeter said pulling out a black fanny pack and a pair of headphones. I figured that you could wear the headphones like your listening to music but you won't be and hear everything going on in the bank.

"Did you get the bag?"

"Yeah," Skeeter said and unzipped the fanny pack and pulled a black plastic disposable shopping bag.

Geezer laughed. I remember everybody wearing those fanny packs in the eighties.

"I see people jogging with them all the time," Skeeter said defensively.

"No, it's good, you did good."

"Last but not least there's this," Skeeter pulled out a box of hair dye. It says it only takes five minutes."

"Perfect we'll dye my hair today."

"When do you want to do the bank?" Donnie asked

"Tomorrow. Sound good?"

Donnie and Skeeter both shook their heads yes.

"Okay then tomorrow it is."

Chapter Twenty-Three

The next day all systems were go. They all met at the park at seven sharp. They went over the plan one last time. Donnie was nervous as hell. He assumed everyone else was too, they had to be.

"Okay you guys head towards the bank and wait across the street until I get there. Once I go in give me a minute. If I get a bad feeling I'll come out and we'll try another day. If it's too crowded I'll just come right back out. I'm going to go straight to the desk in the middle and write my note on a deposit slip. I'll wait until you guys show before I get in line, sound good?"

"Yeah," Donnie and Skeeter said together.

Geezer looked at Donnie and could see he was nervous. "Relax kid this is going to be a piece of cake."

Donnie and Skeeter rode their bikes to the Goodwill parking lot. They waited for Geezer. "My heart is pounding is yours?" Donnie asked.

"A little."

"There he is," Donnie said pointing toward the gas station Geezer was walking in front of. Geezer walked down the sidewalk until he got about 100 yards from the bank then he broke into a slow jog. He ran up the steps and entered the bank. The boys just waited.

"Well he didn't come out, let's go," Skeeter said. They waited for a break in traffic and rode across the street. They stood their bike up by the door so Geezer could easily knock them down on his way out if he needed to. They entered the bank.

"Wait here and watch the bikes," Skeeter said loud enough for the people to hear.

There were only four customers in the bank counting Geezer. There was one person in line and one being helped by a teller. There was another customer sitting at a desk to the right of the velvet rope maze of a line. The boys assumed he was opening an account or getting a loan or something. There was no security guard at all.

Geezer worked his way through the rope maze and waited behind an old lady in line ahead of him. The first customer was just finishing up with the only teller. He gathered his things and headed for the exit. Skeeter got in line behind Geezer.

"Next," The teller called the old lady in front of Geezer. She walked slowly toward the teller.

Another teller pulled a closed sign off the counter. "I can help you over here sir," She said to Geezer. Donnie's heart sank and he swallowed real hard. His eyes darted around the bank. He saw Geezer pull out the plastic bag from the fanny pack and hand it to the teller. She looked scared and rustled around behind the counter. Geezer got the bag from her and turned to walk out the bank. That's when it all went bad.

The customer at the loan desk turned and made eye contact with the teller. She mouthed 'help' to him and pointed to Geezer behind his back. Nothing could have prepared Donnie for what happened next. It all happened so fast it was crazy.

The customer at the loan desk stood up and drew a gun from a side holster under his suit jacket. "Hold it right there!" He yelled pointing the gun at Geezer. Geezer froze like a deer in headlights staring at the gun.

"Run Geezer!" Skeeter yelled and pulled a gun out of his inside pocket. When he raised the gun it went off. There was a pop and the window behind the desk shattered and fell like a waterfall of broken glass. Geezer ran as two more shots rang out. The man in the suit had shot Skeeter two times in the chest.

"Jimmy!" Donnie yelled and ran to him. He knelt down and cradled his head. He had blood coming out of the corners of his mouth. His whole chest was red. "You better run Donnie," He said weakly and closed his eyes and went limp.

"Get down!" The man yelled pointing the gun at Donnie as he picked up Skeeter's gun and put it in his jacket pocket. "Lay down on your stomach and put your hands on your head."

Donnie did as he was told. He could hear the approaching sirens outside the bank. He just laid there and cried. The man sat on Donnie's legs, and held his wrists behind his back. In a matter of seconds the bank was full of cops and paramedics. It was utter chaos. A uniformed officer put handcuffs on Donnie and took everything from his pockets. He just left him there lying on the floor crying.

The paramedics covered Skeeter's body with a sheet. That's when Donnie knew for sure he was dead. Donnie wasn't on the floor long when two police officers helped him up and walked him to a cop car. They sat him in the back and drove off. They took him downtown to

161

Phoenix Police Headquarters. They put him in a room handcuffing one of his wrists to a ring in the middle of a table. Donnie laid his head down on his other arm on the table.

About an hour (Donnie guessed) had passed. A detective entered the room. He placed a can of soda on the table. "I thought you might be thirsty," He said. He pulled a little tape recorder out of his suit jacket pocket. He placed the recorder on the table and sat down. He slid the can of soda closer to Donnie. Donnie reached out and picked it up. He popped the top with his free hand and took a small sip.

"Do you need to use the restroom or anything?" The detective asked.

"No."

"Okay, my name is Detective Hayward. I'm going to record our conversation so there is a record of everything said. That way there is no confusion later and we are both protected legally."

"Okay."

The detective pushed the record button and the wheels on the micro cassette started to turn. "Detective Hayward, Interview with Donald McKay January the second nineteen ninety four," The detective said. "Now I'm going to read you Miranda rights. You have the right to remain silent. Anything you say can and will be used against you in a court of law. You have a right to an attorney, if you cannot afford an attorney one will be provided for you at no cost to you. Do you understand these rights?"

Donnie nodded his head yes.

"Can you please state yes or no for the record," The detective said pointing to the recorder.

"Yes, I understand."

"Can you explain to me what happened today at the Wells Fargo bank on Seventh Street."

"Me and my friend went to the bank to get a roll of quarters and there was a shootout and my friend was shot."

"There was a robbery, correct?"

"I guess so."

"Your friend, what is his name?"

"Jimmy," Donnie said almost starting to cry again.

"What was your other friend's name, the guy in the red sweat suit?"

"I don't know him"

Listen to me Mr. McKay. Don't make this harder than it has to be. The man in the bank, the one who shot your friend is an off duty police officer. He just happened to be in the bank opening an account when the robbery occurred. He already stated your friend yelled 'Run Geezer' before shooting at him."

Donnie just stared at the soda can speechless.

"Who is Geezer?" The detective asked.

"I don't know," Donnie said as tears began to roll down his cheeks.

"Is Geezer a nickname or is his name actually Geezer like Geezer Butler?"

"Who?"

"The bass player for Black Sabbath, his name is Geezer Butler."

"I don't know what you are talking about," Donnie said and took another small sip from the can of soda.

The door opened and another suited man entered the room. He noticed the tape recorder and nodded to the detective. The man handed the detective a folder and left the room. The detective opened the folder and flipped through a couple of pages.

"You said your friend's name is Jimmy?"

"Yes."

"A couple of detectives showed a picture of him around the nearby neighborhoods of the bank. Not one person identified him as Jimmy. The one's who were willing to talk to the detectives all called him Skeeter. Is that a nickname or something?"

"Yes."

"Geezer, that's a nickname too, right?"

"I don't know."

"Look Mr. McKay, you are in a lot of serious trouble here. You and your friends brought a loaded gun into a bank to rob it…"

"I didn't even know he still had that gun." Donnie interrupted.

"But you knew he owned a gun."

"I was with him when he got it," Donnie said without thinking, instantly regretting it.

"Where the hell does a teenage kid get a gun? Can you answer me that?"

Donnie just sat there staring at the can. What was he going to say, they stole it out of a car? He couldn't think of anything that wouldn't get him in more trouble.

"Look we're not stupid. Your friend Jimmy told your other friend Geezer to run when the officer interrupted the robbery. It's pretty obvious you were all there together. Why else would your friend pull out a gun and tell this Geezer fellow to run?"

Donnie didn't answer. He just put his head down and cried.

"You're the one left holding the bag here. One of your friends is dead and the other one disappeared. If you co-operate with us maybe it will help you down the road. Now I'm going to ask you again, who is Geezer?"

"I want a lawyer," Donnie managed to get out between sobs.

The detective reached out and grabbed the mini tape recorder. "End interview," He said into it and pushed the stop button. He put the recorder in his suit jacket pocket. "You're making a big mistake kid," He said as he tapped the folder on the table straightening out the papers inside. He got up and left the room.

It wasn't long and two uniformed officers came in and escorted Donnie to a police car. They put him in back and Donnie laid his head back and closed his eyes. When the car stopped Donnie opened his eyes to a familiar sight, the big metal doors at Madison Street Jail opening.

It was a bit different for Donnie this time around. They took his picture but this time had him change into jail clothes after going through the metal detector. Then they placed him in a cell by himself. The cell was about six by nine on the right side of the hall. It had the usual stainless steel sink/toilet combo and privacy wall. Looking out the window you could see all the other inmates in the cells he went through last time. There was no bunk or mat just a roll of toilet paper.

Donnie got the roll of toilet paper and put it under his head like a pillow. He laid on the floor in the fetal position and cried. All he could think was why did Jimmy bring that gun. That wasn't part of the plan. He was exhausted. He cried himself to sleep.

Chapter Twenty-Four

Donnie was awakened by the sound of the trap in his door being opened. A clear bag with lunch in it was dropped through the trap. The trap was then slammed shut. Donnie was too upset to eat he just rolled over and went back to sleep.

A D.O. came into his cell and woke him up. He was taken to the little room and fingerprinted. That's when he really got upset. Instead of getting one green and white booking slip he had three attached together. He read the first charge and thought he was going to faint. Count 1: Murder in the first degree. He thought to himself, this has to be a mistake.

He didn't even go down the list. If he had he would have seen: Count 2: Armed Robbery, Count 3: Endangerment, Count 4: Endangerment, Count 5: Endangerment, Count 6: Endangerment, Count 7: Endangerment, Count 8: Criminal Damage. He never got passed Count 1 before he started crying uncontrollably in his hands.

The D.O. escorted him back to his cell. When he got there he saw there were now two bag lunches on the floor. He laid down and once again cried himself to sleep. He had no idea how long he was asleep when he was awakened by the trap again. Bang bang bang. "Hello, are you okay in there?" A female voice asked.

Donnie rolled over and looked at the woman's face in the trap. She was an older woman maybe in her forties. She had blondish brown hair tied up in a bun on her head. She wore glasses on the end of her nose. "I see you haven't been eating. Are you alright? I'm Dr. Anderson and want to ask you some questions. Do you feel like hurting yourself or anyone else?"

Donnie just shook his head no.

"How are you feeling? How is your mood?"

Donnie didn't answer. Tears began to roll down his face and he just rolled back over. The woman shut the trap and walked away. Donnie went back to sleep. The next time he was awakened by two D.O.s. They took him upstairs to the sixth floor and sat him at a desk. Dr. Anderson was on the other side of the desk. She asked him another series of questions. She told him she was going to prescribe him an anti-depressant and he was placed in a nearby cell by himself.

After three days Donnie was allowed to come out of his cell and into the pod. It didn't take him long to figure out he was in a psych unit. There were inmates talking to themselves and walking around in circles. He found a book and just stayed in his cell. He only left to get his chow and to take a shower. At least he was eating again. He was still sad but nothing like he was. The anti-depressants seemed to be helping. He slept more than anything. He had Bad dreams of Jimmy being killed. This went on for a month.

Donnie got called to a visit. It was his public defender. He met with him in a small room outside the pod. It was the same as before, divided with a plastic window. Donnie sat down on the metal stool.

"Donald McKay?" The lawyer asked.

"Yes."

"My name is Daniel Turner. I've been appointed to represent you in your criminal matters. How are you holding up?" The lawyer asked. He was a big man. He had to be six foot two or three inches tall. He weighed at least three hundred pounds. His head was shaved clean with a razor. He had a clean shaven face too with the exception of a thick black mustache. He had a double chin that jiggled when he spoke and piercing grey eyes.

"I'm okay I guess."

"Well I'm sure you are aware of the seriousness of the charges you face, however I have some good news for you. I've met with the prosecutor and she has an offer for you. I have never in my career seen anyone get a plea offered this fast in a case involving murder."

"I didn't murder anyone! They are wrong!"

"Under Arizona state law if a person is killed during the act of committing a felony the person or persons committing the felony are responsible for the death."

Donnie just stared through the window at the attorney. He was speechless.

"I have copies of the statues if you'd care to read them for yourself."

Donnie just shook his head no.

"In speaking with the prosecutor I learned quite a bit about why the offer is so fast and good in my opinion. First off are the circumstances. Second she has an overfull case load right now, lucky for you. And third the victim has no family to contest a plea. All this has worked in your favor. Now I can't tell you to take the plea. I can only explain the benefits of doing so. The decision is entirely up to you. Do you understand?"

Donnie nodded his head yes.

"I can tell you, you are looking at a minimum of twenty-five to life if you were to take this to trial and lose. Excuse me thirty-five to life, I almost forgot the victim in under the age of eighteen. That is what you'll get if you go to trial and lose this case. That is just for count one mind you. The armed robbery is a class two felony and a dangerous offense." The lawyer held up a sheet of paper with the heading: General Crimes Sentencing Ranges.

"You would be right here," The lawyer said pointing to a box reading Dangerous Offenses. He pointed to the two and slid his finger across the page under the heading: One Historical Prior 13-704(B), (D). His finger stopped on the box under a 'P' and read 15.75. Due to the fact you were already on probation at the time of the offense an enhancement statue 13-708(C) requires you are to receive no less than the presumptive term. This is just count two alone. Are you with me so far?"

Donnie was numb but managed to nod his head yes. He was basically in shock or he probably would have been crying his eyes out by now.

"That's the bad news. The good news is the offer. The federal prosecutor has agreed to let the state handle the bank robbery. Normally that is handled by the feds because it's a federal crime but they work with Arizona a lot on bank robberies and allow the state to pursue charges. Anyway this is the offer. You plead guilty to second degree murder and the state will drop all the endangerment charges and give you a probation tail of ten years for the robbery. All in all you would serve twenty-two years in prison, that's day for day, flat time. Upon your release you would serve the ten years' probation. They also agree to run any time for your dangerous drug violation concurrent with the probation for the robbery sentence. This is a great deal."

"Twenty two years?" Donnie's voice cracked a little but he still didn't cry. He wanted to though.

"Think of the alternative. You are looking at over fifty years if they stack these charges. Twenty two years is less than half of that. Do you really want to risk it?"

"No."

"I can't think of a defense I could use to defend you in a trial. I've read the police report. A bank teller stated you and the victim had been going to the bank together for weeks. He yelled to the other guy to run and shot at an off duty police officer."

"I didn't even know he had a gun with him."

"I believe you Mr. McKay. I really do. But convincing a jury to believe you is a whole different story. You told the officer in your interview you knew he had a gun."

"I didn't know he had it with him."

"That's not the point. The things you said on tape are bad from a defense attorney's point of view. I can't think of an adequate defense for accomplice liability for the robbery. Being convicted of the robbery means you're accountable for the death because you were committing a felony and someone lost their life in the process. You arrived at the bank with the guy who pulled out a gun and shot at an officer trying to stop a bank robbery. Listen to me Mr. McKay please. I don't see you getting a better deal than this."

"Twenty two years is a long time."

"I know it is. Fifty or sixty is even longer. The probability of you winning at trial is highly unlikely. The officer will testify as well as the tellers. They all saw you two come in together. It's impossible to dispute. You even said yourself you were with…" the attorney flipped through some notes, "Jimmy."

"I know."

"There are cameras in the bank as well."

Donnie sat there in silence. He didn't even think about cameras. It didn't matter he knew his lawyer was right. He could not beat this. Even if he wanted to give up Geezer to get a better deal he couldn't. He knew nothing about him.

"The prosecutor said this offer is only good for seven days. After that it's off the table. I have a settlement conference with her in a week and she expects this signed by then. If it isn't it's off the table and were back to the drawing board. I don't see the next offer getting better. That's if there even is another offer. A plea agreement is not a constitutional right."

"I'll sign it," Donnie said softly.

"Are you positive? I have no problem giving you a few days to read it and think about it."

Donnie just looked at him. This guy has been convincing him how good of a deal this is and when he agrees to sign it he wants him to think about it.

"I have to ask. It is a big decision. I don't want you to rush into it and regret it later. I can't tell you what to do, but..."

"I'll sign it," Donnie interrupted and spoke louder this time. "I don't need any time to think about it."

"Okay," The lawyer said. He handed Donnie the forms through the slot under the window. "Let's go over this so I know you fully understand."

The lawyer went over the whole plea with him line by line. He explained the plea was stipulated that he gets twenty two years flat with a ten year probation tail and no other charges regarding this matter could be filed.

"Now the judge has the final say in this matter. He could throw this plea out. It's rare for a judge to do so. The only time I've seen a judge pull a plea is when the victim's family showed up at sentencing demanding a harsher sentence. Do you understand everything we've gone over?"

"Yes."

"Okay here's a pen. Initial here and here and sign right here," The lawyer said pointing the areas out on another copy of the plea.

Donnie took a deep breath and initialed and signed the documents. He slid them along with the pen through the slot when he was done.

"Here is an unsigned copy for you. Trust me Mr. McKay you made the right decision. The risk was not worth it. Do you have any other questions?"

"No."

"Okay I'll get a hold of the prosecutor right away and we'll set a sentencing date as soon as possible. Sound good?"

"Yes."

"I'll let the guard know were all done here. I wish you the best Mr. McKay and I'll see you at sentencing," The lawyer said as he got up to leave.

"Thanks," Donnie said before the lawyer shut the door. The lawyer waved and flashed a smile before closing the door.

Donnie was escorted back to his pod. He walked to his cell still in shock. He had just signed a big portion of his life away. He didn't want to think about it so he picked up his book. He couldn't concentrate on the words. Tears finally began to run down his face and he fell asleep. The bad dreams had subsided so sleep was welcomed.

Chapter Twenty-Five

Donnie slept most of the time so a month went by fast. Sentencing day arrived and he went through the nightmarish ritual of going to court. It wasn't as bad now that he didn't have to be bused from the Durango Jail but it was still a horrible experience. He was the last person to be seen by the judge. He was all alone in the court room as far as inmates were concerned. Donnie was with his lawyer, the prosecutor and of course the judge. There was a pretty woman in the courtroom also. Donnie asked his lawyer who she was and learned she was the court stenographer, there was also a court clerk and a D.O. acting as bailiff.

"Okay are we ready to proceed?" The judge asked the prosecutor and the defense lawyer alike. The Judge was a chubby man with a round face and a bald head with the exception of salt and pepper stubble on the sides. He wore glasses on the end of his bulbous nose.

"Yes your honor," The prosecutor answered.

Donnie's lawyer just gave a nod and motioned for Donnie to approach the podium. Donnie jingled over there in his leg chains and hand cuffs. The judge started speaking for the record stating the case number. Blah, blah, blah is all Donnie heard. "Will you state your name for the record," The judge said.

"Donald McKay Jr.," Donnie spoke softly into the microphone on a goose neck from the podium.

"You understand you are here to be sentenced and are of sound mind and body?"

"Yes sir."

"You have not consumed any illicit drugs or alcohol in the last twenty four hours?"

"No sir."

"It is my understanding you signed a plea agreement with the county attorney, is that correct?"

"Yes sir."

"Did you have a chance to read the agreement and did your attorney go over it with you and explain it where you were able to fully understand what you were agreeing to?"

"Yes sir."

"Did anyone force you to sign or promise you anything to sign the plea agreement with the state?"

Donnie thought to himself 'Yeah I was promised twenty two years instead of fifty or sixty,' but just said, "No sir."

"Okay Mr. McKay, are you ready to be sentenced on this matter?"

"Yes sir."

"The state of Arizona here by sentences you to twenty two years calendar days on count one murder in the second degree a class one felony and dangerous crime in the state of Arizona. You will be credited the 62 days you have already served. Calendar days means you do flat time, day for day do you understand that Mr. McKay?"

"I do."

"On count two the state of Arizona hereby sentences you to ten years' probation for the crime of armed robbery a class two felony and dangerous crime in the state of Arizona. This probation is to run concurrent with your previous probation for possession of dangerous drugs and possession drug paraphernalia as well as any community supervision you'll serve after the twenty two years in count one. You will serve this probation immediately upon release from the Department of Corrections. Do you understand the sentence that has been handed down to you?"

"Yes sir."

"Okay this concludes the sentencing hearing," The judge said and banged a gavel. "Good luck Mr. McKay. I am fully aware of the unfortunate circumstances involved in your case and believe this sentence to be fair. I hope you take advantage of programs in the Arizona Department of Corrections to better yourself and become a productive member of society upon your release. Please step to the right where the clerk has some paperwork for you to sign."

"Thank you," Donnie said instinctively.

"All rise!" The bailiff yelled and the Judge got up and exited the courtroom.

"Alright Mr. McKay that's it, you should be out of county within the next ten days or so. I have this for you," The lawyer said as he handed him a folder full of paperwork.

"What's this?"

"This is called your discovery. It contains evidence from your case like the police report and such. You will need it in the future if you decide to file any post-conviction relief. I would highly recommend you don't as it may jeopardize your plea. Be sure to keep it anyway. It is my understanding you don't want to go to prison and not have any legal paperwork. Good luck."

"Thanks," Donnie said and put his pink sentencing paperwork in the folder with the rest of the legal mumbo jumbo. The D.O. came and escorted him out of the courtroom and back to a holding cell. Then eventually back to his cell upstairs on the sixth floor.

Donnie's lawyer was right. Six days later he was told to roll up. The D.O. came and woke him at four in the morning and told him. He was heading to prison. "You can't take anything with you," the D.O. said firmly.

"I have legal paperwork," Donnie said.

"Legal paperwork is okay, no food or store items, things of that nature."

Donnie gathered his sheet, blanket and towel and piled them with his mattress by the pod entrance/exit door. He went back upstairs to his cell and got his folder. He waited by the door for the D.O. to return. The D.O. returned and escorted him to a holding cell with other inmates inside also heading to prison. He just sat and waited listening to the other convicted felons talk back and forth.

"I got love. I only got five years," one of them said.

"I'm just happy to get out of county," another said.

"Hell yeah, hit the yard and smoke a cigarette and drink a cup of coffee," said another.

Donnie felt a little out of place. Clearly all these guys had been down this road before and knew what to expect. He didn't know anything and was scared.

A D.O. came and lined them all up in the hall. Another D.O. joined him in cuffing and shackling them. They were all loaded on a bus.

"Alhambra here we come," An inmate in the back said.

"What's Alhambra?" a young inmate in front of Donnie asked someone next to him.

"It's where they process all the men. They make you a medical file and decide what yard they're going to put you on. It sucks but it's a step up from county, you'll see."

A big fat guy was seated next to Donnie. He felt cramped the whole way there. He was relieved when the bus finally reached Alhambra. He was happy to get off the bus and breathe some fresh air.

"Line up on the yellow line!" A corrections officer (C.O.) yelled. "Single file"

"Listen up! As these gentlemen remove your restraints I'm going to instruct you on what to do. Pay attention, I only want to say this shit once. You are going to be handed a big manila envelope. This envelope is going to have your first initial, your last name and your D.O.C. number. Check and make sure your name is correct. Once you have verified your name is correct I want you to place all your legal documents inside. Once your documents are inside fold the flap and bend over the tabs. Anything that doesn't go in the envelope you're going to lose. Do it now!"

Donnie received an envelope from a prisoner that worked at the facility. Down one side in black magic marker it read: D. McKay 102751. He stuffed his paperwork inside and fastened it shut along with the other twenty-five or so inmates.

"Okay guys we're going to head inside. I want you to maintain a single file line. Before entering the door I want you to place your envelope in the box by the inmate worker at the table. No talking! I want to be heard so everybody shut the fuck up!" The C.O. barked as he gave a nod to the mirrored window of the control booth just outside the door. Click, the door popped open. "Alright single file down the hall. You are going to turn left into the open door down the hall." The C.O. stood by the door eyeing the inmates as they passed. He was a big black man with a military haircut and a mean looking face.

Donnie put his envelope in the box and walked past the C.O. into the hallway. He turned left into the room where another C.O. was barking orders. There was a big gray bin on wheels in the middle of the room. To the left there were mirrored windows. Across the good sized room was a counter. Behind the counter there were more C.O.s typing on computers and another inmate worker at a desk sticking stickers on folders and writing on them.

"Everybody pick a spot on the yellow circle on the floor!" The C.O. yelled. The men all formed a circle around the gray bin. "Everything off guys, everything goes on the bin!" He yelled.

The men all began stripping off their clothes and tossing them into the bin. They all stood there naked as jaybirds most of them with their hand over their privates. Donnie felt uncomfortable in a room full of naked men.

A C.O. pushed the bin out of the circle and over by the door they entered. This C.O. was a white guy. He had a muscular build. His gray hair was cut in a flattop. He had a gray mustache to match. His brown eyes seemed to look right through you. He also had a mean looking face. He had tattoos on his forearms. Donnie assumed they were military tats. They looked old and blurry.

"Okay guys listen up! When I step to you I want you to put your pinkies in your mouth and open up and say ah. Lift your tongue and show me you have nothing in your mouth. Then I want you to bend your head down and run your fingers through your hair and behind your ears. Then I want you to grab your dick and your balls and raise them up. Then turn your back to me squat and give me two good coughs. Finally I want you to show me the bottoms of your feet one at a time and wiggle your toes. Everyone got it?"

Some of the men nodded and some said yeah.

"Okay you're first," He said and stepped to Donnie. Donnie did the hokey pokey following all the steps and stood back cupping his genitals. The C.O. made his way around the circle. While that C.O. was conducting his searches another one followed placing jumpsuits, a tee shirt, boxers and socks, and a pair of flip flops on the floor in front of each inmate after his search. When the searches were complete the C.O. yelled, "Okay everybody get dressed!"

Once everyone was dressed a couple of inmate workers were let in and organized the new arrivals in line. The first line was to get shaved. If your hair was long but not all one length it was all shaved off. All your facial hair was shaved off. One inmate refused to have his beard and mullet shaved. He was quickly tackled and escorted off. After that everyone complied.

The next line was to get your picture taken for you prison ID card. Then depending on what line was shorter you got your blood drawn or your teeth X-rayed. After that you were crammed into a chain link fenced cage outside. Before they entered the cage they were each handed a net bag with a blanket and sheet in them along with two more sets of clothes. There they waited to get a physical and be screened by the psych. All in all it was an exhausting process that took most of the day. By the time Donnie was brought to his housing unit he was tired, but it wasn't over

174

yet. Inside he saw the eye doctor who had him read an eye chart taped to the wall. Finally he was told to grab a mat and was directed to a cell.

His cell had two sets of metal bunk beds. In the corner was the famous toilet/sink combo and small privacy wall. Once he entered the C.O. shut the door behind him. He had a magnet about four inches high and two feet wide under his arm. It was white with red letters that read 'MAX CUSTODY'. The C.O. slapped it on Donnie's door and walked away. Donnie put his sheet on his bed, folded the blanket into a makeshift pillow and fell asleep.

Donnie rarely left his cell. His meals were delivered and put through a trap in the door. He was offered recreation time, which was just to go outside in a cage for an hour but he always refused. The good thing about 'rec. days' (which were three times a week) was you could take a shower. The water was always cold but it still felt good to be clean and get a fresh set of clothes. After his third or fourth day a C.O. came to his cell and opened his trap.

"Put your back to the trap and put your hands through it," The C.O. ordered.

"Where am I going?" Donnie asked as he followed the orders.

"Just to the C.O.III's (correction officer class 3) office," The guard said politely as he clicked the cuffs on Donnie's wrists.

Donnie was escorted down the run. It was like a big hallway wide enough for two cars. It was shaped like an 'L'. The showers were across from Donnie's cell with some big cells next to them. Cells lined the side Donnie was on except for in the corner where there were two offices. Directly across from the offices was a control room with large windows. Inside was a C.O. manning a control panel which could pop open any of the cell doors. They could also be opened manually with a key. The C.O. sat Donnie down in a plastic chair in front of a desk in the first office.

"Mr. McKay? The C.O III asked.

"Yes," Donnie said. He was surprised to see the man wasn't wearing a uniform like the other C.O.s wore. He was a short stocky black man dressed in jeans and a polo shirt. He had a Phoenix Suns hat on his head. He didn't have the mean look most of the guards seemed to have.

"I've been assigned as your C.O. III. What I do is classify you to see what custody level you will go to. This is your first time in prison, correct?"

"Yes."

"Normally you'd go straight to the walls with your charges…"

"What's the walls?" Donnie interrupted

"The walls is a five yard. Total segregation and controlled movement. It's not a nice place at all. You get cuffed up just to go take a shower, it's rough. You're in luck though, there's not much room for you and we got some violent inmates that need to be there more than you do. I am putting in for an override so you can go to a four yard instead. It's not entirely up to me we'll have to wait for it to be approved. The only thing I see them turning you down for is you've been STG'd."

"What's that?"

"It stands for Security Threat Group. It's what D.O.C. labels you for gang affiliation and such. You have a swastika tattoo right?"

"Yes."

"Have you ever been affiliated with the Aryan Brotherhood?"

"No."

"Are you a member of any of the various skinhead gangs?"

"No, I was just a young kid when I got the tattoo. I've never been in a gang or anything like that."

"I figured as much. I read your file. I've been doing this job a long time so I'm a pretty good at judging if an inmate is trouble or not. I've been wrong but not often."

"So what are my chances of getting an override?"

"Better than average, like I said there's not a lot of room right now so your timing is good. I'm really going to push for you on this. I can't promise anything but I'll try my best. Now I'm going to ask you a series of questions and I want you to answer honestly."

"Okay."

The C.O. III asked him all the same questions he's been being asked since he was arrested. Are you going to hurt yourself or anyone else? Do you have any enemies in the prison system? Are you in a gang? All the same old crap. He asked question after question and typed Donnie's answers in his computer. Finally he was finished and told Donnie he'd let him know about the override as soon as he heard. The C.O. II escorted Donnie back to his cell and removed his cuffs through the trap.

"Thank you," Donnie said.

The very next day the C.O. III came to Donnie's cell and tapped on the window. When Donnie looked up he saw his face in the narrow window on the door. The C.O. III held his hand up giving Donnie a thumbs up. "You got your over ride, you're going to a four yard."

"When will I go?"

"Anytime now."

"Thanks again," Donnie said happily. He was relieved he wasn't going to the walls. The joy was short lived when he realized he was still going to prison for twenty-two years and still didn't know what to expect.

The next day Donnie was woke up at four in the morning when the C.O. did his count. The C.O. told him to roll up. A C.O. came and cuffed Donnie and escorted him to the processing area where he first came in. He was put in a small phone booth sized cage and un-cuffed. He was told to strip down and push his clothes out the trap. The C.O searched his clothes and had him do the hokey pokey again. His clothes were returned and he was instructed to get dressed. Other Inmates were brought by other C.O.s while Donnie was being searched.

Once all the inmates were searched the C.O. began handing out breakfast. "Eat it quick guys, you can't take it with you," He said as he handed out styrofoam cups of cereal and half pints of milk with plastic spoons. The inmates gobbled down the cereal.Then they were all shackled at the feet. Belly chains were then put on them. They had hand cuffs on the sides of the chains to restrict their arms. The seven inmates were loaded into a white van. Soon they were zooming down the freeway heading south.

The van arrived at the Tucson Prison Complex at about six-thirty in the morning. The van went through several chain link gates ending up at what Donnie overheard a guard call 'The Hub'. The men all exited the van and were split into different groups. They were put into chain link cages in the building. Donnie was only there about a half hour when he and another inmate were put into another van. The van drove them to their unit. Donnie noticed 'Cimarron' written in river rock out the windshield as the van pulled up to a big chain link gate.

The electronic gate opened and the van pulled in to another big chain link gate. The van stopped and the back gate closed. A C.O. walked around the van with a mirror on a stick checking underneath and on top of the van. He then opened the hood and looked in the engine compartment. After the van was inspected Donnie and the other inmate were put into another chain link cage in the sally port. The back gate rolled open and the van backed out. The gate rattled shut again.

Chapter Twenty-Six

Donnie sat on the bench in the cage with the other inmate sitting next to him. They sat in silence for about a half hour. Finally a C.O. opened the cage and escorted them to their buildings. Another C.O. met with them and took the other inmate to a different building.

The C.O. escorting Donnie called on his radio and the door clicked. He pulled the door open and Donnie went inside. To the right were three blue phones mounted on the wall with a sign reading 'Calls are subject to recording and/or monitoring.' To the left was an empty room that was kind of triangle shaped with big windows on the inside wall. All the other walls were gray cement block and there was a concrete floor. They walked past the door to the empty room.

They were standing on a landing. To the left was a door to a control room with officers inside. In front of him Donnie saw a steel railing bolted to the cement floor. On the other side of the railing was about a four foot drop to the floor below. At the end the railing bent down as a handrail for a small set of stairs to the bottom tier. To the right of it was a set of stairs heading up. The pod was a big open cement room with metal cell doors lining the upper and lower tiers. Across the cells by the stairs were three metal doors standing wide open revealing shower stalls. The top tier also had three shower stalls directly above the bottom ones.

The door popped to the control room and the C.O. opened it and told Donnie to 'stay put.' He stepped in and another door clicked open and one of the C.O.s in the 'bubble' as it was called handed him a piece of paper. The escorting C.O. stepped back out and eyed the paper. "Okay, you're going to be in cell 3 upstairs," He said pointing up the stairs. "We'll get you a mat and some bedding along with your property here shortly."

Donnie grabbed the handrail and climbed the concrete staircase and walked to cell three. With a click the door popped open and Donnie stepped inside. He heard the C.O. yell, "Shut that door behind you." Donnie shut the door. Inside the door was that same toilet/sink combo with a little privacy wall. To the right were shelves. Next to them there was a metal desk connected to the shelves. The desk was bolted to the wall and had a metal shelf bolted to the wall above it. Directly across was another desk and shelf they both had plastic chairs tucked underneath them.

The shelf on the left had books across it. At the back of the cell were two metal bunks protruding from the back wall. They each had a metal shelf at the end of the bunk. The bottom bunk had two big metal drawers underneath. Lying on the bottom bunk was an inmate wearing a pair of headphones watching a TV on the shelf at the end of his bed.

"What's your name wood?" He asked.

"No, it's McKay, Donnie McKay."

"Wow, you're a fish," The inmate said with a chuckle.

"A fish?"

"That's what we call new guys who have never been down before. It's not a bad thing it just means you're new. White guys all call each other wood, short for peckerwood."

"Oh," Donnie said a bit confused.

"My name is Eric," His cellmate said as he got up and shook Donnie's hand. Donnie guessed he was about twenty three to twenty five years old. He had a buzz cut so his dark brown hair was only about a quarter of an inch long. He was covered in tattoos. His hands and all the way up both arms were tattooed. His whole neck was also covered. He even had a little star under the corner of his left eye.

"Donnie," Donnie said shaking his hand back.

"So what are you in for Donnie? How much they give you?"

"Twenty two flat for murder."

Eric let out a whistle, "That sucks."

"When do you get out?" Donnie asked.

"Wednesday."

"Wednesday, this Wednesday?"

"Whens day let me," Eric said with a grin. That brought a smile to Donnie's face. He liked Eric already. "I got some coffee, want a cup?" Eric asked.

"Sure, okay."

"Here put some water in this," Eric said and handed Donnie a plastic tumbler. "They didn't give you a bed roll or your property yet?"

"No, not yet, the guard said they would soon. This water isn't very hot," Donnie said filling the cup at the sink.

"That's okay I have a stinger," Eric said as he pulled an electric cord with a curled piece of metal at the end out of his drawer.

"A what?"

"It's an immersion heater. You plug it in and drop it in your cup and it heats the water. We call it a stinger, Eric said as he dunked the stinger in Donnie's cup of water. Just then a voice came over the speaker by the door. "McKay, come to the bubble," The voice said and the door popped. Donnie went out and down the stairs. By the bubble was a mat with a bed roll on top along with his net bag of clothes and his manila envelope. He gathered it all up and hauled it to his cell.

"Oh good you got your stuff," Eric said and took the mat from him to lighten the load. He threw it up on the top bunk. Donnie put the rest of his things up there too.

Eric unplugged his stinger and pulled it out of the boiling cup of water. He put it back in his drawer. He took out a bag of instant coffee and a pink box of sweetener and shut the drawer. He dumped half the hot water into another cup and put a couple of spoonfuls of coffee in each. "Do you want sweetener?" He asked.

"Yeah."

Eric pulled two packets of sweetener out of the pink box, shook them and ripped the ends off. He poured one in each cup and stirred them. He handed Donnie one of the tumblers. "Fill this up the rest of the way in the sink and it should be cool enough to drink."

"Thanks."

"No problem. We're cellies man, we got to look out for each other. Have a seat and drink your coffee and I'll run the place down to you. You can ask me what you need to know. Do you want a cigarette?" Eric asked as he sprinkled some tobacco into a rolling paper.

"No, I don't smoke."

"That's good, I wish I could quit. Hope you don't mind if I smoke," He said and licked the paper and twisted it.

"No, I don't care."

"Good, I need my smokes or I go crazy," Eric said and lit his cigarette and took a drag. He walked to the sink and filled his cup with the cigarette dangling from the corner of his mouth. "Do you got your legal paperwork in that envelope?"

"Yeah."

"Good, Shark is going to want to read it."

"Who's Shark?"

"He's the head. He's an alright dude but you don't want to be on his bad side. When he doesn't like someone it isn't pretty."

"What is a head?"

"Everything is racial in here. Every race has a head, its politics. Say you have a problem with a black guy. You can't just go over there and punch him in the mouth. I mean well you could but I wouldn't recommend it cause it could start a riot if other people jumped in. The heads would talk about it and okay you two to fight. Then you guys could duke it out with no one jumping in. It keeps things from being blown out of proportion and keeps the peace, it really does."

"Why would he want to read my paperwork?"

"To make sure you're not a sex offender or a snitch who told on one of your co-defendants or anyone else. People like that get ran off if they're lucky. More likely than not they're getting fucked up first."

"Does that happen a lot?"

"That's why were locked down right now. The Chicano's fucked up one of their dudes real bad. The cops are investigating it to make sure it wasn't interracial. They don't want a riot on their hands so once they are sure the yard's not going to go off shit will be back to normal."

"What's normal?"

"Well we are usually escorted to chow by pods. They'll bring it to us in Styrofoam trays for now. We go to rec. every other day too, but that won't happen until were off lockdown. White boys under thirty five are required to go to rec. and work out it's mandatory. There are some other rules too. You can't smoke after another race, you know take a drag off their cigarette. I know you don't smoke but if you did. Oh and never call anyone a bitch or a punk unless you're prepared to fight them. If someone calls you that you're going to fight them for sure. Those are like the worst names you can call someone in here."

"Why?"

"Because, a punk is like a prostitute, which is someone's bitch. It's just very disrespectful. You'll see there are punks in prison that are gay. White boys don't allow it so they're ran off if they're white. Some races don't care.

"Man, this place is crazy."

"You'll be alright. Prison is easy. Just don't get in debt and you'll be okay. The only people who have problems are the ones who gamble a lot and do dope. They always seem to get in over their head and its all downhill from there."

"That sounds easy enough."

"It is, trust me."

"How long have you been locked up?"

"I've been in for about seven years including county. I'm doing twenty five to life for murder like you. D.O.C. tries to keep people with like crimes together. They try to keep people with a lot of time together too."

"I guess that makes sense."

"Yes it does. Not much else in D.O.C. makes sense though, you'll see."

"How can I get a job in here? Is it hard to do?"

"Oh, you can get a job easy. I have some applications just fill one out. There are some porter jobs open I think."

"What's a porter?"

"Basically a janitor you clean the pod or the showers depending on where you're assigned. You'll want a job if you don't have money coming from the streets. If you don't have a job you'll want some kind of hustle. I do tattoos, it's hard in here though, were not allowed in the pod, we have controlled movement. I draw cards and stuff for people and that gets me by. I don't need much as long as I have coffee and smokes I'm fine. I was making good money doing tats on the three yard but I got too many tickets and got bumped back up to the four yard. There are some guys that do hobby craft and make some cool shit with craft sticks, you'll see. They sell that stuff for a lot sometimes."

"That's cool, I don't really have skills like that, but I don't mind working."

"Well I have some books if you like to read and I can turn my TV up. There is no speaker but the headphones go pretty loud if you want to watch TV with me."

"Cool man, thanks."

They just watched TV and waited for chow. Eric got up and looked out the narrow window in the door. "Chow is here. I was hoping they would take us to eat but not yet."

"What's for chow?"

"Chicken I think."

That was Donnie's first day in prison. He ate chicken and watched TV and talked with Eric until he finally fell asleep.

The next morning chow was once again served in house. A C.O. came around and passed Styrofoam trays through the traps. The C.O. got to

Donnie's cell and Eric asked, "Hey C.O. how long we going to be on lockdown?"

"I have no idea," He said and pushed a tray through. Eric gave that one to Donnie and got another for himself.

"I don't like that cop, he's a dick."

"Aren't they all?"

"No you'll see some of them don't give a shit. They are just here for the paycheck. Don't get me wrong none of them are your friends but some are better than others."

"This food is not bad."

"It beats county, that's for sure."

After they ate they stacked their trays and sat them on the open trap. A porter came around collecting them. After he put their trays in his garbage bag he stuck his face in the trap. "Is there a new wood in here?"

"Yeah," Eric said.

"Shark asked me to pass him his paperwork."

"Okay," Eric said and looked at Donnie."

"What do I give him?" Donnie asked as he got up and retrieved the manila envelope from the shelf.

"Just give him that whole thing."

Donnie handed the envelope through the trap to the porter. He was a Chicano guy with jet black hair slicked back. He had a thin mustache and a tear drop tattoo under his left eye.

"Alright," the porter said as he took the envelope. "You want your trap shut?"

"No, leave it open," Eric said. "That's another thing about being a porter, people will always be asking you to pass stuff for them. They'll usually kick you down some smokes for doing it if they have them."

"The guards don't care?"

"Some do but most of them don't. You'll learn what cops you can get away with what. They all have their little pet peeves."

Later that day Donnie and Eric were let out to take showers. The guard would let three cells out at a time for an hour. Donnie took a shower and got dressed. When he exited the shower he heard someone call to him. "Hey wood, come down here to cell fifteen," The voice said.

Donnie put his soap and dirty clothes in his cell and went to cell fifteen downstairs. "Here you go man," The voice said as the manila envelope came sliding out the bottom of the door. Then a face appeared in the narrow window of the door. "Tough break youngster, I'm Shark I'll talk to you when we get off lockdown, you alright?"

"Yeah, I'm good."

"Alright I won't waste anymore of your hour out," Shark said and disappeared from sight. Donnie couldn't tell exactly how big he was through the window, but he could tell he wasn't a small guy. Eric introduced Donnie to the guys from cell one and two. He explained that's who they always had their hour out with. It wasn't long and the C.O was telling them to go back to their cells.

"So, you met Shark?" Eric asked.

"Yeah, he introduced himself and gave me my paperwork back."

"Hopefully they'll let us out for rec. tomorrow. If they don't it will probably be a couple more days of lockdown. Lockdown usually only lasts about three days but sometimes it's a week or two."

"I don't mind it."

"I like to get out and get some fresh air. It helps break up the day. I get cabin fever being cooped up too long. It's nice to get a change of scenery, you'll see."

The next day an announcement was made to 'Stand by for chow.'

"Good," Eric said.

"We're off lockdown?"

"Looks like it. You better get ready standby is only for a few minutes."

Donnie jumped down and brushed his teeth and washed his face. He just got done getting dressed when the door clicked and popped open. "Let's go line up." Eric said.

They went down the stairs and waited by the phones. They were soon joined by other prisoners. Eric introduced Donnie to a few here and there. Shark climbed the stairs onto the landing between the tiers. "Good morning woods," He said in a bellowing voice. He was a big guy. He stood about six foot four. Donnie estimated he weighed about 300lbs. and it was all muscle. His head was shaved clean with a razor. His arms were covered in tattoos. He had a silhouette of a hammerhead shark on his neck. Donnie assumed that's why they called him Shark. He also had a little swastika under his right eye where most people had teardrops. He walked up to Donnie. "How you doin' wood? I'm Shark." He said and extended his hand to shake.

"Donnie," Donnie said shaking his hand.

184

"I'd like for you to sit with me at chow so I can go over how shit works around here. You got a new number and I don't want you getting into any trouble. Did your celly give you the gist of it?"

"Yeah, he explained a lot of rules to me."

A C.O. unlocked the door from outside. "Alright guys let's go. Single file you know the drill!" He yelled as he held the door open.

The inmates all marched out single file. They were all segregated. In the front of the line were all white guys then Mexicans, chiefs and blacks. They marched on a cement walkway to another building. There were guards ahead of them keeping an eye on them. A guard stood at about the halfway point and another was at the door of the chow hall.

Shark and Donnie were at the very front of the line. The C.O. opened the door for them and they stepped inside. There was a barrier of bars separating the dining area and the line to the window. They walked down the aisle toward the window. Shark pointed in the dining area and said, "The white boys sit at those three rows of tables."

Shark got his tray and Donnie followed. They filled their cups at a drink dispenser and walked to the back table in the corner. "This is the heads table, after today only sit at this table if all the others are full.

"Okay."

"We never cross into another races eating area. You walk to the end of the row and walk by the fence to dump your tray, understand?"

"Yes."

"When your celly explained the rules to you did he tell you white boys have mandatory workout?"

"He did."

"Do you get high?"

"I did on the streets."

"What did you do?"

"Meth."

"Not in here you don't. Whites are strictly forbidden to do speed. This is going to be considered your first and only warning. If I get wind of you getting high you're getting smashed, got it?"

"Yes," Donnie said and took a bite of his breakfast.

"If you are unsure if you should do something ask your celly or me or any of the white guys they'll let you know, okay?"

"Alright."

"It's alright here wood, you'll see it's a good yard."

Everybody ate and they were escorted back to their housing unit. Eric entered the cell after Donnie and shut the door. "What did you think of Shark?"

"He seems cool."

"Just don't ever get on his bad side, trust me."

"Oh, I believe you."

The next day they were let out for recreation after breakfast. They were all herded out to a fenced in chain link pen. There were workout stations here and there and a full basketball court. "Hey wood, come over here," Shark yelled to Donnie. Donnie walked over to Shark who was standing next to another inmate. "This is Jimmy he has an exercise routine of about four or five guys. You could workout with him until you develop your own routine."

"Hey, nice to meet you, I'm Donnie," Donnie said shaking Jimmy's hand.

"Same here, so you want to work out with us?"

"Yeah, sounds good."

"Cool, we do cardio today jumping jacks, burpees and jog in place in between."

"Okay," Donnie said and fell into line with the other inmates on the basketball court. Jimmy led them through the routine like a professional personal trainer. He seemed like a good guy. He wasn't a big guy only about five-nine or so. He wasn't all muscular like some of the other inmates but he was in good shape. He didn't have any tattoos either and was clean cut. He didn't seem to fit in with the average prisoners.

"They worked out for a good hour straight. After that some of them walked laps. Some of them smoked cigarettes. Eric was one of the smokers. Donnie sat down next to him at the picnic table. "Man, that wasn't as easy as I thought it would be," Donnie said.

"It gets easier. When's the last time you did any exercise?"

"It's been a while."

"Give it a few weeks it will be easy then. Hell I enjoy it now. I used to hate it but now when we're locked down I miss working out. Now I just got to quit these," Eric said holding up his cigarette then taking a big drag. Rec. ended and they were all escorted back to the pod to start the showering routine.

A few weeks went by and Eric was right. The exercise was easier and Donnie felt a lot better. Donnie was a good sized guy. He had grown to six feet tall and had a good build from doing farm work his whole life.

He weighed about 180lbs. and hardly had any body fat. He felt good and slept better now that he was exercising regularly. Routine was making time go by quicker too.

The weather started really warming up. One warm day the group was exercising on the basketball court. They all had their shirts off and were doing their routine. Shark was walking by and looked at Donnie. "Hey wood! Come take a walk with me," He yelled waving Donnie over. Donnie left the line and put his shirt on. He and shark started a lap around the pen.

"What's up?" Donnie asked.

"Is that a swastika on your arm?"

"Yeah."

"Man you can't have that in here unless you earn it. You've had that this whole time?"

"Yeah, I got it when I was like thirteen years old."

"Well I know this is your first time down and you didn't know about political ink in here so I'll let you cover it up, unless you want to put in some work for it?"

"Put in some work?"

"It just so happens I have a situation right now. There is a dude in here, he got here about a week before you. I recognized his name right off but it's a very common name. I looked at his number and was pretty sure he was who I thought he was. His paperwork was fine but I was pretty sure he was the guy who told on an old celly of mine back in the day. I wrote some letters and got my response a couple days ago. He's the guy. I had a feeling it was him. He's been green lighted."

"Green lighted?"

"He's got a hit on him. He rolled over on someone and got them twenty years. He's getting stuck if I have to do it myself. It has to be done he's a snitch. How would you feel about handling this for me?" Shark asked as he stopped walking and looked Donnie square in the eye. "I would never ask anyone to do this unless I was 100% sure it was the right guy. I would never ask anyone to do something I wouldn't do myself. Take a day or two and think about it wood. That guy's not going anywhere. Certain preparations still have to be made anyway. Think about it, there's no pressure you can cover the tat and I'd understand. Let me know what you decide."

"Okay," Donnie said.

"One more thing, this conversation is strictly between us, understood?"

"I understand."

"We are the only ones on the yard who know this situation. I don't want this rat getting wind and going into protective custody on me."

"I won't say a word."

"Good," Shark said and slapped Donnie on the back. "Think it over wood."

Donnie went back to the group exercising but they were just finishing up. He walked to the table with Eric and they sat down. Eric could tell by the look on Donnie's face he had something on his mind. "Are you alright? What did Shark want?"

"I'll talk to you in the cell."

"Alright," Eric said and lit up a smoke.

Once rec. was over and the cons were all herded back to their cells Donnie could finally talk to Eric alone.

"So, what's up?" Eric asked.

"This is what's up," Donnie said lifting the sleeve of his shirt showing Eric the swastika on his arm. "Shark says I have to earn it or cover it up."

"I'll cover it up no problem."

"I don't know if I want to, or if I should. I mean I don't want to seem weak and get fucked with for twenty years."

"Man, that is a rough decision. You got to keep in mind that right now you have a choice though."

"What do you mean?"

"Well if you choose to do some dirt and earn that ink you won't have a choice anymore. If someone tells you to smash somebody you'll have to do it or you'll be the one getting smashed. You know what I mean?"

"I see what you're saying"

"I can cover it up for you no sweat if that's what you want."

"I have some time to think about it. I'll let you know." Donnie thought about it long and hard. He struggled with it the next few days. He thought no one would respect him and his time would be hard if he covered it up. He also thought about what Eric said. Finally he made up his mind. He decided he was going to earn his ink.

Chapter Twenty-Seven

The next time the pod had rec. Donnie took a walk with Shark. He told him he decided to keep his ink. Shark seemed happily surprised and went over the plan with Donnie. Donnie asked questions but Shark explained to him he only needed to know his part in the plan. He explained that people couldn't tell what they didn't know but assured nobody would tell anything anyway. Donnie was nervous about the whole thing but didn't show it. Shark went over the plan a couple times over the next rec. times.

About a week had passed and the day arrived to put the plan into action. Donnie's heart raced as the pod was escorted to rec. Donnie took off his shirt and put it through one of the chain link holes and clipped his I.D. to it. He started his workout routine as usual keeping an eye on Shark. Shark gave Donnie a signal and Donnie walked to a workout station where guys were doing push-ups. On his way another inmate handed Donnie a shirt. In the shirt was a shank, a sharp metal rod with a tape handle it looked like an ice pick but it was wrapped in the shirt. When the mark got down to do his push-ups some inmates stood forming a wall to block the guards view. Donnie leaned down and stabbed the inmate as he did push-ups.

Donnie stuck him in his neck then ribs and once more a little lower as fast as he could. The inmate yelled with the first stab. Donnie walked to the toilet area immediately after the three quick stabs. He was breathing heavy and splashed some water on his face. There was a gunshot and guards started screaming, "Get on the ground! Everybody down!" and all the inmates dropped face down on the rec. yard. The stabbed inmate laid there screaming for help with the shank still stuck in his side just above his hip. The shirt was still wrapped around it soaked with blood.

Guards came rushing in the rec. pen surrounding the stabbed inmate and herding the others to the furthest fence from the inmate. They were all rushed out of the rec. pen with their hands on top of their heads. The inmates were all locked back into their cells. A helicopter was flown onto the yard to fly the injured inmate to the hospital. Donnie could hear it outside, he was breathing heavy standing at the sink splashing water on his face.

"Relax celly it's over." Eric said.

"I know I'm trying."

"Come over here and have a cup of coffee and watch some TV with me. It will take your mind off it."

"What's going to happen now?" Donnie asked as he sat down on the chair next to Eric's bunk.

"Well we'll be locked down a while and they call us in one by one asking everybody what they saw. Everybody will say the same things 'I didn't see anything', 'I was working out', 'I wasn't paying attention,' that kind of shit. Then they'll take us off lockdown and it will be like it never happened." Eric said as he pulled out his stinger from a boiling cup.

"That's it?"

"Yep, they don't give a shit if one of us gets killed. They just have to go through the motions to cover their own asses. They have to show they interviewed everybody and investigated it for when they get audited or whatever the fuck it is they get. It's all just for show, so don't worry." Eric smiled and handed Donnie a cup of coffee.

"Thanks," Donnie said and took a drink. His mind was eased a bit but not much.

They were locked down the next couple weeks. Just as Eric had said the inmates were pulled into an office and interviewed one by one. Then one day out of the blue the speaker came to life calling for stand by for chow. Eric and Donnie got ready and stood by the door. Shark joined them all smiles. "I want you to sit with me at chow today wood," He said looking at Donnie.

The pod was escorted to the chow hall and Donnie sat with Shark. It was just them two at the table. Shark just looked at Donnie and smiled. "You did it wood. You cost me two bags of coffee but you did it."

"Two bags of coffee?"

"I bet my celly you were going to chicken out at the last minute. I'm glad I lost."

"So I can keep my tattoo?"

"Man you put some steel in somebody, you can get some more if you want. Some bolts or whatever I'm proud of you wood. Anybody ever asks you about your ink from now on just tell them Shark approved it."

"Okay."

They ate and the pod was escorted back to their cells. They were called out for their showers and Shark called Eric over to his cell and talked to him a minute, once their hour was up the guard yelled for them to head back to their cells.

"What did Shark say?" Donnie asked.

"He told me if you wanted any ink to do it for you. Do you want some?"

"I'm not sure yet."

"Well let me know. I've been wanting to do some work to keep my hand for when I get back to the three yard. I have a machine already made we'll just need to burn some ink."

"Burn?"

"I burn some hair grease and cover it and make ink from the soot."

"That works? Is it dark?"

"Hell yeah it works and its real dark."

Days went by and Donnie felt like people looked at him differently. He felt like they respected him more. He wondered if it was all in his head. One day he got called to medical and when he got back to his cell there was a TV on his bunk and some headphones. "Where did this come from?" He asked Eric.

"Shark said you could use it, the wood that was using it is going to a three yard any day now."

"Nice, my own TV."

Eric was sitting at his desk drawing. Donnie climbed up on his bunk and started hooking up the TV. Eric held up his drawing. "What do you think?" Eric asked.

Donnie looked at the paper it read 'White Pride' in Old English and was shaded in at the tips. "It looks good," Donnie said.

"I was thinking for your back across your shoulders. I have the ink now if you want to do it."

"I like it." Donnie sat staring at it a moment. "Okay let's do it."

"Alright! I was hoping you'd want it. Drawing this up made me really want to do some work." Eric got everything ready. Donnie sat in a backward chair with his arms folded over the back of the chair as he leaned on them. Eric used deodorant to stencil on Donnie's back. He traced the back of the letters in pen put deodorant on Donnie's back then ran the deodorant stick over the letters. He put the drawing on Donnie's back and rubbed it and peeled it off. "Perfect, check it out," Eric said handing Donnie a small mirror as he held another up behind him.

Donnie positioned the mirror and saw the letters in purple on his back. "Wow, that pen was blue why are the letters purple?" Donnie asked.

"That's just how they come out, they'll be black soon enough," Eric said and plugged in the tattoo machine. It started to buzz. "Are you ready?" He asked Donnie.

"Yeah, I'm ready."

Eric started tattooing. "Feeling alright?" He asked between letters.

"Yeah it's not bad."

"I'll do this outline and we'll take a break and start again after the guard walks."

"Okay."

Eric started tattooing again. Donnie was facing Eric's desk and saw an envelope addressed to Eric on the desk. "Your middle name is Shawn?" Donnie asked and laughed a little bit.

"Yeah, that's my middle name, so what, why's that so funny?"

"Cause it sounds like a French hard-on."

"What? What the hell are you talking about?"

"Eric Shawn like erection," Donnie said erection with a French accent and laughed.

Eric stared off a minute. "I never thought of that before," He said and started tatting some more.

"Oui oui, very good erection." Donnie said laughing in a French accent.

"Stop moving around. You're going to fuck me up, and it's not a real good idea to make fun of someone giving you a tattoo. Especially where you can't see what they are doing. You might end up with a French hard-on on your back." They both started laughing. Eric finished Donnie's outline and they waited for the guard to walk. Once he walked, Eric shaded in the tips of the letters and he was done. He put some triple antibiotic ointment on Donnie's back and gave it a slap.

"Ow, shit what are you doing?"

"Just had to set it in for ya," Eric said and laughed.

"I guess I deserved that one. Mr. Eric Shawn," Donnie said with his French accent and laughed. "Thanks man, it looks good," Donnie said holding his mirror and looking at the mirror over the sink."

"No sweat, think of something else you want I always hook my cellys up with ink."

Donnie kept looking at the tattoo in the mirrors. He liked it.

Chapter Twenty-Eight

Months had gone by and Donnie had befriended another inmate named Dave. Dave was about Twenty-five years old. He had real short buzz cut brown hair and was about five foot ten and had a medium build weighing about 175lbs. He and Donnie started working out together and got along good ever since. Dave had been to prison before when he was Donnie's age he did three years for drug charges. After Dave and Donnie worked out at rec. they always sat at the picnic table and talked while Dave had his after workout cigarette. One day they were sitting at the table with Eric and Donnie heard a faint boom in the distance.

"Did you guys hear that?" Donnie asked.

"Yeah." They said.

"What is it? I've heard it before."

"They are blasting at the mine." Dave said pointing out toward the mountains.

"There is a mine over there?"

"Yeah a big mine and see over there that's Kitt peak there's a huge telescope in an observatory there. I remember going on a field trip to there in school back in the 7th grade."

"You're from Tucson?" Eric asked.

"Oh yeah I was born and raised here. I even lived in that little town right there for a while," Dave said pointing out to the houses in the distance. "I lived there in Sahurita for a year or so, it was a long time ago though."

"That's Sahurita? That little town over there?" Donnie asked.

"Yeah, why?"

"Is the name of that mine Arrow something?"

"Arabaca mine, that's what it's called."

"Holy shit! That's where my girlfriend from Kentucky moved to. Her dad got a job at the mine so they moved out here."

"Wow that is kind of crazy that you end up on a prison yard that you can see the town she moved to." Eric said.

"I know. First I was amazed that she moved to Arizona because that's where my first girlfriend was from and now this."

"Life is a trip sometimes." Dave said.

"Maybe she'll come visit you seeming she lives right there." Eric said.

"I wouldn't even know how to get a hold of her. I'm sure she has a boyfriend by now anyway," Donnie said.

"Hey, my co-worker is getting released next week you should apply for his job." Dave said.

"I don't know." Donnie said.

"Oh it's easy it only takes an hour a day and you get forty hours a week." Dave said.

"What's your job?" Eric asked.

"I'm the downstairs shower porter. The upstairs guy gets out next week."

"There you go celly, you wanted a job."

"I'll think about it," Donnie said.

Shark yelled over to Donnie and waved him over. Donnie walked over to Shark. "Take a walk with me wood," Shark said. They went for a walk around the rec. pen.

"What's up?" Donnie asked.

"I just wanted to let you know you're buddy, you know Mr. Push-ups. He didn't die. He just had a collapsed lung he's on a P.C. yard where he belongs. Thought it might make you feel better to know."

"Okay thanks."

"How are you doing?"

"I'm good, I'm thinking about applying for shower porter. Dave said the upstairs guy is getting out soon."

"Well if you get the job I'll give you my belt. That way if my kids act up you got something to spank them with," Shark said laughing. "Seriously though I just wanted to let you know you didn't kill that dude. I wish you did, but just thought you should know."

"Alright man thanks," Donnie said and walked back over to the picnic table.

"Everything alright?" Eric asked.

"Yeah, I told him about the porter job and he said if I got it he'd give me his belt."

"What?" Eric asked.

"He said to let him know if I got the job that he'd give me his belt so if his kids acted up I'd have something to spank them with."

194

Eric and Dave looked at each other and started cracking up. Donnie just sat there looking at them confused.

"Don't you get it?" Eric asked. "He means sperm from rubbing one out in the shower."

"Oh okay," Donnie said and laughed a little finally getting the joke. He looked out at the small town and thought how Gina was probably over there somewhere right now. What are the odds he thought to himself. Then he thought about the guy he stabbed. He was relieved that he didn't die. The state might call him a murderer but he knew he never killed anybody.

Donnie applied and got the shower porter gig a week later. Dave showed him the ropes. He was right there was really nothing to it. The guys in the pod all cleaned up after themselves so all that was needed was to spray them down with disinfectant and scrub them with a long handled scrub brush that looked like a skinny push broom. Then take the shower curtains downstairs and lay them out and spray and scrub them and clean the little window on the door. It was a piece of cake and he got $14 a week to do it. I know $14 doesn't seem like a lot but you could get a big bag of store from the canteen for $14 in prison.

All Donnie really bought was coffee and sweetener. He'd get some snacks occasionally but not very often. The money slowly added up in his account.

Donnie just did his time and followed his routine of working out, working and watching TV and time went by. There were a few occasions where a younger inmate didn't want to listen to the rules and Shark would have Donnie fight them to put them in line. It was never really a fight more like Donnie punching the other inmate. Giving them a 'hot one' as it was called in prison. Those instances were far and few in between.

Donnie had been in a little over a year now. One day a guard came and got him and took him to the C.O.III's office. He was told he was being re-classed and would be on his way to a three yard very soon. When he got back to the cell he told Eric. "Good for you man, I'm going to miss you though you've been a good celly," Eric said.

The next day at rec. he told Dave he was going to a three yard. Dave was happy for him. Donnie looked at the tattoo on Dave's neck. "I've always wanted to ask you Dave who's Sarah?"

"Sarah's my wife, well my ex-wife now. She left me when I came down the first time. We have a son together. We were high school sweethearts."

"How come you never covered it up?"

"I've thought about it. I just never did. She did give me a son and I couldn't blame her for leaving me. I was a real mess back then." He laughed and said, "But look at me now. But seriously I'll always love Sarah so I don't mind the tattoo."

When rec. was over Donnie and Eric went to their cell. "I want to get another tat from you before they roll me up," Donnie said.

"Cool we can do it tonight after you work if you want."

"Okay."

"What is it you want? I can draw it up while you're at work."

"I want to get Tracy right here," Donnie said pointing to his neck.

"What? Why the hell do you want to do that?"

"What do you mean?" Donnie asked confused.

"After everything you told me I have no idea why you'd want to put her name on you. If it wasn't for that bitch you'd have never run away, never started doing drugs and you sure as hell wouldn't be in here. She put your life on a downward spiral don't you see that?"

"I just love her and I feel like I always will. I always have."

"You're nuttier than squirrel turds if you ask me."

Everyone finished taking their showers and Donnie was let out for work. Against Eric's better judgement he wrote out Tracy in a few different lettering styles. When Donnie came back he showed him the patterns. "Are you sure you want to do this?"

"Yes."

"The only woman's name I'd put on my body would be my mothers or my daughters. You always know you'll love them."

"I'll always love Tracy."

"Alright which one do you like?"

Donnie picked one and Eric tattooed it on his neck for him. Donnie liked it a lot. "Thanks a lot Eric it looks good."

"Well I'm glad you like it. I needed to give you a going away present anyway."

Two days later Donnie was rolled up and on his way to the three yard. It wasn't a far trip. He was only moved to the other side of the fence. Cimarron was split in half South side a three yard and the North side a four yard.

Chapter Twenty-Nine

Donnie was escorted through the gate and onto the South side of the yard. The guard stayed on the North side and locked the gate behind Donnie.

"Go to building Three." The guard said and pointed to the building and turned and walked off. This was strange for Donnie. He was used to being escorted everywhere. He walked to the building door and pushed a button and the door popped open. He walked in the door to the exact same set up as his prior building. The only difference was all the cell doors were open and everyone was freely moving around the pod. Downstairs were a couple of tables where guys were playing dominoes and cards.

A C.O. came out of the bubble with a paper in his hand. "McKay, right?" He asked.

"Yes."

"You're going to be upstairs in the corner cell number 5," The guard said and pointed to the cell. "We'll get you a mat in a few."

"Okay," Donnie said and carried his TV upstairs. Everything else was in his net bag with the draw string over his shoulder like a sash.

"Do you need any help wood?" an inmate asked.

"No, I got it, thanks," Donnie said and walked down the tier and entered cell 5. Nobody was in the cell. The bottom bunk was neatly made and had a TV at the end. Donnie put his TV down on the top metal bunk. He took off the net bag and started unpacking his property on the desk. He was glad he stayed on Cimarron unit or he would have most likely lost his TV because it was not on his property file. He tried to give it to Shark but he told Donnie to keep it that he had three more.

An inmate popped his head in the door. He had bleach blonde hair down to his shoulders and a neatly trimmed mustache. His arms were covered in tattoos. "Hey wood, I'm Eddie, the head of this building."

"I'm Donnie McKay," Donnie said shaking Eddie's hand. Donnie grabbed his folder off the desk and handed it to Eddie.

"What's this?" Eddie asked.

"My paperwork."

"I don't need to see it. Shark already sent a kite (prison slang for a note or message) saying you were coming. He vouched for you, said you were a good wood. Your celly is on a medical run, the dentist I think. He's an alright dude kinda quiet, keeps to himself. He runs a store in here. He'll be back in a few hours. Do you got everything?"

"Yeah, I'm good. I'm just waiting on my mat and bed roll."

"Alright, I'll let you get situated, nice meeting you."

"Same here, thanks."

"McKay!" A C.O. yelled from downstairs. Donnie went downstairs to find a mat and a bedroll sitting by the bubble door. He picked up the mat and threw it over his shoulder and picked up the bedroll and started heading upstairs.

"Hey wood bring it down here," An inmate at one of the tables yelled. Donnie went down the stairs and the inmate grabbed his bedroll, "I'll help you tie up your sheet in between hands." The inmate got the sheet out and laid it across the table as the three other guys stood up. One of them shuffling a deck of cards.

"Thanks man," Donnie said and plopped the mat down on the sheet and started tying his end.

"No problem, my names Danny."

"I'm Donnie," Donnie said and threw the sheeted mat over his shoulder and tucked the blanket under his arm.

"You got it?" Danny asked.

"Yeah, thanks again," Donnie said and went upstairs. He got all his stuff put away and made his bed. He hooked up his TV and started watching a movie. He got about half way through the movie and an inmate came into the cell. He had long red hair in a ponytail and a thick red mustache. He was kind of a big guy about 6' 2" about 200lbs.

"Hey you must be my celly," Donnie said and jumped down from the upper bunk to shake his hand. "I'm Donnie," He said.

"My names Patrick but everyone calls me Red," He said in a muffled voice and shook Donnie's hand. "Sorry I just had a tooth pulled and have cotton in my mouth and am still numb on one side."

"Did it hurt?"

"No, they numbed me up pretty good it was more of a feeling of pressure than anything else. It wasn't half as bad as I thought it would be. You got a hell of an accent, where you from?"

"I'm from Kentucky," Donnie said thinking to himself, I don't have an accent.

"That explains it." Red said. "I run a store in here so sometimes, especially on store day there can be a lot of traffic with people getting stuff and dropping off what they owe. I hope that doesn't bother you."

"I don't care its fine by me. Do you make a good profit running a store?"

"Oh yeah, business is good I give the head 25% and he kicks down some respects to the North side over there ,but the rest is all mine. I do a 50% tax so say you get something from me that costs a dollar. On store day you get me that item back plus something worth 50cents. Cigarettes and coffee are what people are always running out of, but I got a little of everything, I never have to order store myself. Right before we go to shop I make out a little slip for everybody who owes me telling them what to get me. It works real well."

"Nice."

Donnie settled in on the three yard. He got along with his celly. He could be a little grumpy at times but he was cool. He got to meet everybody on the yard little by little. He went to rec. and worked out and started to run a lot and time cruised by once he got a routine down. Before he knew it about four months had gone by. He wrote a letter to his parents. He never got one back but still wrote them every six months hoping one day he'd get a letter back.

One day a fight broke out in the pod and the guards yelled for everybody to lockdown. Donnie was already in his cell watching TV. A guard came around making sure all the doors were shut. He shut Donnie's door on the way by. Donnie got down and looked out the narrow window in the door. He saw a face in cell 3's window. "Chino what happened?" Donnie yelled through the crack in the door.

"Your celly, man. He popped some other white boy in the nose and they started going at it. That shit was dope man, I was right there." Chino yelled back. Chino was a Chicano dude who lived in cell 3.

About an hour later the guards came by and rolled up Red's property. Donnie moved down to the lower bunk. They were locked down the rest of the day.

The next morning Donnie talked to Eddie at breakfast. He told him he wanted to take over running Red's store. Eddie was all for it. "I'll let everyone know to pay you what they owed Red. Did the guards take all his stuff?" Eddie asked.

"Yeah they were tripping on all the store he had. His whole drawer was full plus he had like five property boxes. I have a couple hundred bucks on my books so I'll invest it all in the store."

"Okay with that and what Red was owed it will build up fast."

The next store day Donnie stocked up on cigarettes and coffee. It had been about a week since Donnie had a celly. Eddie told him sometimes they roll you up to a different building or even a different yard. They try to keep the pods and yards racially balanced. They also don't house different races together so If there is no other white guy on the yard with a dangerous crime doing over ten years they move you to where there is one or move one from another yard to you. Donnie was hoping they didn't move him he was settled in nicely and wanted to stay.

Another week went by and Donnie got a pleasant surprise. They were locked down again due to another fight. Donnie's door clicked and popped open. He took off his headphones and looked at the door. Eric pushed it open and stepped inside carrying his TV and net bag. "Oui Oui, Eric Shawn! Where have you been my whole life?" Donnie said in his famous French accent. Eric looked up at him and started laughing.

"Alright! We're cellies again," Eric said happily. Help me get my property boxes from down stairs and make my bed." Eric said.

Donnie jumped down and helped Eric move in. He told him how he had a store and things were going good. Told him how he kind of inherited it from his last celly.

"That's awesome! Between you running a store and me doing tattoos we'll be sitting pretty."

Another month or two went by and Donnie got another surprise. He got a letter from his mother. She sent him $300. She explained to him his father was in town when the mail came one day and she got one of his letters. She said she was sad to find out he'd been writing and she didn't know. She said his father must be throwing his letters away before she ever gets a chance to see them. She told him he isn't the same since he ran away. He drinks and they fight like they never have in the past. She told him she would write him every couple of months or so but told him not to bother writing back because she'd never get them. She said she wished she had more money to send him and told him this was money she socked away from change at the grocery store here and there.

Donnie was happy to hear from his mother. It was bitter sweet though knowing he couldn't write her back. He wanted to tell her so much. He wanted to tell her not to send him any money that he didn't need it. He wished his Dad could find it in his heart to forgive him for running away but he knew his father. If he didn't come around by now he never would. He was shocked to hear his mother and father were arguing. He couldn't remember ever hearing them fight growing up. He felt guilty knowing it was his fault.

Time marched on. Years went by yet everything was the same, to some up prison in one word-boring. There was occasional excitement like fights were pretty common, and sometimes people got killed. Other than that it was the same day, day after day. The only thing that really seemed to change was prison policy and it was never good for the inmates. The first thing Donnie remembered them taking was the weights. There had been rumors the guards were complaining that the inmates were getting too big. When an inmate got his head caved in with a weight that was the final straw.

In 1999 a big change happened. They changed all the inmate clothing to orange. You also could no longer get things like guitars and TV's sent in everything had to be bought from the canteen. The canteen was no longer run by D.O.C anymore it was contracted out so prices were higher. Then in 2001 the attacks on 9/11 happened and there were all kinds of rumors. Everything from they were going to release a bunch of inmates to go to war to martial law was going to be imposed and FEMA was going to kill all the inmates over a level 2 yard. It was crazy. As years went by prison got worse and worse. The food service was contracted out and was bad. The days of three hots disappeared and lunch was replaced with a lunch sack. Donnie watched it all go downhill over the years.

Donnie got a letter from his mom about every four months now. She'd send him money, not always but from time to time. She always sent him a Christmas card with a letter and some money in it. This went on for years. He tried to think of a way he could write her back. He thought of sending letters next door so Jimmy could deliver them to his mother. He didn't know if Jimmy hated him and wasn't sure if his address went up or down from his parents. For all he knew they might not even live there anymore.

Then in 2009 Donnie was called to the Chaplin's office. He was told his father had been in a near fatal car accident. His dad was in intensive care and they were unsure if he was going to live. They let him make a call to talk to his mother. When his mother answered the phone tears started pouring down Donnie's cheeks at the sound of her voice. She told him she loved him and not to worry and that she would write him and let him know what happened. She told him he could write her now that his father was in the hospital so she'd get the mail.

Donnie went back to his cell. He splashed cold water on his face at the sink. When he raised his head up his eyes focused on the tattoo on his neck. He thought of the downward spiral speech Eric had given him and started to get angry. He calmed himself down thinking to himself he made his own decisions and he couldn't blame Tracy when he's the one who decided to run away with her. Eric walked into the cell. "Are you alright?" He asked.

"Yeah," Donnie said and told him about his father's accident.

"Wow, I'm sorry to hear that," Eric said.

Donnie got busy on a letter to his mother. He explained that he loved Tracy and that was why he ran away. He told her all about the bank robbery and everything that happened. He explained that he was trying to get back to Kentucky to patch things up with his father. He knew he had to do it in person. He told her all that happened over the years. The only thing he left out was him stabbing the inmate. The last thing he needed was for a guard to read his out-going mail. He didn't see any reason she should know that anyway.

A few days went by and he got a letter from his mother. She told him that over the years his father's drinking got worse and worse. She called him a 'functioning alcoholic' explaining that he still worked the farm but drank himself to sleep every night and just became a miserable man to live with. She had considered leaving him on several occasions but had no idea how or where she'd go so she just put up with him. She told Donnie what happened the night of the accident. She was writing Donnie a letter. She always wrote the letters at night after his dad got drunk and when he passed out she would walk out to the mail box so he never knew she was writing him. That night she thought he was out for the night but he surprised her walking in while she was finishing up her letter. They got in a huge fight and Donnie's father took off like a bat out of hell in his pick-up. Later the next day in the early morning the police came to the house and told her of the accident.

Donnie sobbed reading his mother's letter. All he could do was think if he didn't leave none of this would have happened. He talked to Eric about it. Without Eric and running at rec. Donnie knew he would be a mess. No matter what Eric told him though he still felt guilty for being selfish and running away without thinking of how it would affect anyone else. As Donnie received more letters from his mother he felt worse.

Donnie learned that not only did his father get hurt in the accident but he ran into a family killing a mother and young boy in the car. His father was hand cuffed to a hospital bed being charged with DUI and two counts of vehicular manslaughter. That was if he lived he was still in a coma and doctors were unsure he was going to pull through. Donnie sometimes dreaded opening letters from his mother because they made him sad. He thought about how ironic it was that after all these years of hoping and praying for a letter from her now he was scared to open them.

As months rolled on he got letters. His dad got out of the coma and was going to live. He was never going to walk again though. He was paralyzed from the waist down. Plus he had his legal problems to deal with. His mother had sold some farm equipment to pay for medical bills and put the farm up to bail him out. She said he was home but still drinking. He was in a wheel chair and as miserable as ever. He was a real chore to take care of and times were hard.

Donnie got more and more depressed and started seeing the psych. doctor who put him on anti-depressants. The doctor recommended he put in to go to a mental health yard and got him an application to fill out. Donnie filled out the application and a week later was told he had been accepted and was put on a waiting list to be moved to Phoenix Complex's Aspen Unit. The only thing that made him not want to go was his friendship with Eric. When he talked to Eric about it Eric told him he needed to go, that he was dealing with so much that anything that could help was worth a try. Eric was always good to talk to, it was like he always knew the right things to say. When Donnie told him he'd miss him and he was his only friend. Eric just told him he'd miss him too but it didn't matter because wherever they were they'd always be friends.

Over the next few months Eric kept Donnie sane tattooing him and talking to him. Donnie didn't run as often but he still did push-ups and other exercises to stay in shape. He took his meds and ran his store and dealt with all the bad news his mother delivered in her letters. Then one day in early 2010 Donnie got rolled up and moved to Aspen. Donnie packed up some of the store and left a majority of it with Eric to take over running. Donnie also left Eric his TV to sell or give away. He had more than enough money to buy a new one when he got to the new yard. Donnie and Eric said their goodbyes and Donnie and his property were taken to the sally port loaded on a van and taken to the hub he was at when they first arrived.

Donnie sat in the chain link cage and waited as he was joined by two other inmates and then another all headed to Aspen. About an hour later they were all loaded into a van and were soon zooming down the freeway toward Phoenix about a two hour drive.

Chapter Thirty

The van arrived at Aspen at about 10:45 AM and the four inmates were unloaded and unshackled in the sally port. They along with their property on carts were escorted onto the yard. It was clearly different. The yard had grass and trees and you could hear the traffic and see the street light at 24th Street and Van Buren. They walked to the visitation area. The walls were all painted with cartoon characters and murals. There they were each given a urine test and were all given a speech how this was a privileged yard and they were lucky to be there. They were told they were required to go to groups on a regular basis, had to have a job and above all there were no politics on the yard. No stores were to be ran on the yard either and if you got a ticket you were gone. The Property Officer inventoried the new arrivals property and they were allowed to take it upstairs to their cubicles. Donnie wished he brought his TV as the property cop didn't check the files.

Aspen was a small unit with only 150 beds. There was a small run downstairs called Able(A) run. Baker(B) and Charlie(C) run were upstairs and were larger. Donnie was housed in B-71 a corner bunk on B run. He met his neighbor Hector. He was a Chicano with jet black hair and a matching mustache kind of short standing around 5' 6". He was stocky and was covered in tattoos. "What's up my names Hector," He said shaking Donnie's hand over the locker/divider between areas.

"I'm Donnie," Donnie replied.

"What yard did you come from?"

"Cimarron."

"I've been there. After chow I'll show you around if you want."

"Cool thanks."

Just before they called chow an inmate came up to Hectors locker and asked for a soda. Hector got one out of his locker and wrote it down on a piece of paper. "That's three Tommy," he said and shut his locker and pad locked it.

"I know." Tommy said walking away.

"I thought there were no stores allowed." Donnie said.

"This is prison holmes. I didn't get locked up for following the rules. You just got to be careful who you deal with on this yard," Hector said. "We're first for chow today."

"First?"

"The runs take turns who goes to chow first, tomorrow will be C run."

Chow was called and Hector showed Donnie where the chow hall was pointing out things on the way. They went through the line and got their trays some people introduced themselves to Donnie here and there in passing and in line. "Let's sit over there I hate being right under the fan," Hector said.

"Where do I sit?" Donnie asked a bit confused.

"Sit right here with me. There's no politics here you can sit with other races it don't matter. I know it's weird at first, but you'll get used to it."

They sat down and started eating. "How long have you been here?" Donnie asked.

"A little over a year, it takes a bit getting used to, you'll see. If you can do your own time and not be concerned with anyone's charges or politics just do you it's a good yard. You just have to learn to ignore a lot of shit it's not for everybody. I like it cause my people live in Glendale so I get a lot of visits. That makes it all worth it to me. I can put up with the petty rules and the wacko inmates and undesirables for my familia dig?"

"Yeah I could see the importance of that."

"Where you from Tennessee or Alabama or something?"

"Kentucky."

"I knew with that accent, it was somewhere like that. You got people here in Phoeniquera?"

"No my folks are back in Kentucky."

"Nobody here to visit?"

"Nope."

"You done Kentucky?"

"Yeah."

They got up and dumped their trays and walked out to the yard. "The yard's open it's kinda like a two yard here but it is a three. There are fours and twos here they override them and everyone here is put on a medical hold so they don't get moved randomly. You got to ask to leave or get in trouble if you want to go."

Donnie noticed guys working out with kettle bells. "You got weights here?"

"Yeah, not a lot of them you got to check them out and you can't have them for more than an hour. People are real good about sharing them though."

"You want a smoke Kentucky?"

"No I don't smoke. Thanks though."

The intercom cracked to life, "New arrivals report to medical, also noon meds guys line up!"

Donnie and two other inmates that came with him were sitting in medical. "Where's the other guy?" Donnie asked.

"He's gone."

"Gone where?"

"They rolled him up. His UA was dirty so he's out of here."

"Wow," Donnie said thinking to himself they don't play. Medical was like a shipping container converted into an office type building called a connex, it stood parallel across from the big red brick building where the dorms and chow hall and visitation were. There were two more container like building next to medical parallel to each other facing the other direction next to medical. Donnie later learned these were the classroom and meeting rooms where groups were held. Donnie and the other inmates were called in one at a time. They had their vitals taken and meds (if they were on any) verified. The nursing staff seemed real nice and everything went a lot faster than other yards.

After Donnie was done at medical he was called to door one. Behind door one (which was in visitation) was where all the staff offices were like the warden and C.O. IV and the counselors or psyche techs (P.T.s) and psyche associates (P.A.s). Everyone was assigned a psyche associate and Donnie was called to meet his.

Donnie stood at door one waiting. A woman popped the door open she was a petite blonde lady a little older maybe 45 or so but still attractive and she smelled good. She asked, "Are you Donald?"

"Yes."

"Follow me," She said and started down the hall, "What do you think of the yard so far?" She asked.

"It's different."

"Different...in a good way?"

"Yeah, it's good," Donnie said with his eyes fixated on her butt as she walked in front of him smelling the pretty aroma trail she left behind her.

"Have a seat," She said pointing to a chair in the office and walked behind her desk sitting in her own chair. "I'm Mrs. Hayes I'm your counselor. I've gone over your file and read your application. I understand you had a family tragedy recently. How are you coping? Are you feeling okay?"

"Yes."

"I'm so sorry. It's bad enough to be in prison but having to deal with that on top. I can't even imagine. Are your meds helping with the depression?"

"Yes."

"Well if you ever need to talk that's what I'm here for. You just ask any C.O. to call me on the radio and I'll see you A.S.A.P. okay?"

"Okay."

"I'm not going to put you in any groups just yet. The session is almost over. So you will be put in groups when the next session starts in about three weeks. Sound good?"

"Yes."

"Well you don't talk much Donald. Maybe that will change when you're settled in. How's your mood?"

"Good."

"You don't feel like hurting yourself or anybody else?"

"No."

"Well okay then, this was just an introduction meeting. You will meet with me once a month unless you need to talk to me sooner. Don't be shy, even if you feel it's not very important talk to me anyway, okay?"

"Okay."

"Well were done then. I'll walk you out." She escorted him back to door one and said, "It was nice meeting you Donald have a good day."

"Thanks."

Donnie went back upstairs to his 'house' as it was called in prison. Hector was there lying in his bunk watching TV. He got up when Donnie walked by. "Man you're lucky you got a good cube right away. Everyone wants a corner bunk."

"There are a lot of empty beds here huh?"

"Yeah none of the double bunks have anyone in them and there's about at least ten cubes empty right now. They rolled up about six guys last week and five or six the week before."

"For what?"

"Different things, a lot of them got tickets for smoking in the bathroom. Some of the graveyard cops will write you up quick for it.

These dumbasses don't have enough sense to wait and see who's on duty before going and lighting up. Where have you been?"

"Medical and meeting my counselor."

"Who'd you get?"

"Mrs. Hayes."

"You lucky dog, she's sexy. I got Collier, he's cool as fuck but she smells better."

"I know she smelt so good."

"You ain't got a TV Kentucky?"

"I had one but I gave it away cause it was a yard TV. If I would have known, I'd have brought it with me."

"Yeah the property officer doesn't give a shit. I guess the last one was a real bitch, she was gone before I got here though. I know someone going home in about eight days if you want to buy another yard TV. If you have the money and he hasn't sold it yet."

"Yeah, check it out for me I got money on my books, but when's store day?"

"We order tomorrow and get it Thursday."

"Wow really?"

"Yeah that's another good thing about this yard, store comes quick. The dude owes me about $15 in store anyway so I'll see what he wants for the TV. If he ain't sold it yet he'll sell it cheap cause I know he don't want to take it home. I'll go talk to him right now."

Donnie was happy. Hector seemed pretty cool and the yard seemed laid back and now he might get a TV. Things were falling in place. He started to write his Mom to give her the new address when Hector came back and started working his combination on his lock. "You got $20 on your books Kentucky?"

"Oh yeah, more than that."

"Alright, I'm going to give him $5 in store and I'll make you a list to order me tomorrow, cool?"

"Yeah."

"You ain't gonna get it until a day before he goes home though."

"That's cool."

"Odela," Hector said and left with a bag of coffee and some honey buns.

They went to chow again. They got lunch sacks for dinner. That's just how it is on three yards lunch and dinner are reversed for some reason it was the same at Cimarron. On two yards you got a sack at noon and a tray for dinner. Three yards were different Donnie had no idea why. Donnie and Hector sat at the same table as before. "We can't take our sacks back?"

"No."

"Why not?"

"Cause these fuckin' morons hoard food in their lockers or get caught feeding the pigeons so we got to eat them in the chow hall."

"That sucks I like to save my sack for later a lot of times."

"Yeah I did too and I like to keep bread for peanut butter sandwiches. You can sneak food out but you don't want to with certain cops."

They finished their sandwiches and went back upstairs. Donnie took a shower and went back to his bunk. He was only wearing his boxers and flip flops carrying his dirty clothes back to his house.

"Kentucky, you can't do that here." Hector said.

"Do what?" Donnie said confused.

"You got to put on pants or shorts, a shirt and have your ID on, going and coming back from the shower they trip out on that here."

"Why?"

"Just some of the petty shit you gotta put up with. I don't have a splitter or you could watch TV with me."

"That's alright I just need to find a book or something."

"Oh, c'mon," Hector said.

Donnie finished putting his shirt on and they walked around the corner and into a little room. Every wall had shelves on it full of books. There was a little desk where an inmate was sitting and a table with four chairs in the middle all kind of cramped. "Man this looks like a good little library," Donnie said.

"The C run library is even bigger. A run has a small one. Well there you go man."

"Right on, thanks," Donnie said as Hector left giving the inmate at the desk a dirty look.

Donnie looked through the books he got to the K's and was happily surprised to find a big selection of Stephen King. He found one he never heard of and was reading the back as he was walking out of the library.

"Hey!" The inmate at the desk said.

"What?"

"You got to check that out."

"Okay."

"Let me see your ID and the book," the inmate said.

Donnie handed over the book and ID and the inmate took out a card from the book and stamped the inside and handed the ID and book back to Donnie. "Thanks come again," He said. Donnie walked back to his cubicle.

"Whatcha find?" Hector asked.

"'From a Buick 8,' I never heard of it before. I like Stephen King though he's my favorite. That dude working the library was kind of weird though."

"I hate that motherfucker. He takes his job too serious, he's a fucking idiot. There's a lot of people I hate on this yard. I just stay away from them as much as I can. I don't like that piece of shit right there," Hector said motioning with his head to the black guy on the other side of Donnie.

"Why?"

"You'll see, he's a fucking weirdo. He goes to Flamenco at least once a month. I keep hoping he won't come back but they bring him back every damn time."

"What's Flamenco?"

"It's a yard over by Alhambra, another mental health yard for people who can't function as well as the ones here. If you flip out here they take you to Flamenco and adjust your meds after three days if you're doing better they bring you back. Usually you go there three times in a little while they keep you there. They keep bringing that asshole back for some reason."

"Where do I send my mail out from?"

"C'mon I'll show you. I was just about to go make a call. The mail box is right by the phones."

They went downstairs and Hector showed Donnie the mail box and made his call. Donnie went back upstairs and cracked open his book. He read it until the lights went out. He stood up and stretched placing the book down on the locker.

"Book any good?" Hector asked.

"It's a weird one. I like it, it's good."

"Cool, goodnight holmes."

"Goodnight."

And that was Donnie's first night at his new yard, where he would likely do the rest of his time. From that day on everyone called him Kentucky. Donnie would joke and say my first name ain't Ken and my last name ain't Tucky and I ain't no fried chicken none neither! With his accent it was funny.

Chapter Thirty-One

Donnie got a job. Everyone at Aspen starts out on the yard crew. After breakfast around 7AM he'd rake or sweep the grounds. It was easy and you got 35cents an hour and forty hours a week even though you never worked past 11AM because the yard closed at 10:45 due to count at 11. Donnie got his TV a week later. So Donnie woke up, ate breakfast, worked 'til the yard closed for count unless he had group that day, ate lunch, ran laps and or worked out, took a shower, ate dinner, went to PM med call and either watched TV or read until he fell asleep. That was his routine and time was flying by. Six months went by like nothing.

He and his mother wrote each other every other month. She would tell him about his Dad and how he was depressed all the time but at least he wasn't mean anymore. He was in a wheel chair but some farm hands built him a ramp to the house. He claimed he wasn't drinking but she knew he was. She knew farmhands had to be buying him bottles and he spent a lot of time in the barn. She didn't say anything to him. She knew he felt terrible about those people dying in the accident and he was stressed about prison. He knew her and Donnie wrote each other regularly now and didn't say anything about it.

His mother would tell him in letters that she can't wait for him to get out. She had it all planned he would move home and help her while his father did his time. She had plenty of farmhands to work the farm during the gap in between. They knew what they were doing without instruction. They did fine on the days Donald Sr. couldn't make it out of bed to supervise. As long as the crop came in and they got paid everything would run smoothly. She explained to Donnie that she still loved his father and always would. She felt awful seeing him like this and knowing the pain and guilt he was going through. She knew killing the woman and especially the child tore him up inside. The court proceedings didn't help. His lawyer was good at finding ways to drag it on with continuances but they can't go on forever.

Another few months passed and everything was going good. Donnie was happy with his routine and the pace time was going and although his mother's letters were depressing at times he was happy to be in her life again even if it was only on paper. Then the bottom dropped out. "Inmate McKay report to door one, inmate McKay door one," said the Chaplin's voice over the speaker. Of course Donnie didn't know the Chaplin's voice at that time. Anyone who has ever been to prison will tell you, unless you are trying to get married or have applied for a religious diet or requested some other kind of business with the Chaplin you don't want to be called by the Chaplin because it's never good news.

Donnie waited at door one not having any idea who called him or why. He knew he didn't do anything wrong so he couldn't be in trouble for anything. He was not too concerned. The door popped open. "Donald McKay?" A man asked.

"Yes."

"Follow me to my office so we can talk. I'm Chaplin Jones," He said as they walked through the hall to his office. "Have a seat," he said. "There is no way to sugar coat this so I'll just come out and tell you, your Father is dead." Donnie's eyes filled up and his throat felt like it was closing.

"How?"

"From what I understand it was an apparent suicide. I've been given permission from the Warden to place a call so you can talk to your Mother. Is that something you wish to do at this time?" Donnie just nodded his head yes. "Is it the same number you have here as an emergency contact?" Donnie nodded yes again. "Okay I can only give you a few minutes. I'll make the call and see if she picks up." The Chaplin dialed the phone. "Hello, is this Mrs. McKay? Hi I'm Chaplin Jones with the Arizona State Prison Complex in Phoenix, Aspen Unit. I'm here with your son who is incarcerated on the unit and would like to know if you'd like to speak with him regarding your family emergency. Okay I'll hand him the phone right now."

"Hello Mom?" Donnie said sobbing.

"Donnie, he's gone your Father is gone," She said crying.

"What happened?"

"One of the farmhands found him in the barn. He shot himself."

Donnie couldn't speak. He didn't know what to say.

"Donnie? Are you there honey?"

"Yes Mom I'm here." He answered crying. "When did this happen?"

"Just a few hours ago, there are still police everywhere investigating."

"Oh, why would he do that?"

215

"I don't know all the details, I'll will write you and let you know everything. All I know is Robert pounded on the door and told me to call 911 that someone was shot. Then the police told me he was dead from a self-inflicted gunshot wound. That's all I know. I have to go though there are police everywhere and I'm sure they want to talk to me some more. I love you Donnie I wish you were here."

"I love you too Mom I wish I was there too."

"I got to go I'll write you real soon, bye Donnie."

"Bye Mom," Donnie said and cried like he never cried before.

The Chaplin took the Phone from Donnie's hand and hung it up. He picked up his radio and called for Mrs. Hayes to come to his office immediately. Mrs. Hayes entered the office and put her hand on Donnie's back. "Donald are you okay?" She asked in her sweet voice. "I know Donald it hurts it's a devastating blow. We're going to get you through this, I promise we'll do all we can," she said and picked up her radio. "Yard Officer, This is P.A. Hayes requesting a medical ICS (Incident Command System) at this time." The intercom cracked to life outside. "ICS the yard is closed. ICS everyone take it inside the yard is closed." Mrs. Hayes got Donnie to his feet and escorted him to medical. There he was given a shot to calm him down. He was transported to Flamenco for three days of observation.

Flamenco was horrible you are locked down in a padded cell and fed sandwiches three times a day. They are pre-made wrapped in paper towels and saran wrap. The C.O. removes the plastic wrap before handing them to you. Basically its suicide watch so they don't want to give to anything you could harm yourself with. The irony is with that treatment you feel more like killing yourself. Mrs. Hayes came to see Donnie every day and talked with him. She was a very nice and caring lady. After three days and a little change to Donnie's medication they felt confident he was going to be okay and he was transported back to Aspen.

Donnie went upstairs and sat at his empty bunk. He was called to the property office to get his things. Hector helped him carry his stuff from property to his cubicle. "How you doing Kentucky? What happened? Did you go off?" Hector asked as Donnie put his stuff away in his locker.

"My dad killed himself."

"Oh shit! I'm sorry man, wow."

"I was sad at first but now I'm just mad that he was such a chicken shit and would do that to my Mom."

Hector didn't know what to say. He felt anything he said would sound bad. "Well as long as you're alright Kentucky and you'll be alright."

"Thanks man."

A few days later Donnie got a letter from his Mother. She told him the police found a letter on his Father's lap. At first they thought it was a suicide note. Once they picked it up they realized it was a certified letter. He must have seen the mailman walking up to the house and yelled for him to come to the barn and signed for the letter. It was from a lawyer stating he was filing a wrongful death suit against Donald Sr. telling him not to liquidate assets and all kinds of legal talk which basically said they are coming after the farm and everything he owned. I guess with the guilt of the deaths and facing prison that was the last straw.

She wrote on. Donnie could see the marks from the tears on the paper. I don't know what I'm going to do. Everything was in your Father's name so all the accounts are frozen. I can't pay the help. Your dad's life insurance is void because it doesn't cover suicide. Luckily I found about $5000 in cash your Dad had stashed in case of emergency. No one could possibly know about that money. But that money is not going to last, between the electric bill, water bill and food I might be able to stretch it six or seven months then what? I'm worried Donnie. I can't afford a lawyer and don't know what to do.

Donnie didn't know whether to be sad or mad so he was kind of both. He went and talked to Mrs. Hayes. She explained to him that certain things we have no control over and to not let news from the outside world destroy him. She said she understands he's worried about his Mother but there is nothing he could do given his situation. She suggested he write her back and tell her to apply for assistance that every state has food stamps and housing assistance and hope and pray for the best. She was right he was helpless in prison and stressing and worrying about everything would only kill him. He started running again and just dealt with it but it wasn't easy. Whenever he got sad or angry he just blamed his Father. When in doubt blame it on the dead guy it works every time.

Donnie wrote his Mother back and told her to apply for help. He told her not to tell anyone about the money she could use it to keep her a float until some benefits kicked in.

He wished he could be there for her but he made some foolish choices of his own and now he had to deal with the consequences. He had been locked up for about seventeen years now and still had five to go. He had to get through that first and foremost before he could do anything for his Mom. He was brushing his teeth one day staring at his Tracy tattoo. He thought about Eric saying she put his life in a downward spiral. Then he thought how he put his Dad in a downward spiral and now his Dad was doing the same to his Mom. Ripple effects he thought when does it end?

A year went by and more devastating news came. His Mother had a stroke and she was in the hospital. All the stress and worrying she did finally caught up to her. Donnie was numb when he heard the news. He knew she was dead and a week later she had another one and she was. One day he was taking a shower and finally cried. He cried so hard but it felt so good to get it out. He dealt with it, what choice did he have? He was never going to get to see her again. In time his thoughts of sorrow about his Mother were replaced by good memories he had of her. That was a welcomed trade, one he'd make any day of the week. It was a real turning point for him.

Hector got in a fight and got rolled off the yard. People came and left Donnie stuck to himself. He didn't hang out with anybody. He talked to people, he wasn't rude. He just didn't allow himself to become friends with anyone. He was the Baker dorm porter now so he was in charge of keeping the floor swept and mopped and throwing out the garbage. He also went to school and got his GED because he ran away before he graduated. He kept busy running, working and reading he didn't even watch TV that much. He just watched it after the lights went out when he couldn't read. He stayed busy all the time. That's the key to doing time, keep your mind occupied and never be in a hurry for anything cause there is always just another line to wait in.

When he got down to a year he started having anxiety about getting out. What was he going to do? He had nobody. Not that he had anybody in prison. He was a total loner. It's not that he didn't want to get out it was just kind of scary. In prison he knew what to expect. He knew he had to be at his bunk at count time. He knew breakfast was at 6AM and lunch at Noon. Out there he didn't know what to do. He never worked anywhere but on the farm. Where was he going to live? How was he going to pay bills?

The months ticked off one by one. When he was 90days from the gate a probation officer came to see him. He explained he was not going to be Donnie's actual probation officer but he was a supervisor of somebody that would be. He told Donnie to get a residence, apply for a halfway house. He said they couldn't keep him any longer if he didn't because his time was up. He was killing his number as they say. But if he gets a residence now he can choose it. When he gets out his probation officer may pick what half way house he goes to and Donnie might not like the one that's picked. Donnie took his advice and applied and was accepted to a halfway house in Sunnyslope right on 11th Ave the same street he lived on with Tracy. They would hold his bed until January 2nd the day after his release if he didn't check in the halfway house by then he couldn't stay there.

Donnie got down to a month then a week and then a day. He had a hard time going to sleep that night before his release date. He didn't fall asleep until 2AM. And they wake you up after 4AM count clears to take you to Alhambra to be processed out. He fell asleep thinking today's the day.

Chapter Thirty-Two

Donnie felt like he had just fell asleep and he was being woken up buy the guard kicking his bunk with his foot. "McKay roll your stuff up so I can inventory it, today's the day."

Donnie wasn't taking much with him. He gave all his stuff away or traded it off during his last week. He put his court paperwork in a property box, his soap dish with his used bar of soap in it, half a bottle of shampoo and his deodorant. He put on his white long john shirt because it was January 1st and he knew it would be cold. The C.O. came back and marked down Donnie's items and took them. He came back and told Donnie to follow him. He walked Donnie downstairs and had him sit in the barber chair and wait. "You're transport's not here yet. They'll come and get you when they get here."

"Okay." Donnie said and waited patiently in the barber chair. He laid his head back and closed his eyes but there was no way he was going to sleep. His mind was racing. He was nervous and excited he hadn't been out of prison in twenty two years. He didn't know how to feel. Donnie waited about an hour and a C.O. came through the outside door that lead out to the sally port. He was a familiar face it was the property officer who inventoried his property when he first came to the yard. "Kick out day McKay! You ready?" The C.O. asked cheerfully.

"Oh yeah I'm ready."

"Let's get the hell out of here then." Donnie got up and followed the C.O., he unlocked the door to the sally port and let Donnie through. There was a white car in the sally port. The C.O. walked over to a storage area and got Donnie's property box and put it in the trunk. He grabbed a milk crate out of the trunk with the leg chains and waist cuffs. "I know it's stupid but technically you're still in D.O.C. custody so I have to cuff you for the ride next door its policy."

"I know."

"At least I checked out a car though and not a van."

"Yeah, I haven't ridden in a car in many years."

Donnie was shackled up and put in the back of the car. The C.O. pulled up to the big gate to the parking lot and got out. He popped the hood and the gate officer looked under the hood and went around the bottom with his mirror and did a visual ID on Donnie comparing his ID. Finally the C.O. got back in the driver seat and a few seconds later the big gate began to roll open. "Here we go," The C.O. said and drove out the parking lot, turned right on to 24th Street went North a short way and right again down a back road that curved around and ended up at Alhambra. The C.O. mumbled something into his walkie talkie and the Alhambra gate opened and he pulled in. He let Donnie out and unshackled him, handed him his box from the trunk and escorted him through the same door where Donnie was first processed. "Good luck McKay," He said and left.

One of the C.O.s at Alhambra took the box from Donnie and locked it in a little cage. "Is someone picking you up?" The C.O. asked Donnie.

"No."

"Well the first bus is going to be here any second so I'm going to have to put you in a cage outside until they are done being processed. There are only 41 coming in today so you're lucky. Yesterday we had 97 from three counties."

Donnie just shrugged his shoulders he didn't care. The C.O. put him out in the small rec. cages where he could have gone to rec. many years ago. He was glad he wore his thermal because it was chilly. Donnie waited in that cage for a couple hours as the Sun came up. Once all the intakes were outside in their cages a female C.O. came and got Donnie. She put him in one of the small cages in back and asked him what size clothes he wore. She returned with a pair of blue jean like pants and a light blue shirt and told him to change. He did and waited some more. She came back and brought him to take his picture.

The C.O. pulled his white street ID out of the machine and fingerprinted him. Then she walked him out to the desk and put his ID and bank card with his bus pass in an envelope. "Who's taking this guy?" She asked another C.O. standing by.

"I am is he ready?"

"He's good to go." She said and handed Donnie the envelope and unlocked the little cage with his property box inside. "Is that all you have," She asked.

"Yes."

"Okay, good luck and don't come back." She said and flashed a smile.

"I won't."

The other C.O. motioned for Donnie to follow him. They walked back out to the sally port and got in a van. Donnie sat in back un-cuffed. The C.O. drove him to the Main bus depot at Central and Van Buren, parked and opened Donnie's door and let him out. He went to the back and opened the back doors and handed Donnie his box. "Here you go you're a free man." The C.O. said and got in the van and drove off.

Donnie looked at the sign with all the bus schedules on it and decided his route and waited for the bus. A guy came up and sat next to him on the bench. He was a black guy about thirty clean shaven and dressed nice in a sports jersey and jeans and new looking Nikes. "You just get out?" He asked.

"Yeah, how'd you know?"

"I've been in those clothes before. Plus the property box is a dead giveaway."

"Oh." Donnie said and took his bank card and ID out of the envelope looking for the bus pass.

"Do you want to use my phone?" The guy asked. "You'll need to activate that card and set up a pin before you can use it."

"Okay thanks." Donnie called the number on the back and activated his card and made a pin.

The bus came and they got on heading North on Central Avenue. The black guy got off a few stops later and Donnie told him thanks again. He just gave him a thumbs up and got off the bus. The bus took Donnie to Sunnyslope Station there he caught the Hatcher bus and rode it to 11th Avenue. He got off and started walking down 11th Ave and found the halfway house. He looked up at the building and thought, I got until tomorrow and walked to the park. He stashed his property box back in the bushes and went and sat at the picnic table. It was about 10AM now. He walked around the neighborhood looked at the old apartment. He went down to Circle K and got some donuts and chocolate milk.

He was kind of lost. He didn't know what to do. He didn't want to go to that halfway house and listen to all their rules. He had about $700 dollars on his card because he never really spent the money his mom sent him. He kicked back in the park and just thought. He thought how he didn't have anybody. His parents were dead. Jimmy was his only friend out here and he was dead. Poor Skeeter he thought. He laid down on the picnic table and took a nap. When he opened his eyes he was surprised to see the sun was going down and it was starting to get a little cold. He walked down to Hatcher and headed East. He stopped at a liquor store and bought tall can of beer. He walked to 7th Street and Dunlap. He wanted to go to Goodwill and buy a jacket or sweatshirt or something. When he got to Goodwill it wasn't there, the building was empty.

It was dark now and getting colder. Donnie sat down and leaned back against the building that used to be Goodwill. He cracked open the beer and took a drink thinking to himself 'good thinking Donnie cold beer will warm you up.' He looked across the street and saw the bank. Memories just flooded his mind he remembered meeting Geezer right here the first time and the robbery. He thought 'What were the odds an off duty cop opening an account that day?' He shook his head and took another drink. Some young kids rolled up on bikes with trailers and parked in front by Donnie. "What happened to the Goodwill?" Donnie asked one of them.

"It's been gone a while," One of them answered. They were probably about eighteen years old twenty at most. "We usually camp right here sometimes you don't mind do you?"

"No, go ahead," Donnie said.

"You look cold. Do you want a sweatshirt," One of them asked.

"I was coming to Goodwill to get a jacket."

"I got something for you," he said digging in his trailer. He pulled out an ASU sweatshirt it was maroon with Sparky on the back and ASU across the front in gold. It was like new. He threw it to Donnie. "This should fit you."

"Wow this is nice. I could give you a couple of bucks for it or something."

"Don't worry about it people give me clothes all the time. That one is way too big for me, I just took it cause I knew I'd find someone who'd want it."

"Thanks man."

"Did you just get out of prison?"

"Yes."

"I could tell by the clothes. Do you get high? Me and my buddy here are going to smoke a bowl of speed. Do you want some?"

"I'll smoke a little with you."

The two boys had laid out their sleeping bags in front of the store. They had their bikes in front of them. They loaded up a bowl and smoked some and passed it to Donnie. Donnie had Déjà vu. He took a hit off the pipe and passed it back. He took a drink of beer and they passed the pipe to him again. He took a big hit and let out a cloud. He sat there a moment staring at the bank after he passed the pipe back. When the kid tried to pass it back Donnie was staring at the bank like he was in a trance.

"Hey Mister are you alright?" The kid asked waving his hand in front of Donnie's face.

Donnie snapped out of it and looked the kid square in the eye. "Do you guys wanna make some money?"

About the Book

The first Twenty-Six chapters were hand written as I served 9.25 years in the Arizona Department of Corrections. I first got the idea of writing a book in 2012. I had never written a book before but decided I wanted it to be about a bank robbery. While I was doing my sentence ideas came to mind here and there and I just thought about them more and more. In 2013 A guy named Don McKay came to Cimarron Unit on a bank robbery charge he was an older guy and I used to play hearts with him and a few other inmates. I told him I might want to pick his brain in the future for a novel I was going to write. He said sure. Tragically he died at Cimarron in a freak accident before I ever asked him much about bank robbing. Years went by and I always thought of little antidotes I thought would be good for a book. In 2016 D.O.C. released me in error, but someone told on me so I was brought back to prison 26 days later. While I was back in prison I decided I should start to put all the ideas I had down on paper and started to write this book on 4/25/2016 at the Whetstone Unit. I used the name Donnie McKay to pay tribute to the inmate who died at Cimarron. I figured it was a somewhat common name and a nice gesture to my old friend. I had picked the name Tracy because my first real girlfriend was named Tracy Stout. She was my first love and I always wondered what happened to her. I found out about a year and a half after my release that she along with her young son and husband were killed many years earlier in a train accident. I had no idea while writing the book. None of the things ever happened to the real Don or Tracy it is all pure fiction.

I was on a yard with a big guy named Dwaine Betts and asked him if I could use his prison number for my books character because it was issued about the right time. I had asked other inmates in the past and they didn't want me to, but Dwaine was cool enough to say yes. I wrote on and off until my release (the real one this time) in November 2018. Once out I typed all I had written fixing things here and there cleaning up my rough draft. Then I wrote the final six chapters finishing it on 5/12/2020. I did not write this book to get rich and famous. My main purpose was to kill time while I was in prison. I do hope people get the anti-racist message and it shows drugs are bad and everything you do in life affects the people that love you. I also hope it will bring awareness to the prison system in America as it does little to no help in "rehabilitating" it is merely a form of punishment and most inmates get out to nothing and just end up re-offending. I hope you enjoyed the book and thank you for reading.

This book deals with some tough issues like drug addiction, mental illness and suicide. If you have any of these issues please seek help.

NATIONAL SUICIDE PREVENTION LIFELINE:

1-800-273-8255

SAMHSA's NATIONAL HELP LINE:

1-800-662 HELP(4357)

This Helpline is for individuals and families facing mental

and/or substance use disorders.

About the Author

Gary Barocsi is 49 years old and lives in Arizona. This is his first novel. He is currently working on his second novel. His second book will be titled 'From Zero to Hero' and will hopefully be out in late 2021.

The following pages contain a sneak peek of

'From Zero to Hero'

An upcoming novel by Gary Barocsi.

Chapter One

Empty beer bottles clanked and rattled as Dave rolled over. He moaned when the Bright Phoenix Sun hit his eyes when he opened them. He quickly covered them with his hand. He felt around by his head with his other hand blindly. He finally felt what he was searching for, his hat. He grabbed the upside down hat with his free hand and placed it on his chest. He reached inside it and pulled out a cheap pair of sunglasses and put them on. He grabbed his wallet from the hat and put it in his back pocket. He felt around by his side and found his cane. He sat up and put his Arizona Diamondbacks hat on. He reached over and grabbed his Styrofoam ice chest and put it on his lap. He pulled the lid off and slashed the cool what was ice, water on his face and it helped wake him up. He took a bandana from his right front jean pocket and dunked it in the cool water. He rung it out and wiped his face and neck down. He rolled the wet bandana up and put it on the back of his neck letting the ends hang down over his chest. It was only about 7 O' Clock and it was already 90 degrees out. The summer heat was brutal in Phoenix.

He got to his feet and started picking up his mess. He put all the empty beer bottles in a plastic grocery bag and tied it up. He folded his blanket he was laying on. He picked up the stuffed teddy bear he used for a pillow and dusted some leaves off of it. He put the piece of cardboard that was under his blanket behind the bushes and placed his folded blanket and teddy bear pillow on top of his cardboard mattress. He got into a shoe box that was already back there and rifled through the junk and odds and ends until he found what he was looking for. He took out a black magic marker and put the cap in his mouth and bit down and pulled the marker off uncapping it. He scribbled on the cardboard bed to see if it still worked. He put the cap back on and picked up a discarded twelve pack box. He ripped a side off the box and uncapped the marker. He wrote:

HUNGRY

HOMELESS

CAN YOU HELP?

He put the sign under his arm and capped the marker and put it back in the shoe box. He bent down and grabbed his cane off the ground. He heard footsteps behind him. He turned and saw it was Kenny his friend. Kenny walked up to him and put a twelve pack of Natural Ice on the ground and ripped the top open. "Have some breakfast Dave," He said and placed three cans on the ground and picked the box back up.

"Thanks, I need a little hair of the dog today."

"I figured when I walked by to get it I had to stop a second and see if your chest was moving. You were out man."

"Can't sleep in with this heat today," Dave said and cracked open one of the cold beers and started chugging it.

"You don't want to sleep in today. People are being generous. I had someone hand me a ten today and two other people gave me fives and I haven't even started counting the cup of change. Get out there and fly your sign before morning rush hour is over." Kenny started walking over to his side of the freeway. He and his wife camped out behind some bushes on the other side. They were nice people, always willing to share what they had.

Dave pounded the two remaining beers and limped out to the esplanade by the turn lane. He put down a milk crate and sat down on it. He was having a bad day, a lot of pain already. He held his sign up and immediately someone gave him two dollars. He thought Damn Kenny you weren't kidding. He sat out there about an hour or so and made about eighteen bucks not counting the cup of spare change. It was hot he had to get out of the sun for a while. He picked up his milk crate and was hit with a half bottle of water.

"Get a job you fuckin' bum!" A voice yelled from a pick-up truck turning onto the freeway.

"How about you give me a job!" He yelled back. "A blow job you asshole," he muttered under his breath as he bent down and picked up the bottle. "Hmmm still cold," he said and uncapped it and smelled it. He took a drink. It didn't taste bad so he drank it down. "Ahh I needed that" he said. "Thanks dickhead," He muttered as he limped across 67th Avenue. He put his milk crate by the bushes where he slept and shouldered his backpack and started limping his way to the corner store. He reached the Circle K and got a Bomb burrito and put it in the microwave for three minutes. He went and got a couple of Gatorades and a twelve pack of Natural Ice. He returned and got his burrito out of the microwave and walked to the cashier.

"How you doing today Dave?" The clerk asked. He was a good kid about twenty five. He was like a punk rock kid or something every month or so his hair would be a different color. This month it was green so far. He had tattoos on his arms and a piercing in his nose like a bull.

"It's a rough one today Joey. I'm hurtin' for certain."

"Eat and get that twelver in you. That should help some."

"You don't have any weed?"

"Nah, I can't smoke you know I'm on TASC." TASC was a place you had to call and drop random UA's (Urine Analysis) when you were on probation or parole.

"That's right I keep forgetting. How long you gotta do that?"

"Two more months and I'm off baby."

"Why don't you get you one of those medical marijuana cards you got a job. You should be able to afford it," Dave said as he put the twelve pack in his backpack. He put one of the Gatorades in there too.

"I ain't spending the money. It'll be $12.94."

Dave gave him thirteen dollars and peeled the wrapper on his burrito and took a bite.

"Here you go," Joey said handing Dave his change.

"Just put it in there," He said pointing to the need a penny take a penny tray on the counter. He took a few drinks of Gatorade and put

231

it in his backpack and put it on. "See ya," Dave said and started hobbling back to his bushes to sit in the shade and eat his burrito. He got back to his spot. "Shit," He said. He forgot to get a bag of ice. He sat there and ate his burrito and drank his Gatorade. Once he finished the two he dumped the water from the ice chest. He dumped the twelve pack in the Styrofoam cooler. He pulled one out and put the lid on. He cracked open the beer.

"Morning Dave," a female voice said. It was Rhonda, Kenny's wife. She was about 5'1" tall with dirty blonde hair. She was a little rough in the face but she had a nice little figure on her. She was a real sweetheart.

"Good morning Rhonda are you headed to the store?"

"Yeah I'm feeling lucky. I'm gonna get me some scratchers. You need something?"

"Yes, could you grab me a bag of ice," He said handing her two dollars.

"Sure," She said taking the two dollars and trotting off.

She came back five minutes later and handed Dave the ice. "Here you go she said and started scratching a lottery ticket.

"Thanks."

"No problem. Woo Hoo! She yelled. "Fifty bucks!"

"Alright, good for you."

"I'm telling you when I get that feeling nine times out of ten I win."

"Well you should be buying a Powerball ticket then, it's over a hundred million."

"Hey yeah maybe I should," She said staring off a minute. Dave turned around to say something to her but she was gone. He looked down the sidewalk and saw she was heading to the store most likely to cash in her ticket and buy some Powerball numbers. Dave chuckled to himself. When she came back she gave Dave a Powerball ticket too. "I got one for you too Dave," She said holding the ticket out to him.

"You hold on to it for me. I'll just lose it."

"Okay, I'm cooking dinner tonight with my winnings. Me and Kenny will be over later on."

"Sounds good, you know where to find me."

Made in the USA
Middletown, DE
21 August 2023

37102602R00142